A WOMAN'S PLACE

Also edited by L. M. Schulman

WINNERS AND LOSERS
An Anthology of Great Sports Fiction

THE LONERS
Short Stories About the Young and Alienated

THE CRACKED LOOKING GLASS
Stories of Other Realities

TRAVELERS
Stories of Americans Abroad

A Woman's Place

AN ANTHOLOGY OF SHORT STORIES

EDITED BY

L. M. Schulman

MACMILLAN PUBLISHING CO., INC.

NEW YORK

Macmillan Publishing Co., Inc.
866 Third Avenue, New York, N.Y. 10022
Collier-Macmillan Canada Ltd..

Library of Congress catalog card number: 73–8575

Printed in the United States of America

10 9 8 7 6 5 4 3 2 1

Library of Congress Cataloging in Publication Data

Schulman, L M comp.
    A Woman's Place

    CONTENTS: Calisher, H. The rehabilitation of Ginevra Leake.—Porter,
K. A. Flowering Judas.—Gallant, M. Sunday afternoon. [etc.]
    1. Woman—Juvenile fiction.   2. Short stories. [1. Women—Fiction.
2. Short stories]   I. Title.
PZ5.S376Wo   813'.01 [Fic]   73–8575   ISBN 0–02–781420–3

ACKNOWLEDGMENTS

"The Rehabilitation of Ginevra Leake" by Hortense Calisher, Copyright
© 1957 by Hortense Calisher, is reprinted by permission of Robert
Lantz-Candida Donadio Literary Agency, Inc.

"Flowering Judas" by Katherine Anne Porter, Copyright 1930, 1958, by
Katherine Anne Porter, is reprinted from her volume *Flowering Judas
and Other Stories* by permission of Harcourt Brace Jovanovich, Inc.

"Sunday Afternoon" by Mavis Gallant, Copyright © November 21, 1962,
by Mavis Gallant, is reprinted by permission of Georges Borchardt, Inc.,
145 East 52nd Street, New York, New York 10022.

"The Puzzleheaded Girl" by Christina Stead is reprinted by permission
of Holt, Rinehart and Winston, Inc., from *The Puzzleheaded Girl: Four
Novellas* by Christina Stead, Copyright © 1965, 1966, 1967 by Christina
Stead.

"Till September Petronella" by Jean Rhys, copyright © 1960 by Jean
Rhys, is reprinted by permission of Andre Deutsch Limited from *Tigers
Are Better-Looking* by Jean Rhys.

Foreword

"It was my life—and it didn't work."
—Pat Loud, wife and mother, on the
TV documentary, *An American Family*

The stories in this collection give the lie to stereotypes of "women's writing." They are not "poetic" or sentimental or vague. If anything, they are almost painfully exact, the product of the most vigorous discipline and finished artistry. Yet in another sense, they are "women's stories." No man could have written them.

No man can truly conceive of the special agonies of an existence in which the central fact of life by which all else is judged is that of being a man's idea of a woman. No man can fully assess the cost of the struggle in which a woman must engage merely to enjoy the right that a man takes to be God-granted—to be master of oneself and one's destiny.

This struggle is all-encompassing—and the picture that emerges from these stories is much like a battlefield strewn with casualties. The moments of triumph are few and mockingly fleeting, like that enjoyed by Nancy Hale's young heroine in "The Bubble." Those who wish to survive with some measure of dignity must learn to live with the weight of their armor, as does Doris Lessing's "Our Friend Judith." Women who attempt to invade male preserves must face the weight of professional hostility as in "The Condemned Librarian," or employ an elaborate strategy of flirtatious deception and subtle trickery as in "Flowering Judas," or simply bear the weight of scorn as in "Sunday Afternoon." Others, who choose to put themselves in the protective custody of men, run the risk of total vulnerability as does the young wife in "Bliss," or else of being turned into one-dimensional creatures of pleasure as does the chorus girl in Jean Rhys's poignant "Till September Petronella."

Always one's angle of vision is essential in adequately assaying the conflict, and at times that point of view may be different from what the author consciously intended. A first reading of "A Domestic Dilemma" might place the beleaguered husband as an innocent victim—until one considers the original spur to his wife's drunkenness. The radical spinster in "The Rehabilitation of Ginevra Leake" might be seen as a figure of pure fun, unless one speculates how a man in a similar situation might be envisioned, or compares Ginevra Leake's career with that of the suburban wife who tells the story. In "The Puzzleheaded Girl," the affection of a hard-headed businessman for a zany young lady begins to seem increasingly patronizing, and tragedy flavors the high comedy, as one wonders at the pressures that could create such eccentricity in the pursuit of freedom and art.

These stories have not been selected for those who demand that characters should be "happy" and that thinking should be "positive." Such people are able to furnish lists of women executives, doctors and lawyers who also are perfect wives and mothers. They keep these lists right beside lists of black millionaires. Such successes, of course, do exist, just as on another level contented housewives and satisfied shoeshine men exist. The exceptional always exists. But though truth is free to be stranger than fiction, fiction does not share that privilege. It is designed to illumine the forces that shape us, to chart the currents upon which our lives move. Above all, it is made to show danger plain. The stories in this volume constitute both messages and warnings, particularly for those who are about to take the helms of their lives in their hands.

"Happy is the age that needs no heroes," wrote the playwright Bertolt Brecht. In the same vein, happy will be the time when a woman need not be a heroine to win her place as a total human being. But as these stories vividly testify, that time has not yet arrived. The heroic age of women is now.

L. M. Schulman

Contents

HORTENSE CALISHER

The Rehabilitation
of Ginevra Leake

Ever since our State Department published that address of Khrushchev's to the Twentieth Congress of the Communist Party, in which he noted the "posthumous rehabilitation" of a number of Russians who had been executed as enemies of the people, I've been nagged by the thought that I owe it to our bourgeois society to reveal what I know about the life of my friend Ginny Doll—or as she was known to her friends in the Party—Ginevra Leake. If you remember, Mr. Khrushchev's speech was dotted with anecdotes that all wound to the same tender conclusion:

On February 4th Eihke was shot. It has been definitely established now that Eihke's case was fabricated; he has been
posthumously rehabilitated. . . . Sentence was passed on
Rudzutak in twenty minutes and he was shot. (Indignation
in the hall) . . . After careful examination of the case in
1955 it was established that the accusation against Rudzutak
was false. He has been rehabilitated posthumously. . . . Suf-
fice it to say that from 1954 to the present time, the Military
Collegium of the Supreme Court has rehabilitated 7,679 persons, many of whom were rehabilitated posthumously.

Being dead, Ginny Doll would certainly fall into the lat-
ter category if anyone chose to rehabilitate her, but since
the manner of her death has elevated her, however errone-
ously, to martyrdom in the American branch of the Party,
it's unlikely that any of her crowd will see the need of
arousing indignation in the hall. The task therefore de-
volves on me, not only as a friend of her girlhood, but as
her only non-Party friend—kept on because I represented
the past, always so sacred to a Southerner, and was therefore no more disposable than the rose-painted lamps, walnut commodes and feather-stitched samplers in the midst of
which she pursued life on the New York barricades, right to
the end. If to no one else, I owe to the rest of us Southrons
the rehabilitation of Ginny Doll, even if, as is most likely,
it's the last thing she'd want.

I first met Virginia Darley Leake, as she was christened,
Ginny Doll as she was called by her mother and aunts,
when she and I were about fifteen, both of us daughters of
families who had recently emigrated from Virginia to New
York, mine from Richmond, hers from the town that, until

I grew up, I assumed was spelled "Lenchburg." My father disliked professional Southerners, and would never answer invitations to join their ancestral societies. However, on one summer evening when he was feeling his age and there was absolutely no prospect of anyone dropping in to hear about it, he succumbed to momentary sentiment and went downtown to a meeting of the Sons and Daughters of the Confederacy. He came back snorting that they were nothing but old maids of both sexes, just as he'd expected; he'd been trapped into seeing home a Mrs. Darley Lyon Leake who'd clung to him like a limpet when she'd found they both lived on Madison Avenue, and he warned my mother that he was afraid the woman would call—his actual phrase for Mrs. Leake being "one of those tiny, clinging ones you can't get off your hands—like peach fuzz."

Mrs. Leake—a tiny, coronet-braided woman with a dry, bodiless neatness—did call, but only, as she carefully explained to my mother, for the purpose of securing a Southern, presumably genteel playmate for her daughter. My mother was not Southern, but she shared her caller's opinion of the girls Ginny Doll and I brought home from school. The call was repaid once, by my mother with me in tow, after which it was understood that any *entente* was to be only between us girls; my parents and Mrs. Leake never saw each other again.

On that first call I had been relieved to find how much the Leake household, scantily composed of only three females—Mrs. Leake, Ginny Doll and Ida, the cook—still reminded me of our own crowded one, in its slow rhythm and antediluvian clutter. Three years spent trying to imitate

the jumpy ways of my New York girl friends had made me
ashamed of our peculiarities; it was comforting to be reminded that these were regional, and that at least there
were two of us on Madison Avenue.

With the alchemic snobbery of her kind, Mrs. Leake had
decreed that the intimacy must be all one way; Ginny Doll
could not come to us. So it was always I who went there,
at first I did not quite know why. For, like many of the
children introduced to me by my parents, and as quickly
shed, Ginny Doll was a lame duck. It would be unfair to
suggest that she and her mother were types indigenous only
to the South; nevertheless anybody down there would have
recognized them at once—the small woman whose specious
femininity is really one of size and affectation, whose im-
perious ego always has a socially proper outlet (Mrs. Leake
wore her heart trouble on her sleeve), and whose single
daughter is always a great lumpy girl with a clayey com-
plexion. At fifteen, Ginny Doll was already extremely tall,
stooped, and heavy in a waistless way; only her thin nose
was pink, and her curves were neither joyous nor warm; her
long hand lay in one's own like a length of suet just out of
the icebox and her upper teeth preceded her smile. One
glance at mother and daughter predicted their history; by
producing a girl of such clearly unmarriageable aspect, the
neatly turned Mrs. Leake had assured herself of a well-
serviced life until her own death—at a probable eighty.
After that, Ginny Doll's fate would have been clearer in
Lenchburg, for the South has never lost its gentle, feudal
way of absorbing its maiden ladies in one family sinecure
or another. But up here in the amorphous North, there was

no foretelling what might happen, much less what did.

Ginny Doll also had manners whose archaic elegance I remembered from down home—it was these that my mother had hoped I would reacquire—but unfortunately hers were accompanied by the slippery voice, with a half-gushy catch to it, that gave her a final touch of the ridiculous. Still, I found myself unable to desert her. It appeared that I was her only friend (although her importunities were always so restrained that it took a keen ear to hear the tremor in them), and after I had gone there a few times I felt guilty at not liking her better, because I felt so sorry for her.

For it appeared also that my father had been accorded a signal honor in being allowed past their threshold. Mrs. Leake was not a widow as we had assumed, but a deserted woman, and it was because of this that nothing more masculine than the old pug, which she sometimes boarded for a rich sister-in-law, was ever allowed past her door. According to Ginny Doll, her mother had done nothing to merit desertion, unless it was having committed the *faux pas* of marrying a Texan. Indeed, her position was so honorable that conscience money from the sister-in-law, the husband's sister, was the means by which she was quite adequately supported. Still, there was a stain upon them—it was the fact that Mr. Leake still lived. Somehow this fact committed them to an infinite circumspection, and was responsible for the exhausted, yet virulent femininity of their *ménage*. It was also to blame for Mrs. Leake's one perverted economy, for which Ginny Doll was never to forgive her—her refusal to get Ginny Doll's teeth straightened. When approached by the sister-in-law, Aunt Tot, on this matter, she would reply that she wouldn't use conscience money to tamper with the work of the Lord. When approached by Ginny Doll, her reply came nearer the truth: "You didn't get them from me." As I came to know the Leakes better, I concluded that the stain was increased by the fact that Mr. Leake not only was, but was happy somewhere. Although Ginny Doll never spoke of him, I saw him clearly—a man still robust, with the slight coarseness of the too-far-south South, a man barreling along somewhere careless and carefree, a man who knew how to get peach fuzz off his hands.

By this time the household had won me, as it was to win so many—in later years I could well understand Ginny Doll's unique position in the Party. How it must have salved Party spirits, after a hot day in the trenches of the *Daily Worker,* to enter an authentic version of that Southern parlor inside whose closed circle one sits so cozened and élite, pleating time's fan! Our famed hospitality consists really of a welcome whose stylized warmth is even more affecting than genuine interest, plus the kind of stately consideration for the trivial that makes everybody feel importantly human—Ginny Doll did both to perfection. In my case, it was summertime when I met the Leakes, and our people do have a genius for hot weather. Inside their living room the shades were drawn cool and gray, white dust covers were slippery under bare legs, and a music box was set purling. No one was ever there long before Ida, a frustrated artist with only two to feed, came in bearing an enormous, tinkling tea which she replenished at intervals, urging us to keep up our strength. When, during the first of my visits, Ginny Doll happened to remark, "Your father is truly handsome; with that ahn-gree hair of his and that pahful nose, I declare he looks just like a sheik!" I took it for more of her Lenchburg manners. It was only later that I saw how the *idée fixe* "Men!" was the pivot from which, in opposite ways, the two Leakes swung.

When I was sixteen, my parents gave me a coming-out dance. After a carefully primed phone call to Mrs. Leake by my father, Ginny Doll was allowed to attend, on the stipulation that he bring her home at the stroke of twelve. At the dance I was too busy to pay her much mind, but later I heard my parents talking in their bedroom.

"She ought to take that girl back to Lenchburg," said my father. "Up here, they don't understand such takin' ways, 'less a pretty face goes with 'em. That girl'll get herself misunderstood—if she gets the chance."

"Taking ways!" said my mother. "Why she followed the boys around as if they were unicorns! As if she'd never seen one before!"

My father's shoes hit the floor. "Reckon not," he said.

The next day, Ginny Doll telephoned, eager for post-mortems on the dance, but I'd already been through that with several of my own crowd, and I didn't get to see her until the end of the week. I found that she had spent the interval noting down the names of all the boys she had met at my house—out of a list of forty she had remembered twenty-nine names and some characteristic of each of the others, such as "real short, and serious, kind of like the Little Minister." Opening her leather diary, she revealed that, ever since their arrival in New York, she had kept a list of every male she had met; my dance had been a strike of the first magnitude, bringing her total, with the inclusion of two doctors, the landlord and a grocery boy, almost to fifty. And in a special column opposite each name she had recorded the owner's type, much as an anthropologist might note "brachycephalic," except that Ginny Doll's categories were all culled from their "library," that collection of safely post-Augustan classics, bound *Harper's,* Thomas Nelson Page and E. P. Roe which used to be on half the musty bookshelves in the Valley of Virginia. There was a Charles Brandon, a Henry Esmond (one of the doctors), a Marlborough and a Bonnie Prince Charlie, as well as several other princes and chevaliers I'd never heard of before. A boy named Bobbie Locke, who'd brought a flask and made a general show of himself, was down as D'Artagnan, and my own beau, a nice quiet boy from St. Mark's, was down as Gawain. My father was down as Rasselas, Prince of Abyssinia.

I remember being impressed at first; in Richmond we had been taught to admire "great readers," even when female, and almost every family we knew had, or had had, at least one. But I also felt a faint, squirmy disquiet. Many of the girls I knew kept movie-star books, or had pashes on Gene Tunney or Admiral Byrd, but we never mixed up these legendary figures with the boys who took us to Huyler's. I was uncomfortably reminded of my father's cousin, old Miss Lavalette Buchanan, who still used more rouge than you could buy on Main Street, and wore gilt bows in her hair even to the Busy Bee.

From then on, my intimacy with Ginny Doll dwindled. Now and then I dropped by on a hot summer day when no one else was around, and I simply had to talk about a new beau. For on this score she was the perfect confidante, of course, hanging breathless on every detail. After each time, I swore never to go back. It was embarrassing where there was no exchange. Besides, she drove me nuts with that list, bringing it out like an old set of dominoes, teasing me about my fickleness to "Gawain." I couldn't seem to get it through her head that this was New York, not "Lenchburg," and that I hadn't seen any of those boys for years.

By the time I'd been away at college for a year, I was finished with her. Ginny Doll hadn't gone—Mrs. Leake thought it made you hard. My mother occasionally met Ginny Doll on the avenue, and reported her as pursuing a round that was awesomely unchanged—errands for Mamma, dinners with the aunts, meetings of the Sons and Daughters —even the pug was the same. The Leakes, my father said once, had brought the art of the status quo to a hyaline perfection that was a rarity in New York, but one not much prized there. Who could have dreamed of the direction from which honor would one day be paid?

The last time I saw her was shortly after my engagement had been announced, when I received a formal note from the Leakes, requesting the pleasure of my and my fiancé's company on an afternoon. I remembered with a shock that long ago, "down South," as we had learned to say now, within that circle of friends whom one did not shuffle but lost only to feud or death, a round of such visits was *de rigueur*. I went alone, unwilling to face the prospect of Ginny Doll studying my future husband for noble analogues, and found the two Leakes behind a loaded tea table.

Mrs. Leake seemed the same, except for a rigidly "at home" manner that she kept between us like a fire screen, as if my coming alliance with a man rendered me incendiary, and she was there to protect her own interests from flame. Ginny Doll's teeth had perhaps a more ivory polish from the constant, vain effort of her lips to close over them, and her dress had already taken a spinster step toward surplice necklines and battleship colors; it was hard to believe that she was, like myself, twenty-three. We were alone together only once, when I went to the bathroom and she followed me in, muttering something about hand towels, of which there were already a dozen or so lace-encrusted ones on the rod.

Once inside, she faced me eagerly, with the tight, held-in smile that always made her look as if she were holding a mashed daisy in her mouth. "It's so exciting," she said. "Tell me all about it!"

"I have," I said, referring to the stingy facts that had been extracted over the tea table—that we were both history instructors and were going to teach in Istanbul next year, that no, I had no picture with me, but he was "medium" and dark, and from "up here."

"I mean—it's been so long," she said. "And Mamma made me dispose of my book." It took me a minute to realize what she meant.

She looked down at the handkerchief she always carried, worrying the shred of cambric with the ball of her thumb, the way one worries a ticket to somewhere. "I wondered," she said. "Is he one of the ones *we* knew?"

The Leakes sent us a Lenox vase for a wedding present,

and my thank-you note was followed by one from Ginny Doll, saying that I just must come by some afternoon and tell her about the wedding trip; Mamma napped every day at three and it would be just like old times. I never did, of course. I was afraid it would be.

Ten years passed, fifteen. We had long since returned from abroad and settled in Easthampton. My parents had died. The vase had been broken by the first of the children. I hadn't thought of Ginny Doll in years.

Then, one blinding August afternoon, I was walking along, of all places, Fourteenth Street, cursing the mood that had sent me into the city on such a day, to shop for things I didn't need and wouldn't find. I hadn't found them, but the rising masochism that whelms women at the height of an unsuccessful shopping tour had impelled me down here to check sewing-machine prices at a discount house someone had mentioned a year ago, on whose door I'd just found a sign saying "Closed Month of August." In another moment I would rouse and hail a cab, eager enough for the green routines I had fled that morning. Meanwhile I walked slowly west, the wrong way, still hunting for something, anything, peering into one after the other of the huge, glass bays of the cheap shoe stores. Not long since, there had still been a chocolate shop down here, that had survived to serve teas in a cleanliness that was elegance for these parts, but I wouldn't find it either. New York lay flat, pooped, in air the color of sweat, but a slatternly nostalgia rose from it, as happens in the dead end of summer, for those who spent their youth there. This trip was a seasonal purge; it would be unwise to find anything.

"Why, Charlotte Mary! I do declare!"

I think I knew who it was before I turned. It was my youth speaking. Since my parents died, no one had addressed me in that double-barreled way in years.

"Why—why Ginny Doll!" Had she not spoken, I would have passed her; she was dressed in that black, short-sleeved convention which city women were just beginning to use and looked, at first glance, almost like anyone. But at the gaspy catch of that voice I remembered everything about her. Here was the one mortal who must have stayed as much the same as anyone could, preserved in the amber of her status quo.

"Why, believe it or not, I was just thinking of you!" I said. It wasn't strictly true; I had been thinking of Huyler's, of old, expunged summers to which she faintly belonged. But early breeding stays with one, returning at odd times like an accent. I can still tell a half-lie, for the sake of someone else's pleasure, as gracefully as anybody in Virginia.

While she extracted the number and names of my children, I revised my first impression of her. Age had improved her, as it does some unattractive girls—this was 1949 and we were both thirty-seven. She still stooped heavily, as if the weight of her bust dragged at the high, thin shoulders, but she was better corseted, and had an arty look of heavy earrings and variegated bracelets, not Greenwich Village modern, but the chains of moonstones set in silver, links of carnelians and cameos that ladies used to bring back from Florence—I remembered Aunt Tot.

Something about her face had changed, however, and at

first I thought it was merely the effect of her enormous hat (how had I missed it?)—the wide-brimmed "picture" hat, with an overcomplicated crown, often affected by women who fancied a touch of Mata Hari, or by aging demi-mondaines. Later, I was to find that this hat was Ginny Doll's trademark, made for her in costume colors by the obscure family milliner to whom she still was loyal, whose fumbling, side-street touch saved the model from its own aspirations and kept it the hat of a lady. At the moment I thought only of how much it was just what Ginny Doll grown up would wear—one of those swooping discs under which romantic spinsters could visualize themselves leaning across a restaurant table at the not-impossible man, hats whose subfusc shadow came too heavy on the faces beneath them, and, well, too late. Here was her old aura of the ridiculous, brought to maturity.

"And how is your mother?" I asked, seeing Mrs. Leake as she still must be—tiny, deathless companion fly.

"Mamma?" She smiled, an odd smile, wide and lifted, but closed, and then I saw the real difference in her face. Her teeth had been pulled in. She had had them straightened. "Mamma's *dead*," said Ginny Doll.

"Oh, I'm sorry; I hadn't heard—"

"Six years ago. It was her heart after all, think of it. And then I came into Aunt Tot's money." She smiled on, like a pleased child; until the day of her death, as I was to find, she never tired of the wonder of smiling.

"But don't let's stand here in this awful heat," she said. "Come on up to the house, and Ida'll give us some iced tea. Oh, honey, there's so much to tell you!"

"Ida," I said, enchanted. "Still Ida? Oh I wish I could, but I'm afraid I haven't time to go all the way up there. I'll miss my train."

"But I don't live uptown any more, darlin', I live right down here. Come on." I gave in, and instinctively turned east. Toward Gramercy Park, it would surely be, or Irving Place.

"No, this way." She turned me west. "Right here on Fourteenth."

I followed her, wondering, used as I was to the odd crannies that New Yorkers often seized upon with a gleefully inverted assumption of style. From Union Square just east of us, westward for several long blocks, this was an arid neighborhood even for tenements, an area of cranky shops being superseded by huge bargain chains, of lofts, piano factories, and the blind, shielded windows of textile agents. Nobody really nobody lived here.

We turned in at the battered doorway of a loft building. Above us, I heard the chattering of machines. To the left, the grimy buff wall held a signboard with a row of company names in smudged gilt. Ginny Doll took out a key and opened a mailbox beneath. I was close enough to read the white calling card on it—Ginevra Leake.

At that moment she turned, holding a huge wad of mail. "Honey, I guess I ought to tell you something about me, before you go upstairs," she said. "In case it might make a difference to you."

In a flash I'd tied it all together—the hat, the neighborhood, the flossy new name, my mother's long-gone remark about unicorns. It wouldn't be need of money. She had simply gone one Freudian step past Miss Lavalette Buchanan. She'd become a tart. A tart with Ida in the background to serve iced tea, as a Darley Leake would.

"I—what did you say?" I said.

She looked down tenderly at her clutch of mail. "I've joined the Party," she said.

Familiar as the phrase had become to us all, for the moment I swear I thought she meant the Republican Party. "What's that got—" I said, and then I stopped, understanding.

"Honey love," she said. The moonstones rose, shining, on her breast. "I mean the Communist Party."

"Ginny Doll Leake! You haven't!"

"Cross my heart, I have!" she said, falling, as I had, into the overtones of our teens. "Cross my heart hope to die or kiss a pig!" And taking my silence for consent, she tossed her head gaily and led me up, past the Miller Bodice Lining, past the Apex Art Trays, to the top floor.

Ida opened the door, still in her white uniform, and greeted me warmly, chortling "Miss Charlotte! Miss Charlotte!" over and over before she released me. I don't know what I expected to find behind her—divans perhaps, and the interchangeable furniture of Utopia built by R. H. Macy —certainly not what confronted me. For what I saw, gazing from the foyer where the abalone-shell lamp and the card tray reposed on the credenza as they had always done, was the old sitting room on Madison Avenue. Royal Doulton nymph vases, Chinese lamps, loveseats, "ladies" chairs, and luster candelabras, it was all there, even to the Bruxelles curtains through which filtered the felt-tasting air of Fourteenth Street. Obviously the place had been a huge loft, reclaimed with much expense and the utmost fidelity, "Lenchburg" Ascendant, wherever she might be. Even the positions of the furniture had been retained, with no mantel, but with the same feeling of orientation toward a non-existent one. In the bathroom the rod held the same weight of ancestral embroidery. The only change I could discern was in the bedroom, where Ginny Doll's nursery chintz and painted rattan had been replaced by Mrs. Leake's walnut wedding suite and her point d'esprit spread.

I returned to the parlor and sat down on the loveseat, where I had always sat, watching, bemused, while Ida bore in the tray as if she had been waiting all that time in the wings. "The music box," I asked. "Do you still have it?" Of course they did, and while it purled, I listened to Ginny Doll's story.

After Mrs. Leake's death, Aunt Tot had intended to take Ginny Doll on a world cruise, but had herself unfortunately died. For a whole year Ginny Doll had sat on in the old place, all Aunt Tot's money waiting in front of her like a Jack Horner pie whose strands she dared not pull. Above all she craved to belong to a "crowd"; she spent hours weakly dreaming of suddenly being asked to join some "set" less deliquescent than the F.F.V., but the active world seemed closed against her, an impenetrable crystal ball. Finally the family doctor insisted on her getting away. She had grasped at the only place she could think of, an orderly mountain retreat run by a neo-spiritualistic group known as "Unity," two of whose Town Hall lectures she had attended with an ardently converted Daughter. The old doctor, kindly insisting on taking charge of arrangements, had mistakenly booked her at a "Camp Unity" in the Poconos. It had turned out to be a vacation camp run, with a transparent disguise to which no one paid any attention, by the Communist Party.

"It was destiny," said Ginny Doll, smiling absently at a wall on which hung, among other relics, a red-white-and-blue embroidered tribute to a distaff uncle who had been Mayor of Memphis. "Destiny."

I had to agree with her. From her ingenuous account, and from my own knowledge of the social habits of certain "progressives" at my husband's college, I could see her clearly, expanding like a *Magnolia grandiflora* in that bouncingly dedicated air. In a place where the really eminent were noncommittal and aliases were worn like medals, no one questioned her presence or affiliation; each group, absorbed in the general charivari, assumed her to be part of another. In the end she achieved the *réclame* that was to grow. She was a Southerner, and a moneyed woman. They had few of either, and she delighted them with her vigorous enmity toward the status quo. Meanwhile her heart recognized their romantic use of the bogus; she bloomed in this atmosphere so full of categories, and of men. In the end she had even found, if briefly, a categorical man.

"Yes, it must have been destiny," I said. Only kismet could have seen to it that Ginny Doll should meet, in the last, dialectic-dusted rays of a Pocono sunset, a man named Lee. "Lighthouse Harry" or "Robert E.," I wondered, but she never told me whether it was his first name or last, or gave any of the usual details, although in the years to come she often alluded to what he had said, with the tenacious memory of the woman who had once, perhaps only once, been preferred. It was not fantasy; I believed her. It had been one of those summer affairs of tents and flashlights, ending when "Party work" reclaimed him, this kind of work apparently being as useful for such purpose as any other. But it had made her a woman of experience, misunderstood at last, able to participate in female talk with the rueful ease of the star-crossed—and wear those hats.

"I'm not bitter," she said. He had left her for the Party, and also to it. Her days had become as happily prescribed as a belle's, her mail as full. She had found her "set."

"And then—you know I went through analysis?" she said. She had chanced upon the Party during its great psychiatric era, when everybody was having his property-warped libido rearranged. Hers had resulted in the rearrangement of her teeth.

"The phases I went through!" She had gone through a period of wearing her hair in coronet braids; under her analyst's guidance she cut it. With his approval—he was a Party member—she had changed her name to Ginevra. He would have preferred her to keep the teeth as they were, as a symbol that she no longer hankered after the frivolities of class. But they were the one piece of inherited property for which she had no sentiment. Too impatient for orthodontia, she had had them extracted, and a bridge inserted. "And do you know what I did with them?" she said. "He said I could, if I had to, and I did."

"With the teeth?"

She giggled. "Honey, I put them in a bitty box, and I had

the florist put a wreath around it. And I flew down to Lenchburg and put them on Mamma's grave."

Something moved under my feet, and I gave a slight
scream. It wasn't because of what she had just said. Down
home, many a good family has its Poe touch of the weirdie,
my own as well, and I quite understood. But something was
looking out at me from under the sofa, with old, rheumy
eyes. It was the pug.

"It's Junius! But it can't be!" I said.

"Basket, Junius! Go back to your basket!" she said. "It's
not the one you knew, of course. It's that one's child. Let's
see, she married her own brother, so I guess this one's her
cousin as well." Her tone was rambling and genealogical,
the same in which my old aunt still defined a cousinship
as once, twice or thrice removed. And I saw that the tip of
her nose could still blush. "Old Junius was really a lady,
you know," she said.

When I rose to leave, Ida followed us to the hallway.
"You come back, Miss Charlotte," she said. "You come
back, hear? And bring your family with you. I'll cook 'em a
dinner. Be right nice to have you, 'stead all these tacky
people Miss Ginny so took up with."

"Now Ida," said Ginny Doll. "Charlotte," she said, "if
there's one thing I've learned—" Her moonstones glittered
again, in the mirror over the credenza. It was the single time
she ever expounded theory. "If there's one thing I've learned
—it's that real people *are* tacky."

I did go back, of course, and now it was she who gave
the social confidences, I who listened with fascination. Once
or twice she had me to dinner with some of her "set," not

at all to convert me, but rather as a reigning hostess invites the quiet friend of other days to a brief glimpse of her larger orbit, the better to be able to talk about it later. For, as everyone now knows, she had become a great Party hostess. She gave little dinners, huge receptions, the *ton* of which was just as she would have kept it anywhere—excellent food, notable liqueurs and the Edwardian solicitude to which she had been born. As a Daughter and a D.A.R., she had a special exhibit value as well. Visiting dignitaries were brought to her as a matter of course; rising functionaries, when bidden there, knew how far they had risen. Her parlor was the scene of innumerable Young Communist weddings, and dozens of Marxian babies embarked on life with one of her silver spoons. The Party had had its Mother Bloor. Ginny Doll became its Aunt.

Meanwhile we kept each other on as extramural relaxation, the way people do keep the friend who knew them "when." Just because it was so unlikely for either of us (I was teaching again), we sometimes sewed together, took in a matinée. But I had enough glimpses of her other world to know what she ignored in it. No doubt she enjoyed the sense of conspiracy—her hats grew a trifle larger each year. And she did her share of other activities—if always on the entertainment committee. But her heart held no ruse other than the pretty guile of the Virginian, and I never heard her utter a dialectical word. Had she had the luck to achieve a similar success in "Lenchburg" her response would have been the same—here, within a circle somewhat larger but still closed, the julep was minted for all. She lived for her friends, who happened to be carrying cards, instead of leaving them.

She did *not,* however, die for her friends. Every news-paper reader, of course, knows how she died. She was blown up in that explosion in a union hall on Nineteenth Street, the one that also wrecked a delicatessen, a launderette and Mr. Kravetz's tailoring shop next door. The union had had fierce anti-pro-Communist troubles for years, with beat-ings and disappearances for years, and when Ginny Doll's remains, not much but enough, were found, it was taken for granted that she died in the Party. The Communist press did nothing to deny this. Some maintained that she had been wiped out by the other side; others awarded her a higher martyrdom, claiming that she had gone there equipped like a matronly Kamikaze, having made of herself a living bomb. Memorial services were held, the Ginevra Leake Camp Fund was set going, and she was awarded an Order of Stalin, second-class. She is a part of their hagiolatry forever.

But I happen to know otherwise. I happen to know that she was on Nineteenth Street because it was her shopping neighborhood, and because I had spoken to her on the tele-phone not an hour before. She was just going to drop a blouse by at Mr. Kravetz's, she said, then she'd meet me at 2:30 at McCutcheon's, where we were going to pick out some gros-point she wanted to make for her Flint & Horner chairs.

I remember waiting for her for over an hour, thinking that she must be sweet-talking Mr. Kravetz, who was an indifferent tailor, but a real person. Then I phoned Ida, who knew nothing, and finally caught my train. We left on vacation the next day, saw no papers, and I didn't hear of Ginny Doll's death until my return.

When I went down to see Ida, she was already packing for Lenchburg. She had been left all Ginny Doll's worldly goods and an annuity; the rest of Aunt Tot's money must have gone you-know-where.

"Miss Charlotte, you pick yourself a momento," said Ida. We were standing in the bedroom, and I saw Ida's glance stray to the bureau, where two objects reposed in *nature morte*. "I just couldn't leave 'em at the morgue, Miss Charlotte," she said. "An' now I can't take 'em, I can't throw 'em out." It was Ginny Doll's hat, floated clear of the blast, and her false teeth.

I knew Ida wanted me to take them. But I'm human. I chose the music box. But as I wrapped it, I felt Ida's eye on me. She knew what *noblesse oblige* meant, better than her betters. So I compromised, and popped the teeth in too.

When I got home, I hid them. I knew that the children, scavengers all, would sooner or later come upon them, but it seemed too dreadful to chuck them out. Finally, it came to me. I taped them in a bitty box masqued with a black chiffon rose, and took them to our local florist, who wired them to a florist in Lynchburg, to be wreathed and set on Mrs. Leake's grave.

Nevertheless, whenever I heard the children playing the music box, I felt guilty. I had somehow failed Ginny Doll, and the children too. Then when Mr. Khrushchev's speech came along, I knew why. I saw that no one but me could clear Ginny Doll's name, and give her the manifesto she deserves.

Comrades! Fellow members of Bourgeois Society! Let there be indignation in the hall! It is my duty to tell you that Ginevra Leake, alias Virginia Darley, alias Ginny Doll, was never an enemy of Our People at all. She never deserted us, but died properly in the gracious world she was born to, inside whose charmed circle everyone, even the Juniuses, are cousins of one another! She was an arch-individualist, just as much as Stalin. She was a Southern Lady.

And now I can look my children in the eye again. The Russians need not think themselves the only ones to rehabilitate people posthumously. We Southrons can take care of our own.

Flowering Judas

Braggioni sits heaped upon the edge of a straight-backed chair much too small for him, and sings to Laura in a furry, mournful voice. Laura has begun to find reasons for avoiding her own house until the latest possible moment, for Braggioni is there almost every night. No matter how late she is, he will be sitting there with a surly, waiting expression, pulling at his kinky yellow hair, thumbing the strings of his guitar, snarling a tune under his breath. Lupe the Indian maid meets Laura at the door, and says with a flicker of a glance towards the upper room, "He waits."

Laura wishes to lie down, she is tired of her hairpins and

the feel of her long tight sleeves, but she says to him, "Have you a new song for me this evening?" If he says yes, she asks him to sing it. If he says no, she remembers his favorite one, and asks him to sing it again. Lupe brings her a cup of chocolate and a plate of rice, and Laura eats at the small table under the lamp, first inviting Braggioni, whose answer is always the same: "I have eaten, and besides, chocolate thickens the voice."

Laura says, "Sing, then," and Braggioni heaves himself into song. He scratches the guitar familiarly as though it were a pet animal, and sings passionately off key, taking the high notes in a prolonged painful squeal. Laura, who haunts the markets listening to the ballad singers, and stops every day to hear the blind boy playing his reed-flute in Sixteenth of September Street, listens to Braggioni with pitiless courtesy, because she dares not smile at his miserable performance. Nobody dares to smile at him. Braggioni is cruel to everyone, with a kind of specialized insolence, but he is so vain of his talents, and so sensitive of slights, it would require a cruelty and vanity greater than his own to lay a finger on the vast cureless wound of his self-esteem. It would require courage, too, for it is dangerous to offend him, and nobody has this courage.

Braggioni loves himself with such tenderness and amplitude and eternal charity that his followers—for he is a leader of men, a skilled revolutionist, and his skin has been punctured in honorable warfare—warm themselves in the reflected glow, and say to each other: "He has a real nobility, a love of humanity raised above mere personal affections." The excess of this self-love has flowed out, inconveniently for her, over Laura, who, with so many others, owes her comfortable situation and her salary to him. When he is in a very good humor, he tells her, "I am tempted to forgive you for being a *gringa. Gringita!*" and Laura, burning, imagines herself leaning forward suddenly, and with a sound back-handed slap wiping the suety smile from his face. If he notices her eyes at these moments he gives no sign.

She knows what Braggioni would offer her, and she must resist tenaciously without appearing to resist, and if she could avoid it she would not admit even to herself the slow drift of his intention. During these long evenings which have spoiled a long month for her, she sits in her deep chair with an open book on her knees, resting her eyes on the consoling rigidity of the printed page when the sight and sound of Braggioni singing threaten to identify themselves with all her remembered afflictions and to add their weight to her uneasy premonitions of the future. The gluttonous bulk of Braggioni has become a symbol of her many disillusions, for a revolutionist should be lean, animated by heroic faith, a vessel of abstract virtues. This is nonsense, she knows it now and is ashamed of it. Revolution must have leaders, and leadership is a career for energetic men. She is, her comrades tell her, full of romantic error, for what she defines as cynicism in them is merely "a developed sense of reality." She is almost too willing to say, "I am wrong, I suppose I don't really understand the principles," and afterward she makes a secret truce with herself, determined not to surrender her will to such expedient logic. But she cannot help feeling that she has been betrayed irreparably by the disunion between her way of living and her feeling of what life should be, and at times she is almost contented to rest in this sense of grievance as a private store of consolation. Sometimes she wishes to run away, but she stays. Now she longs to fly out of this room, down the narrow stairs, and into the street where the houses lean together like conspirators under a single mottled lamp, and leave Braggioni singing to himself.

Instead she looks at Braggioni, frankly and clearly, like a good child who understands the rules of behavior. Her knees cling together under sound blue serge, and her round white collar is not purposely nun-like. She wears the uniform of an idea, and has renounced vanities. She was born Roman Catholic, and in spite of her fear of being seen by someone who might make a scandal of it, she slips now and again into some crumbling little church, kneels on the chilly stone, and says a Hail Mary on the gold rosary she bought in Tehuantepec. It is no good and she ends by examining the altar with its tinsel flowers and ragged brocades, and feels tender about the battered doll-shape of some male saint whose white, lace-trimmed drawers hang limply around his ankles below the hieratic dignity of his velvet robe. She has encased herself in a set of principles derived from her early training, leaving no detail of gesture or of personal taste untouched, and for this reason she will not wear lace made on machines. This is her private heresy, for in her special group the machine is sacred, and will be the salvation of the workers. She loves fine lace, and there is a tiny edge of fluted cobweb on this collar, which is one of twenty precisely alike, folded in blue tissue paper in the upper drawer of her clothes chest.

Braggioni catches her glance solidly as if he had been

waiting for it, leans forward, balancing his paunch between his spread knees, and sings with tremendous emphasis, weighing his words. He has, the song relates, no father and no mother, nor even a friend to console him; lonely as a wave of the sea he comes and goes, lonely as a wave. His mouth opens round and yearns sideways, his balloon cheeks grow oily with the labor of song. He bulges marvelously in his expensive garments. Over his lavender collar, crushed upon a purple necktie, held by a diamond hoop: over his ammunition belt of tooled leather worked in silver, buckled cruelly around his gasping middle: over the tops of his glossy yellow shoes Braggioni swells with ominous ripeness, his mauve silk hose stretched taut, his ankles bound with the stout leather thongs of his shoes.

When he stretches his eyelids at Laura she notes again that his eyes are the true tawny yellow cat's eyes. He is rich, not in money, he tells her, but in power, and this power brings with it the blameless ownership of things, and the right to indulge his love of small luxuries. "I have a taste for the elegant refinements," he said once, flourishing a yellow silk handkerchief before her nose. "Smell that? It is Jockey Club, imported from New York." Nonetheless he is wounded by life. He will say so presently. "It is true everything turns to dust in the hand, to gall on the tongue." He sighs and his leather belt creaks like a saddle girth. "I am disappointed in everything as it comes. Everything." He shakes his head. "You, poor thing, you will be disappointed too. You are born for it. We are more alike than you realize in some things. Wait and see. Some day you will remember what I have told you, you will know that Braggioni was your friend."

Laura feels a slow chill, a purely physical sense of danger, a warning in her blood that violence, mutilation, a shocking death, wait for her with lessening patience. She has translated this fear into something homely, immediate, and sometimes hesitates before crossing the street. "My personal fate is nothing, except as the testimony of a mental attitude," she reminds herself, quoting from some forgotten philosophic primer, and is sensible enough to add, "Anyhow, I shall not be killed by an automobile if I can help it."

"It may be true I am as corrupt, in another way, as Braggioni," she thinks in spite of herself, "as callous, as incomplete," and if this is so, any kind of death seems preferable. Still she sits quietly, she does not run. Where could she go? Uninvited she has promised herself to this place; she can no longer imagine herself as living in another country, and there is no pleasure in remembering her life before she came here.

Precisely what is the nature of this devotion, its true motives, and what are its obligations? Laura cannot say. She spends part of her days in Xochimilco, near by, teaching Indian children to say in English, "The cat is on the mat." When she appears in the classroom they crowd about her with smiles on their wise, innocent, clay-colored faces, crying, "Good morning, my titcher!" in immaculate voices, and they make of her desk a fresh garden of flowers every day.

During her leisure she goes to union meetings and listens to busy important voices quarreling over tactics, methods, internal politics. She visits the prisoners of her own political faith in their cells, where they entertain themselves with counting cockroaches, repenting of their indiscretions, composing their memoirs, writing out manifestoes and plans for their comrades who are still walking about free, hands in pockets, sniffing fresh air. Laura brings them food and cigarettes and a little money, and she brings messages disguised in equivocal phrases from the men outside who dare not set foot in the prison for fear of disappearing into the cells kept empty for them. If the prisoners confuse night and day, and complain, "Dear little Laura, time doesn't pass in this infernal hole, and I won't know when it is time to sleep unless I have a reminder," she brings them their favorite narcotics, and says in a tone that does not wound them with pity, "Tonight will really be night for you," and though her Spanish amuses them, they find her comforting, useful. If they lose patience and all faith, and curse the slowness of their friends in coming to their rescue with money and influence, they trust her not to repeat everything, and if she inquires, "Where do you think we can find money, or influence?" they are certain to answer, "Well, there is Braggioni, why doesn't he do something?"

She smuggles letters from headquarters to men hiding from firing squads in back streets in mildewed houses, where they sit in tumbled beds and talk bitterly as if all Mexico were at their heels, when Laura knows positively they might appear at the band concert in the Alameda on Sunday morning, and no one would notice them. But Braggioni says, "Let them sweat a little. The next time they may be careful. It is very restful to have them out of the way for a while." She is not afraid to knock on any door in any street after midnight, and enter in the darkness, and say to one of these men who is really in danger: "They will be looking for you—seriously—tomorrow morning at six. Here is some money from Vincente. Go to Vera Cruz and wait."

She borrows money from the Roumanian agitator to give to his bitter enemy the Polish agitator. The favor of Braggioni is their disputed territory, and Braggioni holds the balance nicely, for he can use them both. The Polish agitator talks love to her over café tables, hoping to exploit what he believes is her secret sentimental preference for him, and he gives her misinformation which he begs her to repeat as the solemn truth to certain persons. The Roumanian is more adroit. He is generous with his money in all good causes, and lies to her with an air of ingenuous candor, as if he were her good friend and confidant. She never repeats anything they may say. Braggioni never asks questions. He has other ways to discover all that he wishes to know about them.

Nobody touches her, but all praise her gray eyes, and the soft, round under lip which promises gayety, yet is always grave, nearly always firmly closed: and they cannot understand why she is in Mexico. She walks back and forth on her errands, with puzzled eyebrows, carrying her little folder of drawings and music and school papers. No dancer dances more beautifully than Laura walks, and she inspires some amusing, unexpected ardors, which cause little gossip, because nothing comes of them. A young captain who had been a soldier in Zapata's army attempted, during a horseback ride near Cuernavaca, to express his desire for her with the noble simplicity befitting a rude folk-hero: but gently, because he was gentle. This gentleness was his defeat, for when he alighted, and removed her foot from the stirrup, and essayed to draw her down into his arms, her horse, ordinarily a tame one, shied fiercely, reared and plunged away. The young hero's horse careered blindly after his stable-mate, and the hero did not return to the hotel until rather late that evening. At breakfast he came to her table in full charro dress, gray buckskin jacket and trousers with strings of silver buttons down the leg, and he was in a humorous, careless mood. "May I sit with you?" and "You are a wonderful rider. I was terrified that you might be thrown and dragged. I should never have forgiven myself. But I cannot admire you enough for your riding!"

"I learned to ride in Arizona," said Laura.

"If you will ride with me again this morning, I promise you a horse that will not shy with you," he said. But Laura remembered that she must return to Mexico City at noon.

Next morning the children made a celebration and spent their playtime writing on the blackboard, "We lov ar ticher," and with tinted chalks they drew wreaths of flowers around the words. The young hero wrote her a letter: "I am a very foolish, wasteful, impulsive man. I should have first said I love you, and then you would not have run away. But you shall see me again." Laura thought, "I must send him a box of colored crayons," but she was trying to forgive herself for having spurred her horse at the wrong moment.

A brown, shock-haired youth came and stood in her patio one night and sang like a lost soul for two hours, but Laura could think of nothing to do about it. The moonlight spread a wash of gauzy silver over the clear spaces of the garden, and the shadows were cobalt blue. The scarlet blossoms of the Judas tree were dull purple, and the names of the colors repeated themselves automatically in her mind, while she watched not the boy, but his shadow, fallen like a dark garment across the fountain rim, trailing in the water. Lupe came silently and whispered expert counsel in her ear: "If you will throw him one little flower, he will sing another song or two and go away." Laura threw the flower, and he sang a last song and went away with the flower tucked in the band of his hat. Lupe said, "He is one of the organizers of the Typographers Union, and before that he sold corridos in the Merced market, and before that, he came from Guanajuato, where I was born. I would not trust any man, but I trust least those from Guanajuato."

She did not tell Laura that he would be back again the next night, and the next, nor that he would follow her at a certain fixed distance around the Merced market, through the Zócolo, up Francisco I. Madero Avenue, and so along the Paseo de la Reforma to Chapultepec Park, and into the Philosopher's Footpath, still with that flower withering in his hat, and an indivisible attention in his eyes.

Now Laura is accustomed to him, it means nothing except that he is nineteen years old and is observing a convention with all propriety, as though it were founded on a law of nature, which in the end it might well prove to be. He is beginning to write poems which he prints on a wooden press, and he leaves them stuck like handbills in her door. She is pleasantly disturbed by the abstract, unhurried watchfulness of his black eyes which will in time turn easily towards another object. She tells herself that throwing the flower was a mistake, for she is twenty-two years old and knows better; but she refuses to regret it, and persuades herself that her negation of all external events as they occur is a sign that she is gradually perfecting herself in the stoicism she strives to cultivate against that disaster she fears, though she cannot name it.

She is not at home in the world. Every day she teaches children who remain strangers to her, though she loves their tender round hands and their charming opportunist savagery. She knocks at unfamiliar doors not knowing whether a friend or a stranger shall answer, and even if a known face emerges from the sour gloom of that unknown interior, still it is the face of a stranger. No matter what this stranger says to her, nor what her message to him, the very cells of her flesh reject knowledge and kinship in one monotonous word. No. No. No. She draws her strength from this one holy talismanic word which does not suffer her to be led into evil. Denying everything, she may walk anywhere in safety, she looks at everything without amazement.

No, repeats this firm unchanging voice of her blood; and she looks at Braggioni without amazement. He is a great man, he wishes to impress this simple girl who covers her great round breasts with thick dark cloth, and who hides long, invaluably beautiful legs under a heavy skirt. She is almost thin except for the incomprehensible fullness of her breasts, like a nursing mother's, and Braggioni, who considers himself a judge of women, speculates again on the puzzle of her notorious virginity, and takes the liberty of speech which she permits without a sign of modesty, indeed, without any sort of sign, which is disconcerting.

"You think you are so cold, *gringita!* Wait and see. You will surprise yourself some day! May I be there to advise you!" He stretches his eyelids at her, and his ill-humored cat's eyes waver in a separate glance for the two points of light marking the opposite ends of a smoothly drawn path between the swollen curve of her breasts. He is not put off by that blue serge, nor by her resolutely fixed gaze. There is all the time in the world. His cheeks are bellying with the wind of song. "O girl with the dark eyes," he sings, and reconsiders. "But yours are not dark. I can change all that. O girl with the green eyes, you have stolen my heart away!" then his mind wanders to the song, and Laura feels the weight of his attention being shifted elsewhere. Singing thus, he seems harmless, he is quite harmless, there is nothing to do but sit patiently and say "No," when the moment comes. She draws a full breath, and her mind wanders also, but not far. She dares not wander too far.

Not for nothing has Braggioni taken pains to be a good revolutionist and a professional lover of humanity. He will never die of it. He has the malice, the cleverness, the wickedness, the sharpness of wit, the hardness of heart, stipulated for loving the world profitably. *He will never die of it.* He will live to see himself kicked out from his feeding trough by other hungry world-saviors. Traditionally he must sing in spite of his life which drives him to bloodshed, he tells Laura, for his father was a Tuscany peasant who drifted to Yucatan and married a Maya woman: a woman of race, an aristocrat. They gave him the love and knowledge of music, thus: and under the rip of his thumbnail, the strings of the instrument complain like exposed nerves.

Once he was called Delgadito by all the girls and married women who ran after him; he was so scrawny all his bones showed under his thin cotton clothing, and he could squeeze his emptiness to the very backbone with his two hands. He was a poet and the revolution was only a dream then; too many women loved him and sapped away his youth, and he could never find enough to eat anywhere, anywhere! Now he is a leader of men, crafty men who whisper in his ear, hungry men who wait for hours outside his office for a word with him, emaciated men with wild faces who waylay him at the street gate with a timid, "Comrade, let me tell you . . ." and they blow the foul breath from their empty stomachs in his face.

He is always sympathetic. He gives them handfuls of small coins from his own pocket, he promises them work, there will be demonstrations, they must join the unions and attend the meetings, above all they must be on the watch for spies. They are closer to him than his own brothers, without them he can do nothing—until tomorrow, comrade!

Until tomorrow. "They are stupid, they are lazy, they are treacherous, they would cut my throat for nothing," he says to Laura. He has good food and abundant drink, he hires an automobile and drives in the Paseo on Sunday morning, and enjoys plenty of sleep in a soft bed beside a wife who dares not disturb him; and he sits pampering his bones in easy billows of fat, singing to Laura, who knows and thinks these things about him. When he was fifteen, he tried to drown himself because he loved a girl, his first love, and she laughed at him. "A thousand women have paid for that," and his tight little mouth turns down at the corners.

Now he perfumes his hair with Jockey Club, and confides to Laura: "One woman is really as good as another for me, in the dark. I prefer them all."

His wife organizes unions among the girls in the cigarette factories, and walks in picket lines, and even speaks at meetings in the evening. But she cannot be brought to acknowledge the benefits of true liberty. "I tell her I must have my freedom, net. She does not understand my point of view." Laura has heard this many times. Braggioni scratches the guitar and meditates. "She is an instinctively virtuous woman, pure gold, no doubt of that. If she were not, I should lock her up, and she knows it."

His wife, who works so hard for the good of the factory girls, employs part of her leisure lying on the floor weeping because there are so many women in the world, and only one husband for her, and she never knows where nor when to look for him. He told her: "Unless you can learn to cry when I am not here, I must go away for good." That day he went away and took a room at the Hotel Madrid.

It is this month of separation for the sake of higher principles that has been spoiled not only for Mrs. Braggioni, whose sense of reality is beyond criticism, but for Laura, who feels herself bogged in a nightmare. Tonight Laura envies Mrs. Braggioni, who is alone, and free to weep as much as she pleases about a concrete wrong. Laura has just come from a visit to the prison, and she is waiting for tomorrow with a bitter anxiety as if tomorrow may not come, but time may be caught immovably in this hour, with herself transfixed, Braggioni singing on forever, and Eugenio's body not yet discovered by the guard.

Braggioni says: "Are you going to sleep?" Almost before she can shake her head, he begins telling her about the May-day disturbances coming on in Morelia, for the Catholics hold a festival in honor of the Blessed Virgin, and the Socialists celebrate their martyrs on that day. "There will be two independent processions, starting from either end of town, and they will march until they meet, and the rest depends . . ." He asks her to oil and load his pistols. Standing up, he unbuckles his ammunition belt, and spreads it laden across her knees. Laura sits with the shells slipping through the cleaning cloth dipped in oil, and he says again he cannot understand why she works so hard for the revolutionary idea unless she loves some man who is in it. "Are you not in love with someone?" "No," says Laura. "And no one is in love with you?" "No." "Then it is your own fault. No woman need go begging. Why, what is the matter with you? The legless beggar woman in the Alameda has a perfectly faithful lover. Did you know that?"

Laura peers down the pistol barrel and says nothing, but a long, slow faintness rises and subsides in her; Braggioni curves his swollen fingers around the throat of the guitar and softly smothers the music out of it, and when she hears him again he seems to have forgotten her, and is speaking in the hypnotic voice he uses when talking in small rooms to a listening, close-gathered crowd. Some day this world, now seemingly so composed and eternal, to the edges of every sea shall be merely a tangle of gaping trenches, of crashing walls and broken bodies. Everything must be torn from its accustomed place where it has rotted for centuries, hurled skyward and distributed, cast down again clean as

rain, without separate identity. Nothing shall survive that
the stiffened hands of poverty have created for the rich and
no one shall be left alive except the elect spirits destined to
procreate a new world cleansed of cruelty and injustice,
ruled by benevolent anarchy: "Pistols are good, I love them,
cannon are even better, but in the end I pin my faith to good
dynamite," he concludes, and strokes the pistol lying in her
hands. "Once I dreamed of destroying this city, in case it
offered resistance to General Ortíz, but it fell into his hands
like an over-ripe pear."

He is made restless by his own words, rises and stands
waiting. Laura holds up the belt to him: "Put that on, and
go kill somebody in Morelia, and you will be happier," she
says softly. The presence of death in the room makes her
bold. "Today, I found Eugenio going into a stupor. He refused to allow me to call the prison doctor. He had taken
all the tablets I brought him yesterday. He said he took
them because he was bored."

"He is a fool, and his death is his own business," says
Braggioni, fastening his belt carefully.

"I told him if he had waited only a little while longer,
you would have got him set free," says Laura. "He said he
did not want to wait."

"He is a fool and we are well rid of him," says Braggioni, reaching for his hat.

He goes away. Laura knows his mood has changed, she
will not see him any more for a while. He will send word
when he needs her to go on errands into strange streets, to
speak to the strange faces that will appear, like clay masks
with the power of human speech, to mutter their thanks to

Braggioni for his help. Now she is free, and she thinks, I must run while there is time. But she does not go.

Braggioni enters his own house where for a month his wife has spent many hours every night weeping and tangling her hair upon her pillow. She is weeping now, and she weeps more at the sight of him, the cause of all her sorrows. He looks about the room. Nothing is changed, the smells are good and familiar, he is well acquainted with the woman who comes toward him with no reproach except grief on her face. He says to her tenderly: "You are so good, please don't cry any more, you dear good creature." She says, "Are you tired, my angel? Sit here and I will wash your feet." She brings a bowl of water, and kneeling, unlaces his shoes, and when from her knees she raises her sad eyes under her blackened lids, he is sorry for everything, and bursts into tears. "Ah, yes, I am hungry, I am tired, let us eat something together," he says, between sobs. His wife leans her head on his arm and says, "Forgive me!" and this time he is refreshed by the solemn, endless rain of her tears.

Laura takes off her serge dress and puts on a white linen nightgown and goes to bed. She turns her head a little to one side, and lying still, reminds herself that it is time to sleep. Numbers tick in her brain like little clocks, soundless doors close of themselves around her. If you would sleep, you must not remember anything, the children will say tomorrow, good morning, my teacher, the poor prisoners who come every day bringing flowers to their jailor. 1-2-3-4-5— it is monstrous to confuse love with revolution, night with day, life with death—ah, Eugenio!

The tolling of the midnight bell is a signal, but what does

it mean? Get up, Laura, and follow me: come out of your sleep, out of your bed, out of this strange house. What are you doing in this house? Without a word, without fear she rose and reached for Eugenio's hand, but he eluded her with a sharp, sly smile and drifted away. This is not all, you shall see— Murderer, he said, follow me, I will show you a new country, but it is far away and we must hurry. No, said Laura, not unless you take my hand, no; and she clung first to the stair rail, and then to the topmost branch of the Judas tree that bent down slowly and set her upon the earth, and then to the rocky ledge of a cliff, and then to the jagged wave of a sea that was not water but a desert of crumbling stone. Where are you taking me, she asked in wonder but without fear. To death, and it is a long way off, and we must hurry, said Eugenio. No, said Laura, not unless you take my hand. Then eat these flowers, poor prisoner, said Eugenio in a voice of pity, take and eat: and from the Judas tree he stripped the warm bleeding flowers, and held them to her lips. She saw that his hand was fleshless, a cluster of small white petrified branches, and his eye sockets were without light, but she ate the flowers greedily for they satisfied both hunger and thirst. Murderer! said Eugenio, and Cannibal! This is my body and my blood. Laura cried No! and at the sound of her own voice, she awoke trembling, and was afraid to sleep again.

MAVIS GALLANT

Sunday Afternoon

On a wet February afternoon in
the eighth winter of the Algerian war, two young Algerians
sat at the window table of a café behind Montparnasse station. Between them, facing the quiet street, was a European
girl. The men were dressed alike in the dark suits and ma-
roon ties they wore once a week, on Sunday. Their leather
jackets lay on the fourth chair. The girl was also dressed
for an important day. Her taffeta dress and crocheted collar
were new; the coat with its matching taffeta lining looked
home-sewn. She had thrown back the coat so that the lining
could be seen, but held the skirt around her knees. She was
an innocent from an inland place—Switzerland, Austria

perhaps. The slight thickness of her throat above the crocheted collar might have been the start of a goiter. She turned a gentle, stupid face to each of the men in turn, trying to find a common language. Presently one of the men stood up and the girl, without his help, pulled on her coat. These two left the café together. The abandoned North African sat passively with three empty coffee cups and a heaped ashtray before him. He had either been told to wait or had nothing better to do. The street lamps went on. The rain turned to snow.

Watching the three people in the café across the street had kept Veronica Baines occupied much of the afternoon. Like the Algerian sitting alone, she had nothing more interesting to do. She left the window to start a phonograph record over again. She looked for matches, and lit a Gitane cigarette. It was late in the day, but she wore a dressing gown that was much too large and that did not belong to her, and last summer's sandals. Three plastic curlers along her brow held the locks that, released, would become a bouffant fringe. Her hair, which was light brown, straight, and recently washed, hung to her shoulders. She was nineteen, and a Londoner, and had lived in Paris about a year. She stood pushing back the curtain with one shoulder, a hand flat on the pane. She seldom read the boring part of newspapers, but she knew there was, or there had been, a curfew for North Africans. She left the window for a moment, and when she came back she was not surprised to find the second Algerian gone.

She wanted to say something about the scene to the two men in the room behind her. Surely it meant something—

the Algerian boys and the ignorant girl? She held still. One of the men in the room was Tunisian and very touchy. He watched for signs of prejudice. When he thought he saw them, he was pleased and cold. He could be rude when he wanted to be; he had been educated in Paris and was schooled in the cold attack.

Jim Bertrand, whose flat this was, and Ahmed had not stopped talking about politics since lunch. Their talk was a wall. It shut out young girls and girlish questions. For instance, Veronica could have asked if there was a curfew, and if it applied to Ahmed as well as the nameless and faceless North Africans you saw selling flowers or digging up the streets; but Ahmed might consider it a racial question. She never knew just where he drew his own personal line.

"I am not interested in theories," she had taught herself to say, for fear of being invaded by something other than a dream. But she was not certain what she meant, and not sure that it was true.

Jim turned on a light. The brief afternoon became, abruptly, a winter night. The window was a black mirror. She saw how the room must appear to anyone watching from across the street. But no one peeped at them. Up and down the street, persiennes were latched, curtains tightly drawn. The shops were a line of iron shutters broken only by the Arab café, from which spilled a brownish and hideous light. The curb was lined with cars; Paris was like a garage. Shivering at the cold, and the dead cold of the lined-up automobiles, she turned to the room. She imagined a garden filled with gardenias and a striped umbrella. Ve-

ronica was a London girl. At first her dreams had been of
Paris, but now they were about a south she had not yet seen.

She moved across the room, scuffling her old sandals,
dressed in Jim's dressing gown. She dropped her cigarette
on the marble hearth, stepped on it, and kicked it under
the gas heater in the fireplace. Then she knelt and lifted the
arm of the record-player on the floor, starting again the
Bach concerto she had been playing most of the day. Now
she read the name of it for the first time: Concerto Italien
en Fa Majeur BWV 971. She had played it until it was
nothing more than a mosquito to the ear, and now that she
was nearly through with it, about to discard it for something newer, she wanted to know what it had been called.
Still kneeling, leaning on her fingertips, she reread the
front page of a Sunday paper. Is Princess Paola sorry she
has married a Belgian and has to live so far north? Deeply
interested, Veronica examined the Princess's face, trying to
read contentment or regret. Princess Paola, Farah of Iran,
Grace of Monaco, and Princess Margaret were the objects
of Veronica's solemn attention. Their beauty, their position,
their attentive husbands should have been enough. According to *France Dimanche,* anonymous letters might still
come in with the morning post. Their confidences went
astray. None of them could say "Pass the salt" without
wondering how far it would go.

When Jim and Ahmed talked on Sunday afternoon, Veronica was a shadow. If Princess Paola herself had lifted
the coffeepot from the table between them, they would have
taken no more notice than they now did of her. She picked
up the empty pot and carried it to the kitchen. She saw

herself in the looking glass over the sink: curlers, bath-robe—what a sight! Behind her was the music, the gas heater roaring away, and the drone of the men's talk.

Everything Jim had to say was eager and sounded as if it must be truthful. "Yes, I know," he would begin, "but look." He was too eager; he stammered. His Tunisian friend took over the idea, stated it, and demolished it. Ahmed was Paris-trained; he could be explicit about anything. He made sense.

"Sense out of hot air," said Veronica in the kitchen. "Perfect sense out of perfect hot air."

She took the coffeepot apart and knocked the wet grounds into the rest of the rubbish in the sink. She ran cold water over the pot and rinsed and filled it again; then she sat down on the low stepladder that was the only seat in the kitchen and ground new coffee, holding the grinder between her knees. At lunch the men had dragged chairs into the kitchen and stopped talking politics. But the instant the meal was finished they wanted her away; she sensed it. If only she could be dismissed, turned out to prowl like a kitten, even in the rain! But she lived here, with Jim; he had brought her here in November, four months ago, and she had no other home.

"I'm too young to remember," she heard Ahmed say, "and you weren't in Europe."

The coffeepot was Italian and composed of four alumi-num parts that looked as if they never would fit one inside the other. Jim had written instructions for her, and tacked the instructions above the stove, but she was as frightened by the four strange shapes as she had been at the start.

Somehow she got them together and set the pot on the gas flame. She put it on upside down, which was the right way. When the water began to boil, you turned the pot right way up, and the boiling water dripped through the coffee. You know when the water was boiling because a thread of steam emerged from the upside-down spout. That was the most important moment.

Afraid of missing the moment, the girl leaned on the edge of the table, which was crowded with luncheon dishes; pushed together, behind her, were the remains of the rice-and-tomato, the bones and fat of the mutton chops. The Camembert dried in the kitchen air; the bread was already stale. She did not take her eyes from the spout of the coffee-pot. She might have been dreaming of love.

"You still haven't answered me," said Jim in the next room. "Will Algeria go Communist? Yes or no."

"Tunisia didn't."

"You had different leaders."

"The Algerians are religious—the opposite of materialists."

"They could use a little materialism in Algeria," said Jim. "I've never been there, but you've only got to read. I've got a book here . . ."

Those two could talk poverty the whole day and never weary. They thought they knew what it was. Jim had never taken her to a decent restaurant—not even at the beginning, when he was courting her. He looked at the menu posted outside the door and if the prices seemed more than he thought simple working-class couples could pay he turned away. He wanted everyone in the world to have enough to eat, but he did not want them to enjoy what they were eating—that was how it seemed to Veronica. Ahmed lived in a cold room on the sixth floor of an old building, but he needn't have. His father was a fashionable doctor in Tunis. Ahmed said there was no difference between one North African and another, between Ahmed talking of sacrifice and the nameless flower seller whose existence was a sacrifice—that is to say, whose life appears to have no meaning; whose faith makes it possible; of whom one thinks he might as well be dead. All Veronica knew was that Ahmed's father was better off than her father had ever been. "I'm going to be an important personality," she had said to herself at the age of seventeen or so. Soon after, she ran away and came to Paris; someone got a job for her in a photographer's studio—a tidying-up sort of job, and not modeling, as she had hoped. In the office next to the studio, a drawer was open. She saw 100 Nouveaux Francs, a clean bill, on which the face of young Napoleon dared her, said, "Take it." She bought a pair of summer shoes for seventy francs and spent the rest on silly presents for friends. Walking in the shoes, she was new. She would never be the same unimportant Veronica again. The shoes were beige linen, and when she wore them in the rain they had to be thrown away. The friend who had got her the job made up the loss when it was discovered, but the story went round, and no photographer would have her again.

The coffeepot spitting water brought Jim to the kitchen. He got to the stove before Veronica knew what he was doing there. "I'm sorry," she said. "I was thinking about shoes."

"You need shoes?" He looked at her, as if trying to remember why he had loved her and what she had been like.
His glasses were thumb-printed and steamed; all his talk
was fog. He looked at her beautiful ankles and the scuffed
sandals on her feet. He had come from America to Paris
because he had a year to spend—just like that. Imagine
spending a whole year of life, when every minute mattered! He had to be sure about everything before he was
twenty-six; it was the limit he had set. But Veronica was
going to be a great personality, and it might happen any
day. She wanted to be a great something, and she wanted
to begin, but not like Jim—reading and thinking—and not
like that girl in taffeta, starting *her* experience with the two
Algerians.

"I think I could be nearly anything, you know." That
was what Veronica had said five months ago, when Jim
asked what she was doing, sitting in a sour café with ashes
and bent straws around her feet. She was prettier than any
of the girls at the other tables. She had spoken first; he
would never have dared. Her wrists were chapped where
her navy-blue coat had rubbed the skin. That was the first
thing he saw when he fell in love with her. That was what
he had forgotten when he looked at her so vaguely in the
kitchen, trying to remember what he had loved.

When he met her, she was homeless. It was a cause-and-
effect she had not foreseen. She knew that when you run
away from home you are brave—braver than anyone; but
then you have nowhere to live. Until Jim found her, fell in
love with her, brought her here, she spent hours on the
telephone, ringing up any casual person who might give
her a bed for the night. She borrowed money for bus tick-

ets, and borrowed a raincoat because she lost hers—left it in a cinema—and she borrowed books and forgot who belonged to the name on the flyleaf. She sold the borrowed books and felt businesslike and proud.

She stole without noticing she was stealing, at first. Walking with Jim, she strolled out of a bookshop with something in her hand. "You're at the Camus age," he said, thinking it was a book she had paid for. She saw she was holding "La Chute," which she had never read, and never would. They moved in the river of people down the Boulevard Saint-Michel, and he put his arm round her so she would not be carried away. The Boul'Mich was like a North African bazaar now; it was not the Latin Quarter of Baudelaire. Jim had been here three months and was homesick.

"It's wonderful to speak English," he said.

"You should practice your French." They agreed to talk French. "*Vous êtes bon,*" she said, gravely.

"*Mais je ne suis pas beau.*" It was true, and that was the end of the French.

They held hands on the Pont des Arts and looked down at the black water. He wanted to take her home, to an apartment he had rented in Montparnasse. It was a step for him; it was an event. He had to discuss it: love, honesty, the present, the past.

Yes, but be quick, I am dying of hunger and cold, she wanted to say.

She knew more about men than he did about women, and had more patience. She understood his need to talk about a situation without making any part of the situation clear.

"You ought to get a job," he said, when she had been living with him a month. He thought working would be good for her. He believed she should be working or studying—preparing for life. He thought life began only after it was prepared, but Veronica thought it had to start with a miracle. That was the difference between them, and why the lovely beginning couldn't last, and why he couldn't remember what he had loved. One day she said she had found work selling magazine subscriptions. He had never heard of that in France; he started to say so, but she interrupted him: "I used to sell the *Herald Tribune* on the street."

Soon after that, Jim met Ahmed, and every Sunday Ahmed came to talk. Jim wondered why he had been so hurt and confused by love. He discovered that it was easier to talk than read, and that men were better company than girls. After Jim met Ahmed, and after Veronica began selling magazine subscriptions, Jim and Veronica were happier. It was never as lovely as it had been at the beginning; that never came back. But Veronica had a handbag, strings of beads, a pink sweater, and a velvet ribbon for her hair. Perhaps that was all she wanted—a ribbon or so, the symbols of love that he should have provided. Now she gave them to herself. Sometimes she came home with a treasure; once it was a jar of caviar for him. It was a mistake—the kind of extravagance he abhorred.

"You shouldn't spend that way," he said. "Not on me."

"What does it matter? We're together, aren't we? As good as married?" she said sadly.

If they had been married, he would never have let her sell magazine subscriptions. They both knew it. She was not his wife but a girl in Paris. She was a girl, and although he would not have let her know it, almost his first. He was not attractive to women. His ugliness was unpleasant; it was the kind of ugliness that can make women sadistic. Veronica was the first girl pretty enough for Jim to want and desperate enough to have him. He had never met desperation at home, although he supposed it must exist. She was the homeless, desperate girl in Paris against whom he might secretly measure, one future day, a plain but confident wife.

"What's the good of saving money? If they come, they'll shoot me. If they don't shoot me, I shall wait for their old-age pensions. Apparently they have these gorgeous pensions." That was Veronica on the Russians. She said this now, putting the hot coffeepot down on a folded newspaper between the two men.

For Ahmed this was why women existed: to come occasionally with fresh coffee, to say pretty, harmless things. Bach sent spirals of music around the room, music that to the Tunisian still sounded like a coffee grinder. His idea of Paris was nearly just this—couples in winter rooms; coffee and coffee-grinder music on Sunday afternoon. Records half out of their colored jackets lay on the floor where Veronica had scattered them. She treated them as if they were toys, and he saw that she loved her toys best dented and scratched. "Come next Sunday," Jim said to Ahmed every week. Nearly every childless marriage has a bachelor friend. Veronica and Jim lived as though they were married, and Ahmed was the Sunday friend. Ahmed and Jim

had met at the Bibliothèque Nationale. They talked every
Sunday that winter. Ahmed lay back in the iron-and-canvas
garden chair, and Jim was straight as a judge in a hard
Empire armchair, the seat of which was covered with plastic
cloth. The flat had always been let to foreigners, and traces
of other couples and their passage remained—the canvas
chair from Switzerland, the American pink bathmat in the
ridiculous bathroom, the railway posters of skiing in the
Alps.

Ahmed liked talking to Jim, but he was uneasy with
liberals. He liked the way Jim carefully said "A*k*med," having learned that was how it was pronounced; and he was
almost touched by his questions. What did "Ben" mean?
Was it the same as the Scottish "Mac"? However, Jim's
liberalism brought Ahmed close to his mortal enemies; there
were Jews, for instance, who wrote the kindest book possible about North Africa and the Algerian affair. Here was
a novel by one of them. On the back of the jacket was the
photograph of the author, a pipe-smoking earnest young
intellectual—lighting his pipe, looking into the camera over
the flame. "Well, yes, but still a Jew," said Ahmed frankly,
and he saw the change in Jim—the face pink with embarrassment, the kind mouth opened to protest, to defend.

"I don't feel that way, I'm sorry." Jim brought out the
useful answer. In his dismay he turned the book over and
hid the author's face. He was sparing Ahmed now at the
expense of the unknown writer; but the writer was only a
photograph, and he looked an imbecile with that pipe.

Ahmed's attitudes were not acquired, like Jim's. They
were as much a part of him as his ears. He expected intel-

lectual posturing from men but detested clever women. He judged women by merciless, frivolous, secret rules. First, a girl must never be plain.

Veronica was not an intellectual, nor was she plain. She moved like a young snake; like a swan. She put a new pot of coffee down upon the table. She started the same record again, the same coffee-grinder sound. She stretched her arms, sighing, in a bored, frantic gesture. He saw the rents in the dressing gown when she lifted her arms. He could have given her more than Jim; she was not even close to the things she wanted.

Jim knew Ahmed was looking at Veronica. He wondered if he would mind if Ahmed fell in love with her. She was not Jim's; she was free. He had told her so again and again, but it made her cry, and he stopped saying it. He had imagined her free and proud, but when he said "You're free" she just cried. Would the fact that Ahmed was his friend, and a North African, mean a betrayal? It was a useless exercise, as pointless as pacing a room, but it was the kind of problem he exercised his brain with. He thought back and forth for a minute: How would I feel? Hurt? Shocked?

In less than the minute it was played out. Ahmed looked at Veronica and thought she was not worth a quarrel with his friend. *"Pas pour une femme,"* Sartre had said. Jim was too active in his private debate to notice Ahmed's interest withdrawn. Ahmed's look and its meaning were felt only by the girl. She turned to the window, with her back to the room. Suffering miserably, humiliated, she pressed her hands on the glass. The men had forgotten her. They laughed, as if Ahmed's near betrayal had made them closer friends. Jim poured his friend's coffee and pushed the sugar toward him. She saw the movement in the black glass.

She knew that Jim's being an American and Ahmed a North African made their friendship unusual, but that was apart. She didn't care about politics and color. They had nothing to do with her life. No, the difficulty for Veronica was always the same: when a man was alone he wanted her, but when there were two men she was in the way. The admiration of men, when she was the center of attention, could not make up for their indifference when they had something to say to each other. She resented the indifference more than any amount of notice taken of another woman. She could have made pudding of a rival girl.

"The little things are so awful," said Jim. "Look, I was on the ninety-five bus. The bus stopped because they were changing drivers. There were two Algerians, and without even turning around to see why the bus stopped where it shouldn't, they pulled out their identity papers to show the police. It's automatic. Something unusual—the police."

"It is nearly finished," said Ahmed.

"Do you think so? That part?"

In one of the Sunday papers there was a new way of doing horoscopes. It was complicated and you needed a mathematician's brain, but anything was better than standing before the window with nothing to see. She found a pencil and sat down on the floor. I was born in '43 and Jim in '36. We're both the same month. That makes ten points in common. No, the ten points count against you.

"Ahmed, when were you born?"

"I am a Lion, a Leo, of the year 1939," Ahmed said.

"It'll take a minute to work out."

Presently she straightened up with the paper in her hand and said, "I can't work it out. Ahmed, you're going to travel. Princess Margaret's a Leo and she's going to travel. It must be the same thing."

That made them laugh, and they looked at her. When they looked, she felt brave again. She stood over them, as if she were one of them. "I can't tell if I'm going to have twins or have rheumatism," she said. "I'm given both. Actually, I think *I'll* travel. I've got to think of my future, as Jim says. I don't think Paris is the right place. Summer might be the time to move on. Somewhere like the Riviera."

"What would you do there?" said Ahmed.

"Sell magazine subscriptions," she said, smiling. "Do you know I used to sell the *Herald Tribune?* I really and truly did. I wore one of those ghastly sweaters they make you wear. If I sold something like a hundred and ninety-nine, I could pay for my hotel room. That was before I met Jim. I had to keep walking with the papers because of the law. If you stand still on a street with a pile of newspapers in your arms, you're what's called a kiosk, and you need a special permit. Now I sell magazine subscriptions and I can walk or stand still, just as I choose."

"I've never seen you," said Ahmed.

"She makes a fortune," said Jim. "No one refuses. It's her face."

"I'm not around where you are," said Veronica to Ahmed. "I'm around the Madeleine, where the tourists go."

"I'll come and see you there," said Ahmed. "I'd like to

see you selling magazine subscriptions to tourists around
the Madeleine."

"I earn enough for my clothes," said Veronica. "Jim
needn't dress me."

She could not keep off her private grievances. As soon
as his friend was attacked, Ahmed turned away. He looked
at the books on the shelf over the table where Jim did his
thinking and reading. Jim was mute with unhappiness. He
tried to remember the beginning. Had either of them said
a word about clothes?

She could go on standing there, holding the newspaper
and the futures she had been unable to work out. There
must be something she could do. In the kitchen, the wash-
ing up? The bedroom? She could dress. In the silence she
had caused, she thought of questions she might ask: "Ahmed, are you the same as those Algerians in the café?" "Am
I any better than that girl?"

They began to talk when Veronica was in the bedroom.
Their voices were different. They were glad she was away.
She knew it. Veronica thought she heard her name. They
wanted her to be someone else. They didn't deserve her as
she was. They wanted Brigitte Bardot and Joan of Arc.
They want everything, she said to herself. In the bedroom
there was nothing but a double bed and pictures of ballet
dancers someone had left tacked to the walls.

She returned to them, dressed in a gray skirt and sweater
and high-heeled black shoes. She had put her hair up in a
neat plait, and her fringe was brushed out so that it nearly
touched her eyelashes.

Jim was in the kitchen. He had closed the door. She

heard him pulling the ladder about. He kept books and papers on the top shelf of the kitchen cupboard. She sat down in his chair, primly, and folded her hands.

"You are well dressed these days," said Ahmed, as if their conversation had never stopped.

"I'm not what you think," she said. "You know that. I said 'around the Madeleine' for a joke. I sometimes take things. That's all."

"What things? Money?" He looked at her without moving. His long womanish hands were often idle.

"Where would I ever see money? Not *here*. *He* doesn't leave it around. Nobody does, for that matter. I take little things, in the shops. Clothes, and little things. Once a jar of caviar for Jim, but he didn't want it."

"You'll get into trouble," Ahmed said.

"It's all here, all safe," said Jim, coming back, smiling. "I'm like an old maid, you know, and I hate keeping money in the house, especially an amount like this."

He put the paper package on the table. It was the size of a pound of coffee. They looked at it and she understood. She was older than she had ever been, even picking Jim up in a café. There it is: money. It makes no difference to them. It is life and death for me. "What is it, Jim?" she said carefully, pressing her hands together. "What is it for? Is it for politics?" She remembered the two men in the café and the girl with the thick innocent throat. "Is it about politics? Is it for the Algerians? Was it in the kitchen a long time?" Slowly, carefully, she said, "What wouldn't you do for other people! Jim never spends anything. He needs a reason, and I'm not a reason. Ahmed, is it yours?"

"It isn't mine," said Ahmed.

"Why didn't you tell me it was here, Jim? Don't you trust me?"

"You can see we trust you," said Jim.

"We're telling you now."

"You didn't tell me you had it here because you thought I'd spend it," she said. She looked at the paper as if it were a stuffed object—a dead animal.

"I never thought of it as money," said Jim. "That's the truth."

"It's anything except the truth," she said, her hands tight. "But it doesn't matter. There's never a moment money isn't money. You'd like me to say 'It isn't money,' but I won't. If I'd known, I'd have spent it. Wouldn't I just! Oh, wouldn't I!"

"It wasn't money," said Jim, as if it had stopped existing. "It was something I was keeping for other people." Collected for a reason, a cause. And hidden.

None of them touched it. Ahmed looked sleepy. This was a married scene in a winter room; the bachelor friend is exposed to this from time to time. He must never take sides.

"You both think you're so clever," said the girl. "You haven't even enough sense to draw the curtains." While they were still listening, she said, "It's not my fault if you don't like me. Both of you. I can't help it if you wish I was something else. Why don't you take better care of me?"

CHRISTINA STEAD

The Puzzleheaded Girl

Debrett liked his job in the old-
style German Bank in Broad Street, but he soon saw that
the partners' sons were coming into the firm and he could not
rise far; so he joined three friends of his, Arthur Good, Tom
Zero and Saul Scott who had just formed the Farmers' Utilities Corporation. They were all in their early twenties.

It was a new office building, scarcely completed, built
like a factory; everything was in contrast with the German
Bank's offices smelling of old wood, the ink and grease of
ledgers, hair oil and dust, crumbling bindings. Here the
elevator opened into carpeted offices. There was a waiting
room with soft leather seats, photographs of farms, farmers

and machinery, a doorman, a pretty girl receptionist, an outer office with busy clerks. The uniformed doorman, Fisher, was a retired policeman, who looked like a fine old small-town banker; and could be useful as a bouncer. The head clerk was Saul Scott's secretary, Vera Day who was studying law; and the head typist was Maria Magna, business-like, impatient.

One November Saturday afternoon, working overtime, they sent out for lunch; the paper cups were still on the desks when doorman Fisher told Debrett that a girl was waiting for an interview. They still needed a filing clerk. One of the typists, a boyish girl named Charlotte and called Sharlie, went out to look her over. A young seventeen, perhaps, dressed like a poor schoolgirl, she sat reading a small book, her light brown hair over her plain grave face. She looked up, a sweet and wistful expression appeared. Sharlie withdrew, and reported: "She's just a high school kid reading art to impress the customers, an innocent—doesn't know she's alive yet."

Augustus Debrett, a stubby dark man with large hazel eyes, a round head, with pale face turned blue with the winter light, sat between two large windows, behind a big polished desk on which was nothing but a blotter and an inkstand.

She stood for a moment in the doorway looking at the room; the light fell on her. He saw a diffident girl in a plain tan blouse, a tight navy-blue skirt, very short at a time when skirts were not short, round knees, worn walking shoes; she wore no overcoat. "Miss Lawrence, come in."

She had a chin dimple and a dimple in her left cheek, a

flittering smile; and when the smile went, her face returned
to its gravity, its almost sadness. She had a full, youthful
figure. She said she was eighteen. She sat down keeping
her knees together and holding her skirt on her knees with
her brown purse. The little book she placed on the desk in
front of her. It was a book in English on French symbolism.
He looked at her face a moment before he began to question
her. "Surely Honor Lawrence is a New England name? It
sounds like Beacon Hill," and he laughed kindly in case it
was not Beacon Hill. No answer. She said she had experience and wanted a good wage, and then she named a low
wage and said she had no references: "Only my school-
teacher." "Where was your last job?" After a pause, she
said, "I could start now if you liked." Debrett engaged her.
"Come on Monday. If you've been out of a job for some
time, you may be short of money. Do you need money
now? I can give you an advance." "Oh, no, I have money."
She got up and went to the door. There she turned and
said quietly, "Thank you." As she was going out, Tom
Zero, the young lawyer, one of the partners, entered. He
was short, slender, debonair and so swarthy that he was
looked at curiously in restaurants in the South, handsome
and dark-eyed from two olive-skinned parents from southern Europe, fastidious but with a faint sweet personal odor,
like grass and olives: ambitious, bright and selfish.

"I've engaged Miss Lawrence as filing clerk: she's coming on Monday," said Debrett. Zero looked sharply. "Have
you looked at her references? Can she type?" "Yes," said
Debrett. The girl looked straight into Zero's eyes and
moved away. Later, Debrett thought about her, her poverty
and her book.

He had a socialist meeting that night and got home late. No food was laid out for him. His wife who was up early and in the middle of the night with her newborn son was asleep now. He got himself some bread and cheese and a cup of coffee and began to walk about the living room making calculations, repeating his speech at the meeting, the objections and the answers. He baffled professional hecklers by treating them as sincerely puzzled people; and he answered them in good faith. They would sit down, turn away, sincerely puzzled. He wanted to tell his wife what had happened; and he even thought of mentioning the girl to her. Miss Lawrence's address was on the fourth floor of a house in a tenement district far uptown. "A poor, prudish New England family—well-educated, spoke a choice English—New Englanders are poor too—" Such a girl might preserve a girl's primness for years, might be really innocent. "What does a man really know about girls? A man feels he has to be a wise guy and he can misjudge."

Strongest of all were her gray eyes. They looked casually away into the distance, taking her far away, or they looked with hypnotic pinpoint intentness into his eyes, as if someone else were there, not this timid girl; someone indifferent, wise, uncaught.

It was his habit to walk up and down, up and down and go to bed long after midnight. His wife Beatrice was up several times before that with the sickly child. He admired her uncomplaining devotion, he admired her and her mind; but he was irritated by the disorder. He had no sympathy with the child. But his wife had said, "What did we get married for?" This was reasonable, customary. Yet he thought, "If you loved me, you would not need anything else." "My life is empty," she would say; "marriage sucks life out of a woman." She was not happy with the child, but she was busy, her life was not empty; and it seemed to him as if his life was empty. He felt he was not loved and never had been. "She has been very patient with me, since she does not love me," he said to himself.

Miss Lawrence always carried books on art and painters, ostentatiously perhaps, to mark that she was interested in better things than the office; but she read the books; and almost every day, Debrett encouraged her. She would listen in silence, as if not quite in agreement; but when he made social comments or deductions, she would lower her eyes or look out of the window. She was polite and yet odd. She lingered too long when bringing papers to executives; at a glance or word, she went out delicately, gravely or even with a slight smile; sly perhaps? She made few mistakes, typed well; if corrected, she pouted. A spoiled and favored child? A coquette? She rarely spoke to the other girls; liked no one but the senior, Vera Day, who was kind to her. For weeks she wore the same navy-blue skirt; but presently she had a white shirt-blouse as well as the tan, and a beret and a short gray tweed cape; a singular outfit, though she looked neat.

Arthur Good, who originated the Farmers' Utilities Corporation, was dark, pale-skinned, middle-sized, slender, a joyous unprincipled schemer who turned out legal and illegal maneuvres day and night. He saw loopholes everywhere. Arthur was of Italian origin, he had married an Italian girl, had, at twenty-five, already deserted her and was living with a serious French-Canadian girl he would never be able to marry. He was amused at Honor's delicate dawdling and once or twice ran his hand lightly down her hip and touched her stockinged knee. She drew back, ran out of his office. "Like a young cat, lascivious and scared," he said, "not for Artie." As for Tom Zero, he at once realized that she was attracted to him and he was abrupt with her, bored and hostile. He had a fair wife and two small fair children. She was out of place in the commonplace activity of his office.

"I know where you live," said Gus Debrett mildly; "I know that street. I was up there only the other day. I had to go to a meeting near there. I looked in at your place but did not see your name on the letter boxes. Are you a subtenant? A lodger?" She answered indirectly as usual. She lived alone with her father. And then, in an undertone, a spurt of talk. She wanted to live nearer to Greenwich Village. She wanted to find a room in that district, but everything was dear; she hadn't the money and she hadn't friends. She didn't know where to look. Where could she look? She knew no one but her brother, Walter Lawrence, the painter, who shared, with an actor, an old studio at the corner of University Place. They would not take her in.

Debrett listened eagerly now. Her brother was a painter who had just made his name by winning a prize and a fellowship, his was one of the new names in the city. "That is why you are interested in painting! It's your brother's influence? But perhaps you yourself paint?"

No; and she didn't agree with her brother's views. "He gives himself airs, people are running after him; but he hasn't a theory."

"Are your parents very proud?"

Her mother was dead.

"It must be rather difficult for you," said Debrett in a low voice. "I suppose you have to look after the house and your father when you go home from work." She did not reply, sitting up straight, gazing out the window an untranslatable feeling flickering in her face.

"Well, if things are difficult at any time, tell me; I'll do what I can."

She said nothing.

"I wish you knew my wife; she is very understanding, a great friend to women and she would know how to help you. But she's at her mother's at present, as you know," he continued to smile, "since you write my letters to her." The girl listened indifferently; Debrett, supple and enthusiastic, began to talk about his wife's nature, her intelligence and goodness. "She is very loyal and thoughtful; she understands people better than I do . . . In the meantime, perhaps her friend, Myra Zero, cauld have a talk with you. We all want to help you." He talked on and on, quixotically, looking at her with his beautiful dark eyes sometimes gay, sometimes mournful. He paused. After a moment, she said, "My brother talks too much: he has an opinion on everything." "Well, you had better go now, if you want to."

Their business was growing. They added carbide to their commodities and were selling it in quantities in coal mining districts. They had to buy more office machines, including a Moon bookkeeping machine. An instructor was sent along with it. Debrett thought this a good chance for Miss Lawrence to earn more money. She had been with them all the winter; cold spring had come, and she had added very little to her office clothing; the cape but no coat, the same shoes, often sodden, and her hair worn simply as a little girl. Debrett called in Maria Magna who set the girl to the machine. She learned quickly and got it right in an hour or so. Tom Zero coming into the office, glanced over her shoulder and said to Maria Magna, "I see the new girl is getting to work on the bookkeeping." "Yes, I think she'll do it," said Maria Magna, a little warmth in her voice for the first time. But when the instructor had gone, Miss Lawrence rose from the machine and going over to Miss Magna, said she could learn the machine, but she would not, she would have nothing to do with accounts, money machines and sales. "I came here to make a living, but I won't mix in business."

Miss Magna bustled into Mr. Debrett with this story. "Tell her to come in." She appeared at once.

"I understand that you're good on the new machine but you don't want to work it?"

"No. I won't do it."

"Why?"

"I have to earn my living in an office, but I won't mix in business. I hate and despise business and anything to do with making money."

"Do you think it's wrong?"

"It is the enemy of art."

"And you feel yourself an artist?"

"No. But I want to live with artists and live like them. I don't want to be like those earthy girls out there, like Maria Magna and Vera Day. I prefer to die of hunger. Or go away."

"But you have no money."

"No. But it doesn't matter. I can get along without money. In the Village, artists get along without money. They all help each other. It's a different kind of living. This is a terrible world here, everyone working for money, no one working for anything good."

"My God, I think so myself. Things ought to be different; and one day they will be." But, as always, when a word was said that was, however remotely, challenging on social matters, she shut her mind. "You don't think so?" She raised her brown head in its childish hair and he saw the maiden breasts move as she drew in a breath. "You don't think so?"

"I don't think so," she said primly.

"Well, you must feel you're an artist; that you have some other plan for living," he pressed her.

"I don't know; I don't know what these things are," she said vaguely. Tears came into her eyes. "I don't know why I am here."

"You're a good girl," he said, getting up and about to go to her, but glancing at the half-glazed partitions which divided the offices. "Well, go out now and do your work. You do your work well."

"Yes, but I hate it," she said, frowning. She had dried her tears. "It's unworthy. It's not worthy of man."

"Man?"

"Mankind, people. Artists don't think like this; artists don't fight for money."

"That's the old Bostonian highmindedness," he said respectfully. "You don't meet it often in Manhattan."

With a flick of her short skirt she was out of his office. He saw her a few minutes later sitting in the middle of the clerk's room, a high window lighting her hair, as she bent over the telephone book. This surprised him, for she did not like the telephone and made a fuss about taking her turn at the switchboard; although, as at the Moon machine, she was competent. What was she looking at? He also liked to read the telephone book, pictures, data and conclusions forming in his memory as he read. He was stirred by her curious protests which he felt had a meaning; and he was puzzled. Later on, Tom Zero came to him and remarked, "What about this new girl? Let's get rid of her. She's not obliging, she makes too much fuss."

"She's a sort of miracle in our age and town," said Debrett. "She's terribly poor and needs money, but she won't learn the machine because it's too close to gross money making. She can do figures but she despises them. Her brother's Walter Lawrence the painter, supposed to be one of our best painters, and she hero-worships him. We have to be human. Can you imagine a girl who needs fares and clothes and probably even bread, giving up a raise on principle?"

"Well, if you're interested in her, all right, but I hope you're right."

"I'm a happily married man and I'm only interested in my fellow human being, when I see an ingenuous or a pure soul struggling with the world, man or woman; but it strikes me that women struggle oftener. Men don't fight moral battles."

"Moral battles arise when two sets of ethics clash, they're

not in themselves admirable," said Tom Zero. "She'll adjust herself, I suppose. Let her do her work and keep her morals for home. Some buyers are in town today from Market Wheeling, Ohio, the brothers we wrote to. They want to go out tonight, want someone to show them around, the theater, a nightclub, you know? Will you do it?"

"No, I won't," said Debrett. "You know what they want. They want an obscene show; that's what these hicks want in New York."

"Well, someone has to do it," said Zero "I can't. Myra has people to dinner. Scott has an opinion to write and he wouldn't anyway· Good has his father-in-law visiting, trying to patch up his marriage; and the others are tied up, too."

"Well, I'm tied up. Beatrice expects me to be home if she phones. She's not happy. The baby gets her up at six or four; her mother nags her. I'm her only friend. I have to go to my meetings; but she wouldn't understand that sort of night out and I wouldn't understand it myself. Let them hire a guide."

"No, it's a courtesy we owe them. I'd like you to do it. You're a sociable man."

"If that's the price of my staying here, I'll hand in my resignation. I won't do it."

"Don't get heated. Who will though?"

"Try the sales staff, try the carbide men. Why not Big Bill? He's amusing and foulmouthed, known in every whorehouse from coast to coast. They'll like him." said Debrett, already laughing.

"Yes, you're right. If he's in the house."

He went out but turned as he grasped the door handle and shot a sharp glance at the mild man sitting at the desk. Debrett nodded gaily.

When he reached home, Zero said to his wife, "Pity we didn't invite Gus to dinner. He's lonely. Beatie's out of town."

"Oh, she's only gone off to her mother at Morristown." After a moment, she said, "Any particular reason?"

"How does Gus manage?"

"Oh, he scrambles for himself, I guess. He's never home when she is at home. Why, what about Gus?"

"Well, let's ask Debrett some night soon."

"Wait till Beatie comes home."

"All right."

"You have to pick your company for Gus Debrett. He doesn't care what he says. It's all right with us."

"He's diplomatic in business. He's a good wangler."

"But all his outside friends are mavericks."

"Is that what Beatie says?" asked Tom with a smile.

"Oh, Beatie's very loyal."

He smiled. "I see. Just the same. Is that adult? To be always at her mother's?"

"Well, it saves Gus money, Beatie says. And I suppose Beatie's family help them out."

Zero laughed. "I'm sure they don't. More likely, Debrett has to lend them a hundred dollars to eat occasionally."

She said irritably, "Everyone knows how the Honitons spend."

"Yes," said Zero laughing. He added, "I believe if they both died in an accident tonight, God forbid, the Debretts

would have to pay for the funeral expenses and be torn
to pieces by screaming creditors as well."

"Still, it's her mother and she wants to be near her,"
said Myra. "What's your drift? You know how devoted
Gus is."

"Too devoted."

"Explain that, Tom."

The guests began to arrive.

The next day Miss Magna reported that one of the visitors
from Market Wheeling had been idling in the office, jaunty
with the girls, when he passed his hand over Miss Lawrence's shoulder. She sprang at him and hit him with what
she had in her hand—a file. "Send her in to me," said Tom
Zero, holding Miss Magna with his eye. The girl came in
softly. "I hear you hit one of my clients," he said insultingly.
She scowled. He looked at her curiously. "Come here."
She approached. He looked up at her, observing her charm.
"Why?"

"No one can touch me," she said. They were close. His
face flushed. He said gently, "Well, go and behave yourself," and touched her hand with his fingers. She took his
oval fine hand and looked into his face. "I'll have a letter
for you later on," he said. She went. Later he gave the
letter to another girl. She seemed to take no notice.

The Zeros had an apartment on the sixth floor of a new
brick building in the East Eighties. Over the sidewalk was
a blue awning with the number on it in white. There was
a square-tiled entrance hall with palms, behind which two
staircases rose; an elevator, a doorman in blue uniform.

The doorman sat at a small table near the entrance, his back to the radiator. He was supposed to examine callers and announce them through a house-phone, but he let those pass he summed up as respectable; and so he let pass a lady-like girl who said she was expected at Mrs. Zero's.

Myra Zero opened the door. The girl, in a new raincoat and hat, stood there without saying a word, looking at her. "Who do you want?" "I'm Miss Honor Lawrence." "Yes." "Are you Mrs. Zero?" "Yes." The girl stepped eagerly forward and Myra, in surprise, stepped back; the girl was inside. She herself shut the door and began taking off her gloves. "How do you do? You know of me, don't you?" she said politely. "I don't know you." "I work for your husband, Mr. Tom Zero." "Is something wrong?" "Wrong?" "Come in," said Myra with reserve, looking the girl up and down: brown velvet skirt, brown kid shoes and handbag, brown felt hat, no cosmetics, self-possessed. She looked around and said casually, "I didn't think it would be like this." "No? Won't you sit down?" She sat and looked around her critically. "I thought I ought to talk to you." "Why?" Myra said with a slight start. "I have such a long walk to work— my father won't give me the fare. You see, I have to give him everything. Someone gave me a skirt. He doesn't think I ought to have money for myself. He says, What is it for? And I won't explain. I'm too proud. It's a long walk. Then I have to go back and cook all night. If I go out the door afterward, he's angry, very angry. And men do speak to me. I don't like that. If I could find a room, nearer the office, I'd make some friends. I thought you could advise me. My sister's married and doesn't come near us. She sent

me this skirt. My mother died years ago. My brother—"
She was looking at the paintings on the walls, and stopped,
eyeing one of them.

"I'm sorry your mother is dead."

"Oh, she died years ago. She wasn't sick. She was miserable. We used to go and sit with the neighbors. Mother
would never ask for anything, and neither did I. She
wouldn't allow me to. When my father came home, he
unlocked the door and we could go in. Or we sat on the
stairs. But the neighbors asked us in and made us eat something. Father was afraid we would eat before he came
home. My father locked all the windows and nailed them
down. It was hot in summer and I liked sitting on the
stairs. I have to scrub the floor and wash the things with
water and no soap—" She told this in an interested tone.
She then said trustfully, "I never told anyone all this before.
I suppose it's a bit unusual. But I never knew there were
happy families. I thought that was all a lie. I didn't know
there were rich people either." She once more looked
around the room. "Well, you see, he takes my money, to
pay for the food and rent he gave me as a child. The others
have left home, so I will never be through paying. I must
leave. But I don't know where to go. I thought you might
know. Perhaps somewhere here," she continued, looking
out the window toward the other houses. "All the houses in
the city! When I'm walking I look at them all and think,
There are plenty of rooms in there, or at least someone who
could give me a bed. My father takes all my money. He
puts it away somewhere and he doesn't want to buy food.
I don't want to think about it. I never think about it. But I
want to leave."

"You're in trouble," said Mrs. Zero. "I'll make some coffee while I'm thinking about your problem." She went out and presently came back. "Do they know at the office that you're here? Does my husband know?" Miss Lawrence was looking at the paintings. She turned her head slowly, "I asked for the afternoon off." "To visit me, you mean?" "Yes." "Did my husband tell you to come here?" "No. But I heard you were a good woman." "Who told you that?" "They were saying in the office that Mr. Zero is a good man." "And that means I'm good." "Yes." "He's a very good man."

Afterward the wife said, "You want to pay rent, do you?"

"I can't pay much rent. Aren't there people who would give you a bed, just a bed? I could clean the house for them. I do it at home. Sometimes I have to do it over again in the middle of the night."

"Why?"

"He makes me get up. He says it isn't clean enough. So I could easily do two hours a day."

"That wouldn't be necessary, I think."

As Miss Lawrence was going, she hesitated, holding her purse tight and standing upright, looking expectantly at Mrs. Zero. "Is there anything you want?" The girl shook her head. "Are you going back to the office now?" "Yes." "Have you any money?" She did not answer. "You can't walk down to the office. It would take too long. I'll give you your fare." The girl smiled, held out her hand saying, "Thank you for the coffee. You've been very kind," and went toward the stairs. "Wait for the elevator." She did so. When the car had reached their floor, Miss Lawrence said, "Could I see you again?" "Yes, if you like. Come to dinner some night." "Thank you very much. You are really very kind." Holding her empty purse tightly, she passed out of sight. Myra thought about the episode for some time and when her husband came home, she kept the surprise for a while. She was flattered.

"Miss Lawrence came to see me."

"Who is that?"

"From your office."

He thought for a moment and asked, "What for?"

"I am not sure. She said she had the afternoon off to see me. Isn't that odd?"

"Maria Magna wants her to go. Perhaps she gave her time off to look for a job."

"Well, she needs a room and she thought I might know of one."

"Why you?"

"I don't know." They came to no conclusion. "I asked her to dinner."

"Why?"

"She asked to see me again, and so I asked her. Don't ask me why."

"I don't want this," he said casually.

"No date was mentioned. She may not think of it for months," said Myra.

The next evening about half past six, Miss Lawrence came to the door, looking exactly as before, said good evening and remarked, "I know I'm not late, because Mr. Zero was still in the office when I left."

Myra Zero was in a hurry. "What have you come for?"

"You asked me to dinner yesterday."

"I'm getting the children to bed. Come in. Go and sit

where you were yesterday and I'll be in when I can."

When she came back, the girl was sitting in the same chair as before, with her legs stretched out and her eyes closed. As soon as Myra entered, she began to talk trustfully, "I saw my brother and told him you were helping me."

Myra watched her husband when he entered. He was a discreet man. He said, "Oh, it was for tonight, then?" and offered her a drink. "Oh, thank you. I don't drink," she said timidly. She refused a cigarette in the same way, and when he said, "You don't play cards either?" she replied, "I don't know what they are. Do you mean—" she hesitated.

"So your family is religious. But you go dancing?" "Oh, no," she exclaimed with horror. "Do you think dancing is wrong?" asked Myra. "It's such a stupid waste of time." "Then what do you think people should do?" Myra asked, for she and Tom loved dancing and had once won a prize. "I don't know what others should do," said the girl. They had a light meal and the girl soon left, saying she had to be in by nine. "Are you walking home?" "Yes." "Why? Is it for health reasons?" said Zero sarcastically. But Myra went to the door and gave her a dollar. "You can pay me back when you've found a room and have the money. It's our secret." The girl was astounded. "Secret?" She examined the dollar bill. "I mustn't spend it?" She looked at Myra while she explained, a new and astonished understanding on her face. "Or you can have it, keep it." "Oh, no, I'll pay it back."

"I hope this is not going to become a habit," said Myra. "She makes me giddy. She doesn't understand the simplest conventions."

"She's just a young goose. I'll tell Miss Magna to teach

her the elements. But better would be to lose her. It's Gus who's mothering her."

"How old is she?"

"Eighteen."

"She's very immature. But her father keeps her a prisoner."

"Myra, that's not our affair."

"Oh, you're right. But she's touching."

Debrett was a married bachelor. After work he walked the streets, went to a political club, a friend's house, or chess café on Second Avenue, to talk politics and have a cup of coffee. He never drank anything else and ate little. He did not play chess, but there was talk there and a man could sit there the whole evening for only one or two cups of coffee and need not buy a sandwich. A middle-aged woman, living on the ground floor of his apartment building, lent him her daily help for half an hour a day to tidy his apartment. It was never untidy. Debrett was only at home in the evening at times prearranged with a New Jersey friend, born to the name of Goldentopf, recently changed to Seymour. Seymour was a tall thin fair North German type who thought he looked English. He was still living at home with his father, a wholesale butcher who made money; but he despised him, his brothers and sisters, the State of New Jersey and also the United States. "There are natural aristocrats and natural butchers," he said. He kept his gramophone and a large collection of records at Debrett's in New York and often went there to hear new music, and to conduct orchestral records with a baton. He greatly admired Beatrice Debrett and Debrett admired Seymour. Seymour's evenings excepted, Debrett did not return to his apartment till eleven o'clock, or after. There, he would walk up and down working out financial and political problems till very late and then fall into bed. For the newborn child, they had moved out to a street high-banked and bristling with new apartment houses, near the Grand Concourse, in the Bronx. He had to leave his home at half past seven to get to his working place at nine; and an evening appointment brought him home after his wife was in bed. She was an early sleeper, early riser. He ate out, or got himself a bit of bread and cheese when he returned. Now that his wife was away, he telephoned her every day at her Morristown home; or sent daily letters from the office, a husband's love letters, consoling and pleading. If he called at a friend's house, he would take some coffee, talk for several hours, and afterward, he might walk many blocks uptown, thinking and talking excitedly to himself under his breath.

He did not like to have his letters to his wife typed by these earthy girls in the office, and so he dictated them to Miss Lawrence, to whom he could explain everything. Through these letters and talks she knew of his great love for his wife and it seemed to Debrett that they could all be friends. He wondered about her life; she must be lonely. Sometimes he gave her a long look, but there was no response in her eyes. "She is certainly not interested in anyone here. She must be thinking of her talks in the Village with her artist friends." He walked around the Village, too, now, looking in at windows of studios and coffee shops, thinking he might see her; just to add a faint human interest to his evening.

One evening, reaching his street in the Bronx at eleven

thirty, he was surprised to see the light on in his fifth floor apartment. He thought that his wife had returned. In the elevator he had a glad and disturbed face; had his letters brought her home too soon? He had hinted at his loneliness recently. Was it right, when she came home only to his late hours and the distance from the center? She did not make friends easily; she disliked the district. She was the kind of woman who trusted only women; and even those were friends from high-school days, mostly women who had not married. She found comfort in them and their courageous struggle.

When he opened the door, Miss Lawrence walked out of the living room into the small square hall. "What are you doing here?" he called out. "What is wrong?" "I thought your wife was coming and I wanted to see her." "But she isn't coming tonight. How will you get home now?" "I thought she was coming tonight," she said sadly. "It doesn't matter: good night," and she held out her hand. He detained her. "How did you get in?" "A man was here and let me in." "What man?" "I don't know. He was playing records; I sat in the other room." "Have you had anything to eat since you left the office?" "No." He was hungry himself and asked her to eat something with him. She refused. "Have you money for the subway?" She began to walk toward the stairs without answering, her head lowered in thought. At the turn of the staircase, she waved her hand. He ran after her. "Where are you going? Come back. You can't walk home." "I could stay here," she said, raising innocent eyes to him. "With me?" "Yes." "My dear girl—you must take a taxi home." She took the money indifferently. When he got in again, he telephoned Seymour, a dry, unforgiving and ribald bachelor, at the moment sour with disapproval. "I never thought you would do that to Beatie, Gus. It's unworthy of you both. A typist—a typist today is like a servant girl in your father's time. I'd watch my step if I were you. You would forfeit my entire respect." It was hard to explain to a stick like Seymour. Gus explained a little and then said he was tired. "Has she gone?" Seymour persisted. "I must get to bed, Alec. I'm tired out. She came to see Beatrice. She's a very strange girl. I don't understand her myself, but I think she needs help." At this, Seymour laughed drily, told a dirty joke; Debrett laughed and said good-bye.

"In any case," said Seymour, "Beatrice will be home in a day or two, perhaps tomorrow. I telephoned her from your place, while the girl was there and told her she ought to be here." "Perhaps she should, but that's up to her. I don't want her made anxious when she's recovering. She's not very happy and this has been her chance to recover." "If I thought you weren't good to her, I'd have a very low opinion of you," said the bachelor. "I do my best, but happiness is a mystery. One can't manufacture happiness for another human being, especially a sensitive lonely soul like Beatrice."

At the office the next day, he sent for the girl. "What time did you get home last night?" "I don't know. The door was locked. I slept on the landing, until early this morning, when a neighbor took me in, and I got washed." "That is terrible, terrible." She said nothing; looked around. "What did you want to see my wife about?" "Just something private." She seemed as on other days; and he wondered what other nights she had spent on the landing, at a neighbor's. When he reached his street that night about eleven, again he saw his lights on. He walked about anxiously for some minutes, then went upstairs. His wife was sitting in an armchair in the living room wearing a handsome blue dressing gown. She was beautiful, but to him, unlike herself.

"Augustus!" she checked herself; "I have been sitting here, waiting for you for hours." "Why didn't you let me know you were coming?" he cried gladly, rushed over, hugged her. "Did you miss me?" she said, with her usual coolness; but she laughed a trifle and made advances, unlike her and which chilled him. "You know I can't live without you." "Lonely is as lonely does," she said, with pathetic wit. She had no sense of humor. "I'd better go to the kitchen and get a bite; I haven't eaten yet." "I made something for you." "Did you, Beatrice? That was very kind. You are tired. I know this is late for you. But I'm glad you stayed up." He was very glad.

The next day he sent for Miss Lawrence for some letters. "But no more for my wife," he said laughing. "Do you know why? You were remarkably close to the truth. She came home last night unexpectedly. You must go and see her in a few days, when she's a bit more settled. You'll like her. Women like her; and she's very good and understanding."

And one evening the following week, when he got home at ten, his wife was again waiting for him. Presently she said, "Your secretary was here." "Who?" "Miss Lawrence, your secretary." "She was here? I remember—she asked for time off. She said she had an appointment." "And of course what Miss Lawrence wants, she gets," she said pertly. "She's been wanting to talk to you for over a week." "Over a week! You told her to come and see me. Or she seemed to think you did." "Let's not have a misunderstanding over the poor girl." "Let's go to the kitchen and you have your sandwich." "Oh, is there a sandwich? Thank you."

While eating, he searched her face hungrily. "Well, Beatrice, why don't you say what you have to say? What was the problem? I'm interested." She rose. "Frankly, I don't know. I don't know why this insistence. I gather she was here before. Because I know Seymour let her in. Oh, I grant that she wasn't expected. I credit you with that."

He said, "We don't have to spar with each other." "Still, out of all the women in New York she chose me." "You're wrong there: she's been to see Myra and Good's wife." They were standing in the sitting room. "You haven't asked about David." "How is he?" "I think he's better off here than at Mother's." "Perhaps he is. But are you? You have all the work to do here. You can rest there." "Oh, you know how her vulgarity horrifies me: she's a noisy dictator. She has her slaves and maids and her truckling friends and even boy-friends. Essentially, I married you to get away from it; and you keep suggesting I should go back. Why?" "Well, Beatie, so you're glad to be home?" "Yes, I am. It's lonely and miserable and isolated here and I never see you; but I'm not surrounded by drinking, card-playing barbarians screaming like hyenas at dirty jokes, all night." He sat in thought for a moment and then began to read a political weekly which had come by the morning post. He cheered up and presently said, "There's an excellent article here on Brazil."

Much later, she told him about the girl. "She walked in as if expected, said she had been waiting for me to come home and she wanted to talk to me. I was unprepared and didn't know what to expect. I was frightened, I think." She laughed a little. "Why frightened? Did you think she was going to attack you?" "Attack me?" She thought it over. "No. Why should she? Is she paranoiac?" "She's perfectly normal." "Is she? Well, who is? She began to talk and I gathered she was in trouble, but she couldn't come out with it; she was roundabout, hesitant, repressed. She seemed to want to appear too lady-like to say anything definite. At last, I realized that they were overcrowded at home, that she had no money and that she needed clothes." "Did you give her some?" he asked. "You have very few clothes yourself."

"No, not yet. At any rate, I was obliged to ask her to dinner. I just hinted and she took me up on it. She's coming to dinner on Tuesday night." She laughed. "I expect you will be able to make it by eight that night." "Tuesday? Yes, of course I will. I should like you to become friends."

After a silence, she burst out, "Oh, this is intolerable. I can't stand it. I can't stand the problems, the uncertainties. It suffocates me. If only I could die, tonight, and not have to go through with it."

"What is the trouble, my dear? You know I love you and never loved anyone else and that I live for you and I couldn't live without you."

"I don't want it, I don't want it, I don't want it."

"I don't understand, I don't understand."

"It's the intolerable anguish of living, the intolerable doubt about everything."

"Surely you don't mean Miss Lawrence?"

"Oh, no, of course not," she said scornfully. "You don't suppose I suspect you?"

"There is no reason to."

When he got home at seven that Tuesday evening, his wife took him into the bedroom and said, "I thought you'd come together. She's been here while I've been putting the baby to bed and I've had not time to prepare anything: just sitting there. She won't take a drink—"

"She's a teetotaler," said Debrett proudly.

"——and she has no conversation."

"You should have talked to her about art—she considers that the only subject fit for a human being."

"What do I know of art?"

"Well, she seems to think you're a kindred spirit," he said, with pleasure.

"You go and entertain her; she's probably used to you. I have nothing for dinner. I felt too happy to go out and shop."

But though the girl behaved with lady-like gravity, then and throughout the meal, she never once looked at Debrett, turning her head always to Beatrice, hanging on her words, smiling and bending her head to her plate, glancing critically at the pictures or curtains, or even at the table service. She smiled at the wife's few jokes and when Beatrice got to her feet, Miss Lawrence jumped up and helped her silently. The meal did not take long. Beatrice had opened a can of salmon and had made some salad. Miss Lawrence had never eaten salmon; instead she ate a boiled egg with relish.

"Do you like boiled eggs?" asked Beatrice.

"I haven't had a boiled egg for years, since mother was there; but I like them."

"What do you like to eat?" said Beatrice with curiosity.

"We have vegetables—oatmeal, cheese," she said, musing as if she had never considered it.

"Are you vegetarians, also?" Beatrice said with a smile.

The girl looked at her, puzzled.

"No meat or fish, I mean."

"No."

"You have many principles, haven't you?" said Debrett. She looked at his wife, questioning.

"But you eat dessert?" said Beatrice. "Milk puddings, I suppose? I'm afraid I only have ice cream."

"Oh," she exclaimed, delighted, "I've never had ice cream."

She left immediately after the plates were cleared. When she was going, Beatrice offered her some clothes she had set aside. The girl went through them carefully, selected a blouse, left the other things lying there, said good-bye suddenly and left, with the blouse in her hand.

Beatrice herself spoke as if she were musing all the time and her words were the product of serious thought; it had always attracted him. But Beatrice objected to the girl's slow spokenness: "Why does she pull each word off her teeth as if it were taffy?"

Debrett had not liked the blouse being given away, it was Beatrice's. He spoke to Tom Zero about raising the girl's wages. He began wondering if he could spare her a little out of his own salary. Impossible. He gave all but a few dollars, for lunches, to his wife; and indeed, they were beginning to need more money at home. He had worries. The firm had begun honest and gained repute, was taking a short cut to riches, selling its stock and increasing the stock when necessary. It had entered upon fraud. Farmers, investors, small towners, countryfolk who had invested in the firm, bought the stock and could not sell it back; this was illegal. But the company paid good dividends, kept straight accounts and the legal situation, handled by Tom Zero and Saul Scott, was always unassailable. All these talented young men could have made money honestly; crooked money seemed gayer and cleverer. Debrett had no heart for it. He did not care for money at all. He could make money for others, invent schemes of any color, but never for himself. "The firm's making money; if you hang on, you bunch of crooks, you can sell out for a big price to the Chicago Farmers' Supplies," he said, with a laugh. But they hung on for quick profit and an early bankruptcy. He had no stomach for fraud or financial investigations; he decided to move. He was looking about, both for a new job with good pay and a new home downtown, so that he could see his family early in the evening. Beatrice was very unhappy.

When he had decided to move he realized that he would be leaving Miss Lawrence on her own. He took her to lunch to try to work out her problems and give her some advice.

Not to be misconstrued, he mentioned it to Tom Zero. He went to a lunchroom pleasing to New York women, intending to spend more money than he ever did for himself. There was a lofty room with decorated walls, menus, flowers, a lot of small tables and he expected her to be delighted. But she looked about slightly in her dignified way; and he admired her, though he was disappointed. Halfway through the meal which he selected to suit her limited tastes, he was greeted by a woman passing close to the table; it was Beatrice. Miss Lawrence looked up, smiled and put out her hand, "Oh, I am glad you came, too." Beatrice behaved with the good and distant manners he admired, greeted them both and walked out. When he got home, she said, "Augustus, I would not do that again, if I were you." "Beatrice, you must understand—" "Let us say no more about it." For days he did not ask for Miss Lawrence.

She had been there nearly a year: it was August. She had refused her holiday, asking to be allowed to work during the fortnight. "And you can pay me the money extra." Debrett was also working, his wife having gone to Morristown to her mother's. Three engineers arrived from the Middle West to test a new piece of apparatus, a gas generator, which the firm wanted to market. Two of them were busy in town; the third, hanging about the office, found the young filing clerk interesting. He was nearly sixty, had a long soft red nose, and often he would sit down at one of the empty desks and begin designing a piece of apparatus. "And what do you do?" "I file the letters, I fill in at the switchboard, I type personal letters." "You're new, aren't you?"

"I've been here since November." "I'm going to a little restaurant near here for a bite of lunch. Would you like to go with me?" "Yes, thank you." "What time do they let you out?" "What do you mean?" She seemed hurt. "What time do you lunch?" "Half past twelve." He took her to a large old-fashioned restaurant on the ground floor of a warehouse. "Oysters?" "What is that?" "Tomato juice?" "Yes, please." "Chicken a la king?" "What is that?" "You don't get around much, do you?" "Oh, I go around a lot; but I eat with friends, at their homes." "You have a lot of friends, then. Boy friends, too, I expect." "Boys? I don't like boys. I like men. I have a lot of men friends." It doesn't surprise me." He touched the hair on her shoulder; and she gave a loud cry and bounded out of her chair. "Good grief, don't do that! What did I do?" he said, looking about. "I don't want men to touch me." He was frightened. "I didn't mean any harm; don't you understand? I admire you. I respect you." She was very sweet. "I forgive you. I know you didn't mean any harm." He said, "I'm a real honest man, girlie; if you scream at me again because I happen to touch your arm I think I'd fall through the floor. I don't go out with girls. I just like to talk." And he went on to talk. He told her about Celinda his wife, a farm girl who was a good bit younger than himself, a fine wife and mother, and could do anything. She ran the farm and had the children obedient and doing the chores. He talked about his children, two girls and a boy; and his well-managed little farm, ten acres, with fruit, poultry and vegetables, a tractor, horse and cow, near Hamilton, an Ohio village, some distance from Cincinnati. "My wife's as good as two hired men." He had to travel about the country; his wife put up with it and was good to him, very good. "I wish you knew her; you'd like her and she'd like you. But this is all about me."

She told him what she was interested in: modern painting, painters, new trends in poetry. "That's very unusual and advanced for a filing clerk." "I won't be there long. It's temporary. I'm looking for the right place for me." "Aren't they good to you there?" "Yes, they're good to me, but it means nothing. It's an ugly dreadful life."

"You're a country girl, I suppose." She did not answer. "Well, if you're a country girl, I know how you feel. When you look up at all those tall buildings, you think, but in what corner do they grow the corn and the potatoes; and where do they keep the hens?"

On the way back to the office he said he'd like to buy her a little gift, what would she like? She said, a book about Gauguin, small and comparatively cheap. "You meet me at Brentano's, and I'll give it to you; no strings to it. I think a lot of you. You remind me of my wife."

The next day, a Saturday, the office was working overtime again. There was an unpredicted storm, with a fiery sky; a fireball bumped over the skyscrapers into the street. No one had a raincoat. They sent the office boy out for coffee and sandwiches; but Miss Lawrence went out into the downpour. She said she had an important appointment. She returned at the end of lunch-hour, drenched, her wet face absorbed. They got her partly dry; they fussed around her, asked, laughing, "How was your appointment? How did it turn out?" She did not answer. A new job, a boy, a runaway match? She did not come to work the next Monday, nor during the week. She was not seen again in the Farmers' Utilities Corporation.

During the week, Walter Lawrence, her brother, telephoned and when he heard she was no longer working for them, he seemed relieved. "That's good, then." "It's good?" said Tom Zero, surprised. "I mean, I know where to look." But on the following Monday a wornout bent old man asked to see Mr. Zero. His name was Tommaseo. Miss Magna sent him to Mr. Debrett. "An old man here insists that his daughter works for us. He hardly speaks any English and I don't understand him," she said proudly, for she was the daughter of an Italian immigrant and spoke no Italian. Debrett knew no Italian but his sympathy with strange human beings enabled him to understand that Mr. Tommaseo bought fruit and vegetables early in the morning in the Gansevoort Market, east of Twentieth Avenue, and took them to a small shop he had near Bleecker Street, where he had a cut-rate trade. His daughter had stolen money from him and run away to the streets; his wife, son and other daughter had also taken money from him and never paid him back. Now he had nothing but debts and nothing to look forward to. The firm, the Farmers' Utilities, owed him money, his daughter's pay, which was his, because of what she owed him. Debrett explained that his daughter had never worked for him. "She did, she did, and you owe me her wages," cried the old man. Debrett was ashamed to call for the bouncer and eventually persuaded Tommaseo to leave; but he left crying bitterly and exclaiming, "All thieves, all cheats." Debrett turned back shaking his head. "Crazed poverty; it tears your heart," he said to Tom Zero who was looking at this scene.

"Gus, you'll never be rich," said Zero. "I hope not," said Debrett. "That is a wish always granted," said Zero, without smiling. "But he did know something about us," said Maria Magna, "though he got all the names wrong. He's an old crook, I think; wanted to frighten you, pretend you'd stolen his daughter. The old men think up all sorts of tricks. I know them." "Why say that, Maria? All he said to me was, I've always worked hard and starved." And as he walked home that night, Debrett wished he had given five dollars to the old man, bent, grasping, perhaps a crook or deluded, casting his eyes about furiously, calling out names, "Dibretti, Seer, Scotti, I know, I know—" Debrett, Zero and Scott, names on the doorplate.

Later, Walter Lawrence called to see Debrett. His name and his sister's, was Tommaseo; they had changed to Lawrence. Their father was an Italian immigrant, at home a mason, here a man with fruit and vegetables on a barrow, who by hard work and cruel pinching had been able to rent a small store, where he sold seconds and rejects. This man had become a miser, a man who watched every bite they took, and shrieked, "You're killing me, you're ruining me, don't eat so much"; horrible scenes, frightful gestures. When he went out he took the key with him and they waited for his return; either on the staircase or in neighbors' apartments. They scarcely ever bought anything. They dressed in the cast-offs of tenement neighbors. It was not only that he would not give the money, it was the unbearable scenes he made on a shopping expedition. He would trudge ahead, muttering, even shouting at them. If they stopped at a window, he would slowly come back, look in, say, "Why are you stopping here? Is there anything else you can think of to ruin me? What else do you want?" When they reached the store, no one, not even the storekeepers and assistants, though they were used to haggling, could stand the horror of his cries and insults. "I know it was poverty, but every slum father does not do that; I simply can't forgive him. My mother put up with it. My mother was afraid we would die of exposure to hunger and cold; and when the last of us could earn a living, she put an end to it. He had to pay for the gas she used then. He sold the stove and all their cooking was done on a gas ring. My sister Honor's name was Rosina. She never had any clothing till she went to school. She was wrapped up in a shawl or a skirt. She actually does not know even now, I think, what it is to go into a shop and buy something for herself. As for hair, face, any feminine thing, she knows they exist, but does not think they are for her. It doesn't matter much yet. She's not sixteen yet; and in spite of the life she's led, or because of it, she's austere, pure and high-minded. She believes in what she says."

"But where is this child?" cried Debrett.

"In a way, I don't care; anywhere is better than that inferno. But I expect she will knock at my door in a day or two."

"You take it very calmly. I can't be so cool. I'm worried about a girl of fifteen—you say she's not sixteen?—alone all night in the streets."

"Oh, I know Honor. She's found herself some hole or

corner. She's a surprising girl. She has a memory as long as your arm for people and addresses. She may even be with one of our neighbors up at home. But I know she will come to no harm—or the sort you mean—she's as safe as a saint; she's quite a rare human being."

"I wouldn't be so calm if it were my sister. I had a sister once. She died of tenement life; and I've never forgotten it. It haunts me."

"I know she'll come to me," said the brother. "I know she will be all right."

Not long after this, Farmers' Utilities began to break up. Debrett was the first to go. He found a job in Wall Street and was able to move his family downtown. Tom Zero quit and set up his own law firm. Scott went to work with a judge. Palmer, the old engineer, was in Chicago doing business with his old firm, when he got a letter from his wife Celinda, on the farm near Hamilton, Ohio. "A slip of a girl, not more than sixteen, I am sure, has come to stay with me here. She says she worked for you in New York and that you raved about me and said she should live on a farm. She had not eaten or slept decently for five days, but I cannot get out of her how she got here. She has no money. She said, I thought I'd like to forget everything; but she had no object, just to wander, and she found out in a day or two that she is not strong enough for the hobo life, so she came to the nearest home."

Celinda, a strong smooth-boned girl with thick bronze hair, who looked ten years younger than she was and was twenty years younger than her husband, accepted the visitor with curiosity. "My husband says you have a family and a job in New York." "I can't go back there." "Why?" "My father shut me out—I got home late." "Where had you been?" "To see—a friend of mine, for dinner; and I had to walk home." "What sort is your father?" She was apparently thinking it over. "Well—your father?" "I don't know," she said at last, sitting in her chair serenely and as if amused. "What does he do?" "He sells things, I suppose, things like you have here, vegetables." "Well, and where were you working?" But there the visitor was quite clear. She gave the name of the office, the address, the private addresses of all the partners and senior employees, the salesmen on both sides of the house (that is, for goods and for stock); and very vivaciously, she gave the names of the various firms Celinda's husband, Palmer, worked for. "What a wonderful memory you have!" The girl was startled and became quiet. "How do you remember all that?" "I don't remember them—they were in the files and the telephone book." "And you can't go back there?" "Where?" "To the firm, Farmers' Utilities." For a long time she was silent, pondering. "Did something happen there?" "Where?" "In the firm? Did something happen to you? Were they disagreeable to you? Did someone hurt your feelings?" "I don't think about them." No matter how much Celinda questioned her, she got this kind of answer.

At first Honor did nothing and Celinda thought her too weak to work. She very rarely spoke about herself, but she would volunteer remarks suddenly, such as, "My brother is not as fine as he thinks; there are other painters too." "Is he a painter?" "I suppose he is. Yes, he is. But he's overrated, particularly by himself. He's an architect of his own fame, the same kind of architect as a woodworm." After such tart, unexpected sentences, she would retire into herself, sit peacefully. And as suddenly, "My brother is a mean, slobbery little man. I don't like him at all. He is all for himself. He left my father. He never paid him back the money he owed him for his keep." "Did he owe him money?" "My father paid for his food and rent when he was a child." Once or twice, sitting in the chair Mrs. Palmer had put out for her under an apple tree in the rough grass at the side of the house, she spoke about herself. "I have finer perceptions than my brother. He will use anyone. I won't have anything to do with stupid people. My senses are delicate. I'm an artist by nature, but I haven't the means, my brother says. He says it's a complex type of human being. People worry me. I need this country quiet. I feel better than I ever did in my life. Your husband said I was to stay here and forget the city; see where the corn grows. I'll never get home again."

The farmhouse in Ohio suited her and she was going to stay with them a long time, she said. "Don't you think you should help me with the chores to cover your keep?" Honor stared at the woman. "Are you like my father?" The Ohio wife wrote again to her husband and waited. Here was a young unfortunate, she thought; so young that she could not send her out onto the roads. She measured her hospitality, but was not unkind. Honor did almost no work in the house or farm. She sat on the dry grass or the veranda, moping. She ate sparingly, drank water and milk and had her share of things that were quite different, she said, from any she had had before; fruit, vegetables, eggs. She did not want to be a nuisance and insisted upon sleeping rolled up in a quilt on the floor. "I'm used to it; and I read somewhere that it is good for the nerves." She played with the children and told them stories of town life.

"My brother stabbed himself in the foot with a railing and nearly died. In our house was a little boy who lived by himself in the daytime. His parents went to work. He climbed up and down the stairs all day, rubbing his hands on the wood and crying. My father nailed up the windows in our room so that the sparrows could not get the crumbs we put out. One day I got a prize at school and my father sold it for two dollars. My brother kept a rat in a can in the yard; but a dog got it. My mother and my brother and I used to sit on the landing and my mother told us stories about her home. It was very cold in winter and hot in summer and there were miles of stone arches to keep the sun and snow off you. Arcades they are. And in the arcades are stores with lace, and diamonds and money, stores with money in the windows, you can go in and get it; and cakes and things like that; roast chickens, too, and shoes, with red and green stripes and leather lace on them. My mother said if she ever had the money she would take us home with her. If she had had the money we would be there now. But I'll go one day."

In this way, Honor stayed till autumn. The husband returned home once. The day before he returned, Honor went away; she returned after he left, without saying where she had been, or how she knew he had gone. The second time, he was coming home for a longer stay. This time she went and did not return. She did not say good-bye, or thanks, and they never heard of her again. In the spring, they found traces of her in a shed full of lumber; but they did not know when she had stayed there. No one in the East heard of Honor again for two years or more, that is, till she was nearly eighteen.

It was then that Augustus Debrett received a message in his Wall Street office that a woman wanted to see him in the waiting room. "No, not your wife." At first glance she seemed as before, the sweet sober face, the swinging skirt, and then he saw that she was older; she was thin and nervous. She held herself withdrawn, standing as usual away from the center, using the shadow for her mystery. She was dressed with taste. "Miss Lawrence!" She looked at the two people doing business in the outer office, at the machine, through the half-glazed partitions. "Not here! Can you meet me in the front hall of the New York Public Library, where we used to meet?" "We used to? Can't you speak to me here? I'm very busy, Honor." "No, not here. I must see you. You must come." "I'm busy at lunchtime, Honor." "Well, at six then. I'll wait for you there." "All right, but are you sure there's nothing now? Have you money?" "Yes, plenty of money." They glanced at him in the office and he did not like that. He was always kind to girls, treated them as equals, made no coarse jokes, never flirted or took them to drinks after work, was devoted to his wife. But the girl attracted attention.

After work there was a summer storm and he did not have his coat. Still, he went up to the library. She was there. They walked about around the halls and staircases; and she was casual, made no excuse. "Where are you living now, with your brother?" "Oh, no, he's married. I went there"—for the first time she seemed to be complaining—"they had only one bed. I can sleep on the floor. It's good for the nerves. There was another room, a boxroom, or larder, something. I could have slept there." "And where are you now? Are you at home?" "Home?" "At your father's?" "I never see my father; he moved, I think," she said, after a pause. "But you have somewhere to stay?" Another pause. "Yes, kind people. I like it there." "Where are you then?" "At the YWCA." He was relieved. She continued, "It's too dear for me. There are other places I've heard of." With his grimy handkerchief, he had a ten-dollar bill he had borrowed from the cashier. He turned and twisted it in his pocket. The thunder and lightning continued. The city steamed and the water poured straight down, flushing the streets. "You have no coat or umbrella, Honor?" "Yes, I left it at the door with a parcel." She walked about with him confidently. He listened to the steps on the marble floor. "I like it here," said Honor. The storm began to clear; streaks of sunlight were seen. "Did you want to ask me something, Honor?" She looked straight into his eyes. "No, I am all right." He could return the ten dollars tomorrow to the cashier; but he would not mind going into debt for the girl, if she needed it. "You had no request to make?" He had these old-fashioned words, got from his immense reading of the old books, as a boy. "Oh, no. The rain's over now. Good-bye." She shook his hand, made a sort of half curtsey and ran down the steps, did not look back. He was relieved, thrust the ten dollars back into the handkerchief and went home.

An old house in Eleventh Street had been transformed into apartments. He had the ground floor, two lofty rooms separated by a sliding door; and in the back, a small kitchen and bathroom. They slept and ate in the back room, which had iron bars on its tall windows and overlooked an old garden. They would have to move again soon because of the baby.

Dinner was ready. "I'm sorry I was late. A funny thing happened. Do you remember that girl who worked in Farmers' Utilities, Honor Lawrence?" "She came back? Does she want a job?" "I don't know what she wanted. It wasn't money." "Does she look well off?" "Hard to say. Older, but quite well; you might say elegant. It isn't money spent on clothes: she wouldn't do that. It's style, a personal style." "What did she want?" "She said she had to see me. The office wouldn't do. I met her at the library." He recounted the episode fully, gaily and anxiously. "I assure you, I was as taken aback as you are now." "Oh, I'm not taken aback," said Beatrice in her hollow, soft and husky tones; "you'll see her again. If she came back after two years, you'll keep on seeing her." "I won't. What has she to do with me?" "I don't know," said the wife.

They ate and the wife began to worry. "There's no air in this apartment; the old trees cut out any light or air even when those windows are open. I owe it to David to go to Morristown in this weather, and Mother wants me there. This apartment has no air, only a through draught. The kitchen isn't hygienic; there's no real place to bathe the baby out of a draught and the sink gets stopped up because the pipes are laid so flat. There are roaches coming up the pipes."

"Well, go to Morristown if you must."

"You know how I hate it. What do you get out of this marriage? I know you never wanted a child," she said crankily and full of doubt.

He sighed. "I don't know, Beatrice. I do my best."

"How long can we go on like this? Is this life? Oh, this is awful."

"I'm afraid you're very unhappy."

"Your only dream is to be happy!" she said in anguish. "The word makes me shriek."

Six months later, in winter, he was again called to the waiting room in his office and there was Miss Lawrence; though now she wore a dark gray coat, well cut but too large for her. " Can I see you privately?" But he was afraid of office gossip. She said, "Will you meet me in the Public Library?" "I could meet you downstairs in this building in about twenty minutes. Take a seat and wait and I'll come." He was taken by surprise: she had come for a loan. "Enough to buy some clothes—you may be sure, I'll pay you back. I met a lady in San Francisco who is interested in me and who is taking me to Italy tomorrow. You know my mother was in Italy as a girl. Italy is very interesting now, it's an age of youth. I want to study art and painting. I think I can do something real in Italy. I need twenty dollars for clothes." "Twenty dollars! Can you get clothes for that sum?" "Oh, yes, I can." Debrett had to take her upstairs, to ask the cashier for a twenty-dollar loan. People were about and two or three customers, men standing by, heard her further frank remarks. A big man said, "Twenty dollars—I'll lend you that, little lady; but what will I get for it?" He took money out of his pocket; the others began to laugh. She said gravely, "Give me a piece of notepaper, please." The man picked a sheet off a memo pad and gave it to her. "And a pencil, please." She went over to the desk, wrote and handed him the sheet of paper. He looked, looked at her, handed it to the others and burst out laughing. "Big day in my life!" She had written, "I will give you a kiss." He looked around with a big gay laugh, a popular man's man, the kind trusted to take out-of-towners around New York. He screwed up an eye, stared at her, looked her up and down, stopped laughing, turned back and pulled money out of his pocket, and handed it to her gravely, "I'll do a good deed, they can put my name in after Abou ben Adhem." She took the money and before another word was said, ran out of the office. "Who is that?" "Debrett's friend." "Your friend, Gus?" "She worked for me once, years ago. She's only a kid." "Is she crazy or what?" "Just a nice girl." One of the salesmen showed the notepaper; "Nice girl or smart girl." Debrett took it and threw it in the trashbasket. "I know her history. For her it hasn't the implication it has for you."

An hour later, she was at Saul Scott's asking for a passport in her assumed name of Honor Lawrence. "Can I alter my birthplace? I want to make it Boston. I am going with a rich woman who likes me and she thinks I am from Boston."

Saul Scott's solid red face smiled kindly. "I'll tell you your rights. Put that money in your purse; you can't pay me. I'm too dear. And Vera Day, on your way out, will give you all the help you need. She'll fill out the forms."

But, with the forms filled in, she hurried out of the office; and then, with the news of her Italian journey, she visited Tom Zero, Arthur Good and others unknown. Zero refused to see her, but she was in his office before he knew it. He refused to lend her money, but in the end did so: "Twenty dollars to buy clothes to go to Italy." "Thank you, you will be repaid," she said and was gone in her usual way.

Tom told his wife Myra. "How did she know your address?" "I don't know. She went to see Saul Scott and others." "Gus Debrett?" "Yes, for one." "Beatrice won't like it!" "Why?" "You know how everything depresses her. Where has the girl been all this time?" "California apparently. That's where she met this woman. She's traveling with a monied woman." "How these tramps get around," said Myra. "They spend in traveling the money we spend in rent and comforts," said Tom. "Very simple." Myra telephoned Beatrice, who was very gloomy. "Of course Gus lent her money and of course she'll keep coming back. According to Gus, she's painfully honest, never told a lie. How does she create that impression?" "It's the New England look." "And she's an Italian," cried Beatrice. "Well, she's gone to Italy, Beatrice. It sounded final to me. Don't think about it any more." "Oh, she'll be back, we're haunted," said Beatrice. "We have no luck." When she turned to her husband, she said sharply, "What's this trip about then?" "Search me: self-improvement, I think." "I envy her. She's free and she can get away from her local entanglements whatever they are." "We can do it too, Beatrice. She's got the courage to go and try her luck; why not us? She hates this money world, so do we. I have been thinking about it, as I walked home. If a slip of a girl who knows no foreign language has the courage to rise out of that hard cruel poverty where she was starved and humiliated, why not us? I could find a job, France or Italy." "To Italy—" cried Beatrice. "France. Or England or Germany. I know all the chief cities as I know my own East Side." Beatrice was silent. At last, she said quietly, "If you want to go—I'll go. I must get away from Mother and the others. I can't stand family quarrels. How can people live like that? Among total strangers there must be calm." "*Calme, luxe et volupté*—" said Debrett with a radiant expression. "Mother likes a good fight; it gives her tone and she looks radiant. I hate it. I could cut my throat. When you're there, they expect you to take part. If you don't, you're selfish. *When the whole family is at each other's throats, there you are with your nose buried in a book.* I often wanted to go and throw myself in the East River as a child." "Instead, we'll throw ourselves into the Atlantic; but we'll swim to the other side." He came toward her, "I'm so glad, I'm so happy you want to go. It will make all the difference to us. You'll see, you'll be happy over there." "You are right, perhaps. Your girl friend has no husband or child, so it's rather different; and apparently she has found someone to look after her. It was bound to come to that," she said mournfully. "What future is there for that puzzleheaded girl?" "Beatrice," said Debrett solemnly, "never mind about Honor Lawrence. She is out of our lives for good. Our lives are now in the future; and I swear you will be happy. You have me to look after you."

The following afternoon, Miss Lawrence came again to see Debrett in his office; she looked tired. "Why didn't you go to Italy?" "I couldn't go." "Has the boat sailed?" "Yes. The lady went but she took someone else." "Oh, Honor! Poor girl! She let you down." "She said I let her down." "How is that?" "I'm afraid I can't tell you here. Something dreadful happened. Can I see you alone?" "Not here, Honor." "In the Public Library tonight at six." He was put out. He telephoned his wife and explained why he would be late. The line was silent. "Beatrice, what is it?" "Oh, that girl, that gadfly—" "I thought you were sorry for her." "I'm sorry for women—for the struggle, without hope—" "Yes, so am I, Beatrice. Don't you want me to see her? I'll get a message to her somehow." "Oh, see her, see her," she said with bitter hopelessness. "I can see she's going to be with us for the rest of our lives." "Oh, no, she is not. I am going to see what is wrong, and if I can fix it up for good. I will tell her she can't keep calling upon me. You see, it's her innocence; she doesn't see it as hurtful, as a nuisance. She's in trouble; and like a lost child, she cries out to the first person she meets." "I understand, Gus. I know you; I know you mean well." "Yes, I do."

When he met the girl he was tired. "Why didn't you go? How could you have been deceived like that? I thought you were eager to go and were great friends." "I couldn't go in such circumstances." "You'll have to be more explicit, Honor. I don't understand you."

"It was terrible. She's a dreadful woman, mad I think. She got me a room in a hotel, down there," she said vaguely. "Last night she came to call on me. She brought something to drink. I don't drink. Then she put her hand around my waist. I don't like that. I stopped that. She kept on and I slapped her. Then she turned into a fiend, her face was all screwed up, all in wrinkles, she looked like a bird and she flew at me, saying things in a little voice—and she threw me out, wouldn't let me stay in the hotel, wouldn't pay for me, she said." He waited. "What really happened, Honor?" "I don't know. I said to her, that's a nice blouse, where did you get it? What's wrong in that? She began to behave so wildly. She ground her teeth, her eyes opened, she glared at me and said in a rude voice, I made it myself; and did you make that yourself? And she pulled at my dress and tried to tear it off me. Then I knew she was mad. She was such a wonderful woman," said Honor slowly, turning her head away. She never cried. "I thought she liked me. She used to come and see me in California, when I had a little room with some friends, and she brought me presents and she took me to the art shows. People didn't like me in California and she was good to me." "People didn't like you? I thought you made friends easily." "Eva, this woman, took me everywhere, and I stayed with her. She gave a party for me; but they never spoke to me and if I spoke to them, they'd turn their heads away pretending not to hear; or they would get up and go away. So she said, she'd take me to Italy, where people were old and civilized and hadn't little suburban ideas; and we would see new people. And I told her what I had never told anyone, all about my father and mother; and she said, she would be father and mother to me."

"Yes, now I see," said Debrett; and he asked her if she

had a place for the night. She had, she said; and after a long pause, looking into his face, she touched his hand and left him. He went home and told his wife the story. "You see, I am right about her. I know her. She is utterly innocent and unsophisticated. What do you make of it?" "Myra Zero has just telephoned me to say that your child-woman called on Tom at his office and told him she had not gone to Italy, but could never tell him why; and he gave her ten dollars for a place for the night. Of course, she is going to pay him back." "She always does, Beatrice. She is completely, painfully honest. She always tells the truth." "Perhaps she does," said Beatrice.

It was four months before Debrett heard of her again. She telephoned him at his office. "What is it this time, Honor?" "I must see you." "No, no, I'm too busy. Tell me now." "No, I can't speak about it like this; I must see you." "I can't see you, Honor." She was in the waiting room in five minutes. He heard her calling his name. He was alone; the reception clerk had gone to lunch. She had no need of money, she said at once. She looked older, even dissipated. Her dress, usually neat, was untidy. She no longer wore short skirts and high blouses and had lost some of her charm: her thick hair was uncombed. She was in disorder and even dirty; but was still grave and prudish. "I just wanted to see you, Mr. Debrett, to tell you my troubles are over. I know you worry about me. I have a home now. I tried for a job but didn't get it. I went to a business college and told them to give me a certificate, but they wouldn't give me one." "Did you study at the college?" "No. But I told them I had all the skills: they could take my word."

"Well, you say you have a home, Honor?" She smiled triumphantly. "Yes, I have been invited to live as companion in the home of a lady in charge of a mental rest home." "Will that suit you?" "Oh, yes, she understands me. She says I will be a tonic to her after all those sick minds. She says I am quite unusual." She stood in front of him, upright, looking into his face with a sweet self-pleased look, waiting for him to be pleased. "I see. And what can I do for you?" "Nothing. I just thought I ought to see you." As he turned, she put her arm around him. "I need friends," she said.

He looked at her profile. She upset him; he was puzzled. "I was just going out for a snack. Would you share a sandwich with me?" She agreed and they went to a cheap lunchroom, where he often ate. She ate greedily, but accepted only one sandwich and a glass of milk. While he paid the bill, she walked out; and when he reached the sidewalk he saw her hurrying, almost running down the street; she skipped once, twice, on the curb. Was she just a child; or a free soul? He remembered what a friend had told him, "Once going down Eighth Street I saw a girl do the splits and then walk on as if nothing had happened." He did not call after Honor or try to follow her. She had left him in the middle of a conversation.

During the brief meal he had said, "When did you meet this woman?" "A week ago." "You want to be careful; she may be a Lesbian." "Oh, no, she's an American, she's from New England, just as I—" "You didn't understand what was wrong with that woman who was taking you to Italy, did you?" "Oh, yes: she was mad." "Honor, go and see my wife. She'll explain. I'm going back to the office—" She had gone. He went back to the office where he was finishing up the week's work; and he telephoned Beatrice.

"I know," said his wife, "she's here now. I'll take her to the park with David and we'll talk."

He went home troubled and could not eat his dinner. His wife, a keen, solid but morbidly uneasy woman rested on his face those large, gloomy, beautiful eyes which had always held him spellbound. She said at last, "Well, I saw that girl, Gus. You're worried about her, aren't you? You can't eat. Every time she comes into our lives, you don't sleep. Watch out, Gus. I can see you in a mess." "Over the poor suppliant? Don't be silly. To her I'm a kindly uncle, someone she worked for. She has a high opinion of herself and probably thinks I didn't pay her enough. I was her first job. She's not interested in men. But I am worried. Don't laugh at me, I feel she partakes of a sacred character, those the gods love, or hate: it's the same. If the suppliant demands and you don't give, you're accursed. That's an old idea. You can see the same thing in *Cuore,* by Edmondo de Amicis. At least in the old countries there is this idea that the sick and maimed are sent for your especial care."

"I know you can't resist lame ducks. I spoke to this girl in the park. That kind of talk is better done outdoors. She sat awhile watching David play. She seemed to like that. She listened to me and then she smiled, shook hands and wandered away, just as if she had not understood. I did what I could but I very soon came to the conclusion that she knows nothing at all of the physical side of love, to give it a name." "Do you think that's possible?" "It seems indefeasible," she said: her eyes searched the room anxiously. "Unlikely?" She stiffened. "It doesn't seem likely, but it's the result of a subconscious tabu. It's a real part of feminine nature, Gus. Such girls exist everywhere. I understand it. What have the coarse facts about men and women to do with nice manners, a soft voice, correct speech, polite ways, feminine delicacy? A girl is pretty and sweet and naturally chaste; people tell her she's charming. How should she know it's all a masquerade?" "But she spends her evenings in Greenwich Village." "Oh, she listens and doesn't hear. If you haven't the key! A woman doesn't want to spoil another woman's life. She may be lucky; she may never get tangled with a man. There are plenty of happy bachelor girls: it's a good life."

Debrett said nothing. Beatrice concluded, "Men can't understand it, even the best of them. Women are terrified not to get married; everyone's at them; and then they get married to eat and have a child; and so they find themselves shackled like an imbecile in a little room, with no money and no freedom." "It sounds a pretty miserable world for women," said Debrett. Beatrice sat down in an armchair with a tragic face.

Five days later in the afternoon the doorbell rang at the Debretts'. Beatrice went, stood back from the door, crying, "Oh!" Honor Lawrence was there, untidy, hardly decent; she looked as if she had been running through the streets. "I want to tell you something: let me come in!" She walked in, stood in the middle of the hall, looked around. "You had better sit down." "No." Beatrice looked at her without sympathy. In spite of their words about her, she thought

the girl an awkward booby. It was herself she had pity for:
she was unhappy, in a trap. She had not wanted to marry,
but to live like brother and sister with Debrett. When that
became intolerable, she had agreed to an ordinary marriage,
to avoid the disgrace of a break-up; but she could not en-
dure married life, could not shut her eyes to the boredom
and unfairness. "You don't like me," said the girl, "but
that is nothing. Your husband is kind to me and is my
friend; and I want you to tell him what happened to me. He
warned me." "Well, go and tell him yourself," said Beatrice.
"I'm sorry you find me so unresponsive, but I have my own
troubles; I am not as absorbed in your problems as you are."
"Surely, you must be a very selfish woman," said Honor,
"but you can't imagine what happened to me, or you would
want to help me. Don't you know that things are happening
all the time that are never mentioned anywhere? All newspapers and all written things are lies, because they don't tell
what really happens." "Well, sit down and tell me. I suppose
I must listen. I don't sleep. I'm exhausted. I'm walking in a
dream; but I know I can't escape this story of yours. Sit
down, sit down." The woman who was to help her had
treated Honor as a mad woman, and more cruelly, perhaps, than she dared to treat the patients. Honor had es-
caped by her suddenness, simply running out of the room
in the state she was in; and had fixed herself up somehow
on the way to town. "Where did you get the clothes?" "I
took some clothes out of the nurses' room." Near the end of
her tale, Honor seemed overcome by her sufferings. She got
up. "Let me go now; I can't stay here any longer." Beatrice
tried to keep her; she gave her a half-worn coat. The girl

set out, doubtless on one of her long inexplicable wanderings, her multitude of painful visits to all the strangers she called her friends. "I suppose she calls me her friend, too," said Beatrice to herself; "I ought to be; I am. I wish I had her naïveté."

At home, that night, the wife, slightly warmed now by thinking over Honor's miseries, retold the story. "I'm not surprised. The matron is a sadist who thought she had to do with a weak shade of lunatic; and I think she is one," said Debrett. "Saul Scott was always very sweet and tender with her because he held she was insane. Let's not worry about her. She's unfortunate; and in the end they'll have to gather her in." "That remark isn't like you and should never be made. She is just a repressed girl who is hunted by lechers, criminals and hags. And the only protection she has from life is that in herself she concentrates all the horror and misery which is life itself. She frightens off the dark side of life." "That is a morbid view, Beatrice." "I am morbid because I see." "I can't see life like that: I can see hope, especially for us."

Honor was at the Wall Street office the next day. Still untidy and unclean, she brushed past people in the outer office to see the president of the firm, a man she did not know. He was indignant and wanted to force her out. She did not resist it. She said in a low purring voice, "I came to see Mr. Debrett, but he can't give me advice; he hasn't the information; and I thought you could help me." She smiled at him. He was a kindly man who did not mind those who did not get in his way. "Is it about an account?" "Oh, no, nothing to do with money. I don't need money. I have plenty." He was disarmed. "Come here, sit down and tell me what I can do for you." "No, there is nothing you can do for me. I am going now." She shook hands; and she went. A week later, Tom Zero met her on 42nd Street. She was flushed, her frayed skirt slipping, and buttons missing from her blouse. Zero was a clean, ultrafashionable dresser. This looked like utter distress and abandon. "When did you get back from Italy?" She muttered something of her story. "I don't know what to do. I never guessed women were so horrible." "Didn't you know? I thought you always knew," and he laughed a little. She turned to run. He took a step and came close without touching her. "Be a sensible girl; I'll help you, but be sensible." "Oh, that word: sensible! She said that; be sensible. Everyone says it to me. Why? What do they mean? I don't know what they mean." She put a hand up to her face—real tears had started. She left him, went on her wanderings, and time passed.

Debrett sent his wife and child to Nice, where they lived in a poor pension; and when he had the money, he himself started for Europe, living at first on milk and cheese dishes, to save. His mother and a cousin, hearing of his move, also wished him to bring them abroad. Debrett worked in London and then in Berlin. He was at the Hotel Adlon and in his lonely style was walking up and down the room, working out business problems, when he received a late long-distance call from his correspondent in London, from a certain Abraham Duncan born in the East End and now, by his own efforts, a rich man. "How in the world did you know I was here, Duncan? Even my wife has not got my address yet."

"Listen, dear boy, time's short; there's a Mrs. Hewett here: she says you know her very well." The voice was discreet, peremptory, a little gay. "She says she's living in a room in Islington—that's a poor district—" "Yes, yes, I know." "She says she's starving and by gum, she looks it; she wants ten pounds and she says you'll guarantee her. What shall I do my boy?" "Hewett? Is she a woman about fifty: there was one had a ground-floor apartment in my house in New York—" "No, no, this one's maybe twenty-five, thirty, hard to tell: looks downtrodden, beat. Here, she says her name was Lawrence." "Honor Lawrence!" "Hurry up my boy: you know her? What shall I do?" "My goodness, I suppose give her the money. Ask her how she traced me." "No time now. All right. I'll call you at the office tomorrow. Lucky I was in the office—she got here at ten at night!" "That certainly is Honor Lawrence." Debrett sat down and sweated a cold salt sweat. He started to write to his wife and changed his mind. "The gadfly of fate," she had said once, an unimaginative woman, too; but an oppressed and persecuted woman, haunted by fate, or so she felt. She was now unhappy in her pension, the child boarded out; Beatrice leading an aimless, poor life. "Mrs. Hewett?" He thought she must have found out his old house, simply borrowed the name of the ground-floor tenant. Mrs. Hewett had sent her maid to clean the rooms when Beatrice was away at Morristown; and had kept his keys. He told Beatrice nothing about it.

When he returned to London, his first call was on Duncan and after business was settled, he asked for the ten pounds to be put on his account. "I've sent everything to Nice."

Duncan said, "I was very curious, in fact, inquisitive, my boy. It was late at night, a Saturday. I was working late, nearly ten. And she called on that day at that hour at a business office in the City. I was just going home. I don't know how she found her way through the City at that time of night: no one about. My word, she looked bad; hungry and poor. She wouldn't tell me where she lived and set off to walk home. I followed her, offered her a ride. Nothing doing. I lost her at Kensal Green, near the cemetery." He laughed. "My word! I'm not superstitious, not very; but she went into the cemetery." "You're joking!" "No—there I lost her. Made me think of the ghosts of the city of Prague; ghouls. But ghouls don't take money; proved she was human." They burst out laughing, but uneasily. "What did you think of her?" said Debrett, "Thought she must be —someone—you knew in the States; but then I saw— wasn't sex: touchy girl. Something you know at once. Or I know," he said with a warm troubled laugh. "Saw she was a Presbyterian." "She isn't." "Puritan," he amended; "if you hadn't said to give the money, I should have given it. She looked so miserable. A good deed." "I am worried about her," said Debrett; "she's such a miserable wanderer, a sort of wraith. She gives Beatrice the willies. She worked for me once. But Beatrice understands." "There's a letter for you she left." Debrett took it, looking at the envelope, "The Piccadilly Hotel! Was she staying there?" He read:

Dear Mr. Debrett

I had no notepaper and so I walked into this hotel to get some. I wish I could stay in a place like this. It is warm here and they have good clothes and are having food. This place is

not for me. I am sorry to be going to do what I am. I know
I owe you twenty dollars. But I am reduced to beggary and
need ten pounds, not for myself. I am now Mrs. Hewett. I
married Jay Hewett who was at school with me. I wanted to
come to Europe. So did he. He pretended he loved me and I
married him; but he didn't love me. I found that out now. I
can't imagine what his motives were. He's a dreadful person. Do not speak to him if he comes to see you. I think he
must be partly mad. I am afraid a lot of people are mad. I
trust you, but I could never speak about this madness. I
am afraid to tell what I have found out about people; I won't
be believed. They will think I am lying or even worse. I am
in a terrible position. Don't try to see me. I don't know what
I'll do. It was a dream, a lie; the reality is monstrous; perhaps
all things are monstrous. Perhaps this is hell.

Honor Lawrence

Duncan read the letter, asked her age and said, "It's the
marriage shock, she means. She looked innocent. If a
woman doesn't know, it must be an awful shock. I can
understand a girl going out of her mind over it. We don't
think; it means nothing to us. She looked distraught. She
told me she had just married. Who is she? Looked a nice
enough girl."

Debrett told him about her. "Is her story true, do you
think?" Duncan asked. "I've never known her to lie." Duncan glanced at him, said, "Well, some girls don't. Hard for
them. Hard is life for those who can't eat dirt."

Perhaps five years later, Debrett saw her one afternoon
walking along the Boulevard du Montparnasse, at some distance. She looked well and was stylishly dressed in a velvet
dress, her hair loose and shining. She had a youthful figure
and style.

"Let's go down the Rue Vavin," he said to the woman he was with; "there is Honor Lawrence, a girl who used to work for me and who married and came to Europe when I did; but she may need money and I am short at present."

Debrett had now left his wife for this woman, a gray-eyed woman with loose brown hair: her name was Mari. "Astonishing how she keeps her youth and girlish beauty," said Debrett. Mari looked and saw a plump, dark-haired woman, rakishly and carelessly dressed in green material, the blouse pulled down tightly between her full breasts, the skirt untidy. Mari had once been married to a dark thin young man who had led her a dance and in the end deserted her for an old schoolfriend of his, who looked not unlike the woman in green. This woman in green, prancing and bounding along the pavement, looked a little mad, self-satisfied and singing to herself. "I heard that she married again and went to South Africa," said Debrett. "I don't know if it's true. She came to Beatrice one afternoon some years ago. She found her out in Nice and when the door was opened, she threw twenty dollars at her, so that they lay inside the door. She said she owed it to me; so she did. I don't want it, said Beatrice, why do you haunt me now? He's left me, as you knew he would." "Why did she say that?" "Beatrice never understood Honor's simplicity and straightforward ways. She saw something eerie in them. She is honest herself, but never believed that Honor was truthful and pure."

A few years later, Debrett and Mari were living in one room in a building in London let out in what are called one-room flats. Downstairs lived the busy, noisy, greedy but kindhearted landlady who was putting her three children through Oxford and Cambridge on her slum rents.

Naturally generous, she would at times think of the condition of her tenants and try to fatten them up with a can of tomatoes, soup or oil bought wholesale.

For some time she had a stout, dark, stormy woman tenant who went in and out at odd hours, morosely; and at the end left quietly, owing four weeks' rent. "She was hard up and looking for a job," explained the landlady. "It is the first time I have let anyone run on like that; and see what has happened." There was some talk about the defaulting lodger. "I often noticed her," said Debrett to Mari, "because she reminded me of someone you don't know; Honor Lawrence, a girl who worked for me." "But I noticed her too, and she reminded me of your wife Beatrice." "No, no, Honor Lawrence."

At the end of five weeks, the dark woman brought the rent. "I owe it to you and you must have it." "You see, I knew," said Debrett. "She is exactly like Honor Lawrence, the same woman, you might say."

And five years later, when they were living in the country, a visitor came to see them, Mari's cousin Alice, a demure, self-contained girl of twenty-one, with long fair hair and a velvet skirt, who sat all day doing nothing and answered all questions after a pause. She was out of a job and looking for one. "If you had had a bed I could have stayed here, had a few days in the country," she said looking around; "it would suit me. You see I have a job offered me in town, but I can't take it; they want me to bind myself for three months. I could never do that. I must be free."

"I hope," said Debrett, "that you won't invite that girl Alice to stay with us. When I saw her coming up the stairs,

I felt the hairs rise along my spine. She is so exactly like Honor Lawrence; it is the same girl. If she ever got in here, she'd never leave. I don't want her here; let her go. Never invite her."

And Mari became uneasy, and discouraged the odd, charming, long-haired girl with the soft wooden face in which was a dimple.

It was more than three years later than that, that Debrett was on a business visit to New York; and having half an hour to put in, he went toward the 42nd Street Public Library, which he had visited every afternoon in his youth and remembered fondly. On the first steps below the portico someone pulled his sleeve—Honor, the real Honor. She was now about thirty. But she looked much younger, he thought. Were his eyes getting worse? And he saw now that the others, the one on the Boulevard du Montparnasse, the one in the slum, and the young one, had not looked like her. Was she real? he thought for a moment. Did she shuttle between youth and age, inhabit and divest herself of other women's forms? "The ghouls of the city of Prague."

"Mr. Debrett! I thought I would see you here."

"It's almost a miracle that you do, Honor. I've just come back after many years away. I've come from London. You were the last person I expected to see. How are you? Where are you living?"

"I don't know," she replied quietly. "I have just come back from South Africa. I married a South African I met in an art gallery in Europe and went out with him."

"So you divorced Jay Hewett?"

"I was never married to Jay Hewett. It was no marriage

and I didn't consider it one." She still had charm, her self-centered, stiff-necked enigmatic manner, but she seemed less inhuman; no ghoul.

"Would you like a cup of coffee, Honor?"

"I should be glad of a sandwich and coffee. I've had nothing to eat all day. I have no money and no home yet. If you could lend me ten dollars I will pay it as soon as I get money from Derek."

"Where is your husband?" She did not answer. "Don't tell me about your husband, if you don't wish to."

In the cafeteria he brought her the food he knew she preferred. "I wrote you a letter in London," she said; and told him his European addresses, those of his partners and of his wife. She continued, "I told you about Jay. I was unfair to Jay. It was all my fault. What he tried to do was natural; that's what marriage is. One day I met a man in an art gallery. I was waiting for you there. I thought you'd be sure to know where I was. This man took me to lunch and gave me wine to drink. Then he took me to his hotel. I had more to drink and something happened. We went out to dinner and I had more to drink and we went back again, and I woke up the next morning with him and then I suddenly knew that that was marriage." She looked into Debrett's face. "So I was married to him. I went out to South Africa with him and I had his child, my child. It's still there, but I don't know where. The family wouldn't have me. They deported me. They gave the child to an orphanage. They wouldn't tell me where it was; and I went around everywhere knocking at doors. They had taken it away. They said it was a colored child." "Eh?" "They said that to get me deported. They were rich. They could do anything they liked. I was quite wrong about Jay. I thought we would get married and study modern art."

"Did you get a divorce from Jay? That was quick."

"Oh, I never told Derek anything about Jay. We weren't married, were we?"

"You mean you married Derek bigamously?"

She looked puzzled, "That was years ago."

"And what now, Honor?"

"I must find someone and get some money for the trip back. Derek loves me. He will meet me and convince his family. Will you take me to Pennsylvania Station? I must get a train to the country, to a woman who will be kind to me."

"Honor, what woman?"

"Come with me," she said; and he went, anxiously and unwillingly.

When they reached the environs of Pennsylvania Station, she said, "Won't you come and see me in my present home; it's a room nearby. We can have coffee there."

It was a small dark room with upholstered chairs and a blue-covered divan, of good appearance. She sat there in the half-dark on the divan quietly telling him her story; how she had gone to Europe with Jay, each of them traveling steerage in a six berth cabin, men and women separated; how they landed in London, where she expected to find Debrett; they had only a few dollars and they had gone to a shelter suggested by the American Embassy. There in a miserable room without even a washbasin and with an iron cot, there had been a horrifying scene. She and then Jay had run out into the streets. From then on they had lived in the streets, under bridges, in parks, even in a cemetery for a night or two. "I never used the money you gave me, I gave it to Jay to go away. He followed me about. And then I found Derek and I never saw Jay again. Besides I know you will always be not far from me."

Debrett looked at her uneasily. She went on calmly, "I am ill, I can never be intimate with a man. Derek made me ill. They said it was I who did it. You must go now. I had to see you to tell you the whole story, but you must go now. I cannot have men in my rooms; it's not allowed. Of course, if Derek doesn't send me money, I will be put out of here. Where will I go? Give me your address." But Debrett, though he was very much upset, did not give the address. He said he was leaving town.

It was a few months later that he walked into a coffee shop near Central Park Plaza. There sat a woman who looked fifty, in clothes dirty and unbuttoned, gray-haired, face creased and yet with a self-possession and simpering, and the tender smile of former beauty. She came over to Debrett and said her name, "I have been waiting for you here. I knew you would come."

He drew back. "I had no intention of coming here; you couldn't have known." He looked at her with dislike.

"I know, Augustus Debrett; I have ways of knowing."

"You just wait, don't you, and then say things like that?"

"That's not it. It's you. I know where you will be."

She was about thirty-one, not older; but she smiled like an aged prostitute, cunningly and coarsely using the remains of once potent charm to get some last hesitant cus-

tomer. She handed him a piece of paper. "Read it." On it
was written, "I feel that Mr. Augustus Debrett will be at
57th Street this afternoon."

"I suppose you saw me come in and wrote it," he said
handing back the paper.

"No! Don't you know I always know where you are?"

"I don't believe in things like that, Honor. I suppose you
know a lot of people and you wait till you see them."

"I went back to Capetown, but the immigration au-
thorities kept me out. Someone had sent a letter against me,
saying I had married an African, a black African."

"Had you?"

"It was Derek's family said that, because he would never
do anything like that to me. And they won't let him answer
me; and now I have no money."

"Here's some money," he said, getting up hastily and
putting the money into her dirty hand. She opened a handbag and put it in. "I found this handbag on the street," she
said; "I was not waiting for money. I wanted to tell someone
my story."

He hurried into the street. A few days elapsed. He was at
an art show, a Walter Lawrence exhibition in a midtown
gallery, with Mari, when he stopped her in front of a drawing and said, "Look there! Do you recognize that? You've
seen her: that's Honor Lawrence; that pencil sketch."
"Is that Honor Lawrence? Well, it's not like the women
you've pointed out several times." "Yes, yes, you've forgotten. I know who it is. No one who knew her could ever
forget her."

A slight dark man of about thirty-five, with thinning

hair, wearing glasses and poorly dressed, turned around and said, "Who are you? You're Debrett, aren't you? Do you know who I am? I'm Jay Hewett, Honor's husband. Can I speak to you alone for a minute? I know that she went to South Africa, but I consider myself her husband. I know that you had an appointment with her a few days ago, in a coffee shop." Debrett described what had happened. "I know businessmen. I know she worked for you. I know you influenced her and she idealized you. I know she followed you to Europe." "What are you saying? Let's sit down; and then you talk like a rational man." Mari had moved on around the exhibition. "Who is that?" "That's Mari, my wife." "You met Honor in Europe and you introduced her to that South American who made such a mess of her life." "Hold on there; you've got a lot of stories tangled. I didn't introduce her and it wasn't a South American." "I know what Honor told me and she never lies."

Debrett stared at Jay Hewett with a soft open mouth. Jay continued, "I know what she told me and Honor never lies: she's incapable of it. She doesn't know why one should."

"You are quite wrong, I assure you, about following me to Europe. Why, you were married here, weren't you, and went to England together?" "I just want to say something to you. I can sense that you don't care for Honor any more. I've got to explain things to you. I've got to tell you the whole story. I knew Honor when she was thirteen, when she was telling people she was fifteen or eighteen; to protect her own childhood, she did it. I was seventeen and I loved her. I hardly had a decent night's sleep then. She was so young and innocent, untouchable innocence, such an austere fragility, such a child. She behaved like a coquette and tease, but I knew she was really a naïve child. You see I knew all about her, I have always known. I've hardly had a whole night's sleep in my life, or at least since I knew her. I wake up at four or five and begin to wonder about her. She's my joy, I rejoice in her; and I've learned you don't need much sleep. But I've had night jobs, too. I have discipline. I don't coddle myself. I've learned to like work; so I wake up and think of my work. I've done all kinds of things. I went out West. I got a job in a pool parlor. Anything real you see, to meet people. I went on the stage in a road company, painted scenery, did all kinds of jobs. I enjoyed overcoming the difficulties. I made myself meet all kinds of women; no fretting and mooning, you see. But all the time I knew I was going to marry Honor; she must have known too, although for years she treated me like dirt —why use such an expression? She didn't know what she was doing. You don't say a bird or a cat treats you like dirt. It was just a sort of innocent and ignorant wildness. She used to go about with other boys, and men, but she never even kissed them. I know that. They talked about it. But only I understood why. She'd leave a boy suddenly, while they were walking down the street. She could not bear to be touched. I knew this; I never touched her, so she got to trust me. She always knew where I was. And one day she called on me: just knocked at the door and walked in and said to me, Jay, today I think we'd better get married; I want to go to England and I think we'd better go. You see, she knew a lot about me; she knew my whole life. I had nothing to hide ever. I had always lived for her; so I felt it was a natural development. I knew she couldn't marry till she was ready; and I thought she was ready. Anything that happened was my fault, because I was the only one who understood her; and I didn't question her; I allowed my feelings to take over. She knew I had been writing to painters in Paris and London and was quite friendly with them; I had very good letters from them, not the usual brush-off letters. She knew all about this. So I was glad, and thought she was thinking of me. I was living for it; and it happened. How wonderful it was! That day paid for all. She understood me and others in an extraordinary way. She was inspired; she is inspired. You would not credit what shrewd, keen, and inspired observations she makes about people. There are people with great gifts who want to create, but are not self-centered enough. The glory of creation is in them. They end by creating themselves; and they are miraculous creatures. People fall in love with them, because they've made something new. I don't blame you, Debrett—" he broke off, "not really."

"I sympathize with all you say; but let me set your mind at rest. I was never in love with Honor."

"Yes, you couldn't understand Honor as I could. Because she was a work of art I was born to understand; for others, the misunderstood masterpiece. I nearly called on you several times. I just wanted to clarify your relations to Honor. At first, in London, I blamed you for what happened."

"How could you?" said Debrett, with cross patience.

Hewett rested for a while. They walked along the lines of drawings and paintings. He had an unpleasant color, earthy, and an unpleasant attitude, aggressive with a grating voice; so that though his words carried conviction, Debrett felt no sympathy. Debrett's eyes stared at him, wide open, his mouth too was slightly open; his breathing could be heard. His hands were cold.

Hewett said, "Life's very short, isn't it? We don't understand many people in a lifetime. We don't love many people in a lifetime. It's a dreadful thought. Life rushing past, populations of people and we're indifferent, blind; we might be asleep or dead. We are dead when we don't love. I am sure there are people who don't understand one human being in a lifetime. A lifetime! What a word! What it means! Think of the people, towns, plains, forests—it fills me with love to think of it. But for some, just habits and quirks. I suppose she borrowed money from you, too, the other day?"

"Eh?" said Debrett.

"It doesn't matter. If she owes you anything I'll pay it back. I assure you, you never meant anything to her; only one man ever did." He smiled. "Don't look so sympathetic; it wasn't me."

"I never actually spoke to Honor in Europe."

"She got money from you and gave it all to me. That was like her. She never thought of herself. If she goes about like a beggar and a tramp, with her stockings around her ankles, it's because she doesen't understand the conventional life of a woman. She's a spirit in a dress of rags. I understand poor wandering women now; I cry for them, not laugh at them. Do you know the Spanish never laugh at monsters, idiots and poor creatures? They call them creatures of God like everyone else, more so, they think. What wonderful people the Spanish are; that is love. I don't believe in God, but their heart is great. Honor told me she went to Europe to pay you back some money she borrowed from you. Isn't that incredible? And yet I believe it."

"How did you think you would live in Europe? How could you take her into that unspeakable misery. What way out was there?"

"Yes, the man of accounts! You wouldn't understand! I was too crazed with happiness to think. I thought the road was up, from there. I remember sitting in the subway and looking at some faces opposite, I've forgotten them now, and I was thinking, Well, that's something accomplished, that's done. One can't say that, I know now; especially about another human being. One must leave them free. She had despised and insulted me for years—terribly insulted; been cruel to me, and then without being asked she came and said, We'll marry. It was a reward for all those years. My fault. I thought of her as a reward." After a slight pause, he said, "It was all misery; but that is the story of my happiness and joy. Some people haven't had so much."

"Do you know where she is now, then?"

"Yes, I have an appointment with her this afternoon. I was at this exhibition yesterday. I saw the head of her and I found out from the artist where she is."

And it was from Walter Lawrence, who was beginning to fall in love with Mari, that they heard the rest.

In the afternoon, Jay met her in the Square.

"You said you wanted to see me," she said, politely offering her hand. She looked tired and old, untidy.

He had a few words with her, about where she was living, about helping her. She said, "Could we go and have some milk? I wish there were milk bars here as there are in London. I used to walk along the street looking at the milk bars, beautiful places with white tiles and clean glass, so healthy and pure. I used to go into as many as I could. Milk is good for you, you know. You oughtn't to drink beer and whisky, Jay."

"I haven't drunk beer or whisky for years. I have no money for such things. I have a job that enables me to pay the rent of a hall bedroom; and I could manage for us both if you were willing."

"I had a baby," she said quickly; "and I drank milk for the baby's sake. His family sent my baby to an orphan asylum and I went everywhere asking for it, but they said I had no proof. I was its mother, but there were no papers. And he divorced me; he told me to leave. I can never go back and I don't know if my child is alive or dead."

"You look very sick to me, Honor. Let me look after you. Never mind the past."

"No one wants me now. You don't want me. I am very sick. I can't do anything for you. I know what you want."

"Oh, Honor, Honor—you know me—" He took her arm. "I'll take care of you. I will. I am yours. I don't want your love, or anything you could never give me. But I'd rather die than live without you; you are life. It's quite simple; you're so real. What's there in me, if not you? Your terrible sorrows are real. It's that, and the beauty of your mind and sorrows that I care for. They're my hope, my fire, my salvation. I love you."

She pushed him away roughly and spat. "Love! I spit, I spit it out," she cried out. "It was all lies. It kills you. It's to get you. There's no love at all."

She got up and he got up. "Don't come near me again and don't follow me." She went down Washington Place, disappeared into a large apartment house. She probably went out again through a courtyard, for he could not find her. She knew the city like a beggar, like a small boy.

It was three years later that he heard of her death in winter, in a half-covered doorway, up three steps, of a loft building not far from Union Square. And he too disappeared. Perhaps he died. No one asked after him, for he had never made an impression. It was only when people mentioned Honor's name, later, "Walter's sister," that it was sometimes said, "Did you know that she was actually married to a man named Hewett; but they said it was not a real marriage."

Debrett thought he saw her from time to time, but as a young woman. "Is she eternally young?" he said to himself. Then he heard of her death. "But I don't really believe it," he said to Mari. "It's too *faits-divers*. It's not like her. I expect she's turning up somewhere at this moment, asking for help. She's a wraith, a wanderer. What is she?" "She's the ragged wayward heart of woman that doesn't want to be caught and hasn't been caught," said Mari, in her beautiful metallic voice. "She never was in love." He looked at her in doubt. "She never loved anyone," said Mari. Debrett thought of this. He did not believe it, but walking up and down under the trees in someone's garden, he bent his head a little, saw nothing, wiped his eyes with his hands.

JEAN RHYS

Till September Petronella

There was a barrel organ playing
at the corner of Torrington Square. It played *Destiny*
and *La Paloma* and *Le Rêve Passe*, all tunes I liked, and
the wind was warm and kind, not spiteful, which doesn't
often happen in London. I packed the striped dress that
Estelle had helped me to choose, and the cheap white one
that fitted well, and my best underclothes, feeling very
happy while I was packing. A bit of a change, for that had
not been one of my lucky summers.

I would tell myself it was the colour of the carpet or
something about my room which was depressing me, but it
wasn't that. And it wasn't anything to do with money either.

I was making nearly five pounds a week—very good for me, and different from when I first started, when I was walking round trying to get work. *No* Hawkers, *No* Models, some of them put up, and you stand there, your hands cold and clammy, afraid to ring the bell. But I had got past that stage; this depression had nothing to do with money.

I often wished I was like Estelle, this French girl who lived in the big room on the ground floor. She had everything so cut-and-dried, she walked the tightrope so beautifully, not even knowing she was walking it. I'd think about the talks we had, and her clothes and her scent and the way she did her hair, and that when I went into her room it didn't seem like a Bloomsbury bed-sitting room—and when it comes to Bloomsbury bed-sitting rooms I know what I'm talking about. No, it was like a room out of one of those long, romantic novels, six hundred and fifty pages of small print, translated from French or German or Hungarian or something—because few of the English ones have the exact feeling I mean. And you read one page of it or even one phrase of it, and then you gobble up all the rest and go about in a dream for weeks afterwards, for months afterwards—perhaps all your life, who knows?—surrounded by those six hundred and fifty pages, the houses, the streets, the snow, the river, the roses, the girls, the sun, the ladies' dresses and the gentlemen's voices, the old, wicked, hard-hearted women and the old, sad women, the waltz music, everything. What is not there you put in afterwards, for it is alive, this book, and it grows in your head. "The house I was living in when I read that book," you think, or "This colour reminds me of that book."

It was after Estelle left, telling me she was going to Paris

and wasn't sure whether she was coming back, that I struck
a bad patch. Several of the people I was sitting to left London in June, but, instead of arranging for more work, I
took long walks, zigzag, always the same way—Euston
Road, Hampstead Road, Camden Town—though I hated
those streets, which were like a grey nightmare in the sun.
You saw so many old women, or women who seemed old,
peering at the vegetables in the Camden Town market,
looking at you with hatred, or blankly, as though they had
forgotten your language, and talked another one. "My
God," I would think, "I hope I never live to be old. Anyway, however old I get, I'll never let my hair go grey. I'll
dye it black, red, any colour you like, but I'll never let it
go grey. I hate grey too much." Coming back from one of
these walks the thought came to me suddenly, like a revela-
tion, that I could kill myself any time I liked and so end
it. After that I put a better face on things.

When Marston wrote and I told the landlord I was going
away for a fortnight, he said "So there's a good time coming for the ladies, is there?—a good time coming for the
girls? About time too."

Marston said, "You seem very perky, my dear. I hardly
recognized you."

I looked along the platform, but Julian had not come to
meet me. There was only Marston, his long, white face and
his pale-blue eyes, smiling.

"What a gigantic suitcase," he said. "I have my motorbike here, but I suppose I'd better leave it. We'll take a
cab."

It was getting dark when we reached the cottage, which

stood by itself on rising ground. There were two elm trees in a field near the verandah, but the country looked bare, with low, grassy hills.

As we walked up the path through the garden I could hear Julian laughing and a girl talking, her voice very high and excited, though she put on a calm, haughty expression as we came into the room. Her dress was red, and she wore several coloured glass bangles which tinkled when she moved.

Marston said, "This is Frankie. You've met the great Julian, of course."

Well, I knew Frankie Morell by sight, but as she didn't say anything about it I didn't either. We smiled at each other cautiously, falsely.

The table was laid for four people. The room looked comfortable but there were no flowers. I had expected that they would have it full of flowers. However, there were some sprays of honeysuckle in a green jug in my bedroom and Marston, standing in the doorway, said, "I walked miles to get you that honeysuckle this morning. I thought about you all the time I was picking it."

"Don't be long," he said. "We're all very hungry."

We ate ham and salad and drank perry. It went to my head a bit. Julian talked about his job which he seemed to dislike. He was the music critic of one of the daily papers. "It's a scandal. One's forced to down the right people and praise the wrong people."

"Forced?" said Marston.

"Well, they drop very strong hints."

"I'll take the plates away," Frankie told me. "You can

start tomorrow. Not one of the local women will do a thing for us. We've only been here a fortnight, but they've got up a hate you wouldn't believe. Julian says he almost faints when he thinks of it. I say, why think of it?"

When she came back she turned the lamp out. Down there it was very still. The two trees outside did not move, or the moon.

Julian lay on the sofa and I was looking at his face and his hair when Marston put his arms round me and kissed me. But I watched Julian and listened to him whistling—stopping, laughing, beginning again.

"What was that music?" I said, and Frankie answered in a patronizing voice, "*Tristan,* second act duet."

"I've never been to that opera."

I had never been to any opera. All the same, I could imagine it. I could imagine myself in a box, wearing a moonlight-blue dress and silver shoes, and when the lights went up everybody asking, "Who's that lovely girl in that box?" But it must happen quickly or it will be too late.

Marston squeezed my hand. "Very fine performance, Julian," he said, "very fine. Now forgive me, my dears, I must leave you. All this emotion—"

Julian lighted the lamp, took a book from the shelf and began to read.

Frankie blew on the nails of one hand and polished them on the edge of the other. Her nails were nice—of course, you could get a manicure for a bob then—but her hands were large and too white for her face. "I've seen you at the Apple Tree, surely." The Apple Tree was a night club in Greek Street.

"Oh yes, often."

"But you've cut your hair. I wanted to cut mine, but Julian asked me not to. He begged me not to. Didn't you, Julian?"

Julian did not answer.

"He said he'd lose his strength if I cut my hair."

Julian turned over a page and went on reading.

"This isn't a bad spot, is it?" Frankie said. "Not one of those places where the ceiling's on top of your head and you've got to walk four miles in the dark to the lavatory. There are two other bedrooms besides the one Marston gave you. Come and have a look at them. You can change over if you want to. We'll never tear Julian away from his book. It's about the biological inferiority of women. That's what you told me, Julian, isn't it?"

"Oh, *go* away," Julian said.

We ended up in her room, where she produced some head and figure studies, photographs.

"Do you like these? Do you know this man? He says I'm the best model he's ever had. He says I'm far and away the best model in London."

"Beautiful. Lovely photographs."

But Frankie, sitting on the big bed, said, "Aren't people swine? Julian says I never think. He's wrong, sometimes I think quite a lot. The other day I spent a long time trying to decide which were worse—men or women."

"I wonder."

"Women are worse."

She had long, calm black hair, drawn away from her face and hanging smoothly almost to her waist, and a calm, clear little voice and a calm, haughty expression.

"They'll kick your face to bits if you let them. And shriek with laughter at the damage. But I'm not going to let them —oh no . . . Marston's always talking about you," she said. "He's very fond of you, poor old Marston. Do you know that picture as you go into his studio—in the entrance place? What's he say it is?"

"The Apotheosis of Lust."

"Yes, the Apotheosis of Lust. I have to laugh when I think of that, for some reason. Poor old Andy Marston . . . But I don't know why I should say 'Poor old Andy Marston.' He'll always have one penny to tinkle against another. His family's very wealthy, you know."

"He makes me go cold."

I thought, "Why did I say that?" Because I like Marston.

"So that's how you feel about him, is it?" She seemed pleased, as if she had heard something she wanted to hear, had been waiting to hear.

"Are you tired?" Marston said.

I was looking out of the bedroom window at some sheep feeding in the field where the elm trees grew.

"A bit," I said. "A bit very."

His mouth drooped, disappointed.

"Oh, Marston, thank you for asking me down here. It's so lovely to get away from London; it's like a dream."

"A dream, my God! However, when it comes to dreams, why shouldn't they be pleasant?"

He sat down on the windowsill.

"The great Julian's not so bad, is he?"

"Why do you call him the great Julian? As if you were gibing at him."

"Gibing at him? Good Lord, far be it from me to gibe at him. He *is* the great Julian. He's going to be very important, so far as an English musician can be important. He's horribly conceited, though. Not about his music, of course—he's conceited about his personal charm. I can't think why. He's a very ordinary type really. You see that nose and mouth and hear that voice all over the place. You rather dislike him, don't you?"

"Do I?"

"Of course you do. Have you forgotten how annoyed you were when I told you that he'd have to *see* a female before he could consent to live at close quarters with her for two weeks? You were quite spirited about it, I thought. Don't say that was only a flash in the pan, you poor devil of a female, female, female, in a country where females are only tolerated at best! What's going to become of you, Miss Petronella Gray, living in a bed-sitting room in Torrington Square, with no money, no background and no nous? . . . Is Petronella your real name?"

"Yes."

"You worry me, whatever your name is. I bet it isn't Gray."

I thought, "What does it matter? If you knew how bloody my home was you wouldn't be surprised that I wanted to change my name and forget all about it."

I said, not looking at him, "I was called after my grandmother—Julia Petronella."

"Oh, you've got a grandmother, have you? Fancy that! Now, for Heaven's sake don't put on that expression. Take my advice and grow another skin or two and sharpen your claws before it's too late. *Before it's too late,* mark those words. If you don't, you're going to have a hell of a time."

"So that I long for death?"

He looked startled. "Why do you say that?"

"It was only the first thing that came into my head from nowhere. I was joking."

When he did not answer, "Well, good night," I said. "Sleep tight."

"I shan't sleep," he said. "I shall probably have to listen to those two for quite a time yet. When they're amorous they're noisy and when they fight it's worse. She goes for him with a pen-knife. Mind you, she only does that because he likes it, but her good nature is a pretence. She's a bitch really. Shut your door and you won't hear anything. Will you be sad tomorrow?"

"Of course not."

"Don't look as if you'd lost a shilling and found sixpence then," he said, and went out.

That's the way they always talk. "You look as if you'd lost a shilling and found sixpence," they say; "You look very perky, I hardly recognized you," they say; "*Look gay,*" they say. "My dear Petronella, I have an entirely new idea of you. I'm going to paint you out in the opulent square. So can you wear something gay tomorrow afternoon? Not one of those drab affairs you usually clothe yourself in. Gay— do you know the meaning of the word? Think about it, it's very important."

The things you remember. . . .

Once, left alone in a very ornate studio, I went up to a

plaster cast—the head of a man, one of those Greek heads —and kissed it, because it was so beautiful. Its mouth felt warm, not cold. It was smiling. When I kissed it the room went dead silent and I was frightened. I told Estelle about this one day. "Does that sound mad?" She didn't laugh. She said, "Who hasn't kissed a picture or a photograph and suddenly been frightened?"

The music Julian had been whistling was tormenting me. That, and the blind eyes of the plaster cast, and the way the sun shone on the black iron bedstead in my room in Torrington Square on fine days. The bars of the bedstead grin at me. Sometimes I count the knobs on the chest of drawers three times over. "One of those drab affairs! . . ."

I began to talk to Julian in my head. Was it to Julian? "I'm not like that. I'm not at all like that. They're trying to make me like that, but I'm not like that."

After a while I took a pencil and paper and wrote, "I love Julian. Julian, I kissed you once, but you didn't know."

I folded the paper several times and hid it under some clothes in my suitcase. Then I went to bed and slept at once.

Where our path joined the main road there were some cottages. As Marston and I came back from our walk next morning we passed two women in their gardens, which were full of lupins and poppies. They looked at us sullenly, as though they disliked us. When Marston said "Good morning," they did not answer.

"Surly, priggish brutes," he muttered, "but that's how they are."

The grass round our cottage was long and trampled in places. There were no flowers.

"They're back," Marston said. "There's the motorbike."

They came out on to the verandah, very spruce; Frankie in her red frock with her hair tied up in a red and blue handkerchief, Julian wearing a brown coat over a blue shirt and shabby grey trousers like Marston's. Very gay, I thought. (*Gay—do you know the meaning of the word?*)

"What's the matter with you, Marston?" Julian said. "You look frightful."

"You do seem a bit upset," Frankie said. "What happened? Do tell."

"Don't tell her anything," said Marston. "I'm going to dress up too. Why should I be the only one in this resplendent assembly with a torn shirt and stained bags? Wait till you see what I've got—and I don't mean what you mean."

"Let's get the food ready," Frankie said to me.

The kitchen table was covered with things they had brought from Cheltenham, and there were several bottles of white wine cooling in a bucket of water in the corner.

"What have you done to Marston?"

"Nothing. What on earth do you mean?"

Nothing had happened. We were sitting under a tree, looking at a field of corn, and Marston put his head in my lap and then a man came along and yelled at us. I said, "What do you think we're doing to your corn? Can't we even look at your corn?" But Marston only mumbled, "I'm fearfully sorry. I'm dreadfully sorry," and so on. And then we went walking along the main road in the sun, not talking much because I was hating him.

"Nothing happened," I said.

"Oh well, it's a pity, because Julian's in a bad mood today. However, don't take any notice of him. Don't start a row whatever you do; just smooth it over."

"Look at the lovely bit of steak I got," she said. "Marston says he can't touch any meat except cold ham, I ask you, and he does the cooking. Cold ham and risotto, risotto and cold ham. And curried eggs. That's what we've been living on ever since we came down here."

When we went in with the food they had finished a bottle of wine. Julian said, "Here's luck to the ruddy citizens I saw this morning. May they be flourishing and producing offspring exactly like themselves, but far, far worse, long after we are all in our dishonoured graves."

Marston was now wearing black silk pyjamas with a pattern of red and green dragons. His long, thin neck and sad face looked extraordinary above this get-up. Frankie and I glanced at each other and giggled. Julian scowled at me.

Marston went over to the mirror. "Never mind," he said softly to his reflection, "never mind, never mind."

"It's ham and salad again," Frankie said. "But I've got some prunes."

The table was near the window. A hot, white glare shone in our eyes. We tried pulling the blinds down, but one got stuck and we went on eating in the glare.

Then Frankie talked about the steak again. "You must have your first bite tonight, Marston."

"It won't be my first bite," Marston said. "I've been persuaded to taste beef before."

"Oh, you never told me that. No likee?"

"I thought it would taste like sweat," Marston said, "and it did."

Frankie looked annoyed. "The trouble with you people is that you try to put other people off just because you don't fancy a thing. If you'd just not like it and leave it at that, but you don't *rest* till you've put everybody else off."

"Oh God, let's get tight," Julian said. "There are bottles and bottles of wine in the kitchen. Cooling, I hope."

"We'll get them," Frankie said, "we'll get them."

Frankie sat on the kitchen table. "I think Julian's spoiling for a fight. Let him calm down a bit. . . . You're staving Marston off, aren't you? And he doesn't like it; he's very disconsolate. You've got to be careful of these people, they can be as hard as nails."

Far away a dog barked, a cock crew, somebody was sawing wood. I hardly noticed what she had said because again it came, that feeling of happiness, the fish-in-water feeling, so that I couldn't even remember having been unhappy.

Frankie started on a long story about a man called Petersen who had written a play about Northern gods and goddesses and Yggdrasil.

"I thought Yggdrasil was a girl, but it seems it's a tree."

Marston and Julian and all that lot had taken Petersen up, she said. They used to ask him out and make him drunk. Then he would take his clothes off and dance about and if he did not do it somebody would be sure to say, "What's the matter? Why don't you perform?" But as soon as he got really sordid they had dropped him like a hot brick. He simply disappeared.

"I met an old boy who knew him and asked what had happened. The old boy said, 'A gigantic maw has swallowed Petersen . . .' Maw, what a word! It reminds me of

Julian's mother—she's a maw if you like. Well, I'd better take these bottles along now."

So we took the four bottles out of the bucket and went back into the sitting-room. It was still hot and glaring, but not quite so bad as it had been.

"Now it's my turn to make a speech," said Marston. "But you must drink, pretty creatures, drink." He filled our glasses and I drank mine quickly. He filled it up again.

"My speech," he said, "my speech. . . . Let's drink to afternoon, the best of all times. Cruel morning is past, fearful, unpredictable, lonely night is yet to come. Here's to heartrending afternoon. . . . I will now recite a poem. It's hackneyed and pawed about, like so many other things, but beautiful. 'C'est bien la pire peine de ne savoir pourquoi—' "

He stopped and began to cry. We all looked at him. Nobody laughed; nobody knew what to say. I felt shut in by the glare.

Marston blew his nose, wiped his eyes and gabbled on: " 'Pourquoi, sans amour et sans haine, Mon coeur a tant de peine. . . .' "

" 'Sans amour' is right," Julian said, staring at me. I looked back into his eyes.

" 'But for loving, why, you would not, Sweet,' " Marston went on, " 'Though we prayed you, Paid you, brayed you In a mortar—for you could not, Sweet.' "

"The motorbike was altogether a bit of luck," Frankie said. "Julian had a fight with a man on the bus going in. I thought he'd have a fit."

"Fight?" Julian said. "I never fight. I'm frightened."

He was still staring at me.

"Well then, you were very rude."

"I'm never rude, either," Julian said. "I'm far too frightened ever to be rude. I suffer in silence."

"I shouldn't do that if I were you," I said. The wine was making me giddy. So was the glare, and the way he was looking at me.

"What's this young creature up to?" he said. "I can't quite make her out."

"Ruddy respectable citizens never can."

"Ha-hah," Frankie said. "One in the eye for you, Julian. You're always going on about respectable people, but you know *you* are respectable, whatever you say and whatever you do and you'll be respectable till you die, however you die, and that way you miss something, believe it or not."

"You keep out of this, Phoenician," Julian said. "You've got nothing to say. Retire under the table, because that's where I like you best."

Frankie crawled under the table. She darted her head out now and again, pretending to bite his legs, and every time she did that he would shiver and scream.

"Oh, come on out," he said at last. "It's too hot for these antics."

Frankie crawled out again, very pleased with herself, went to the mirror and arranged the handkerchief round her hair. "Am I really like a Phoenician?"

"Of course you are. A Phoenician from Cornwall, England. Direct descent, I should say."

"And what's she?" Frankie said. Her eyes looked quite different, like snake's eyes. We all looked quite different—it's funny what drink does.

"That's very obvious too," Julian said.

"All right, why don't you come straight out with it?" I said. "Or are you frightened?"

"Sometimes words fail."

Marston waved his arms about. "Julian, you stop this. I won't have it."

"You fool," Julian said, "you fool. Can't you see she's fifth-rate. Can't you see?

"You ghastly cross between a barmaid and a chorus-girl," he said; "You female spider," he said; "You've been laughing at him for weeks," he said, "jeering at him, sniggering at him. Stopping him from working—the best painter in this damnable island, the only one in my opinion. And then when I try to get him away from you, of course you follow him down here."

"That's not it at all," Marston said. "You're not being fair to the girl. You don't understand her a bit."

"She doesn't care," Julian said. "Look at her—she's giggling her stupid head off."

"Well, what are you to do when you come up against a mutual admiration society?" I said.

"You're letting your jealousy run away with you," said Marston.

"Jealousy?" Julian said. "Jealousy!" He was unrecognizable. His beautiful eyes were little, mean pits and you looked down them into nothingness.

"Jealous of what?" he shrieked. "Why, do you know that she told Frankie last night that she can't bear you and that the only reason she has anything to do with you is because she wants money. What do you think of that? Does that open your eyes?"

"Now, *Julian!*" Frankie's voice was as loud and high as his. "You'd no right to repeat that. You promised you wouldn't and anyway you've exaggerated it. It's all very well for you to talk about how inferior women are, but you get more like your horrible mother every moment."

"You do," Marston said, quite calm now. "Julian, you really do."

"Do you know what all this is about?" Frankie said, nodding at Julian. "It's because he doesn't want me to go back to London with him. He wants me to go and be patronized and educated by his detestable mother in her dreary house in the dreary country, who will then say that the case is hopeless. Wasn't she a good sort and a saint to try? But the girl is *quite impossible.* Do you think I don't know that trick? It's as old as the hills.

"You're mean," she said to Julian, "and you hate girls really. Don't imagine I don't see through you. You're trying to get me down. But you won't do it. If you think you're the only man in the world who's fond of me *or* that I'm a goddamned fool, you're making the hell of a big mistake, you and your mother."

She plucked a hairpin from her hair, bent it into the shape of pince-nez and went on in a mincing voice, "Do Ay understend you tew say thet *may* sonn—" she placed the pince-nez on her nose and looked over it sourly "—with *one* connection—"

"Damn you," said Julian, "damn you, damn you."

"Now they're off," Marston said placidly. "Drinking on a hot afternoon is a mistake. The pen-knife will be out in a minute . . . Don't go. Stay and watch the fun. My money on Frankie every time."

But I went into the bedroom and shut the door. I could hear them wrangling and Marston, very calm and superior, putting in a word now and again. Then nothing. They had gone on to the verandah.

I got the letter I had written and tore it very carefully into four pieces. I spat on each piece. I opened the door—there was not a sign of them. I took the pieces of paper to the lavatory, emptied them in and pulled the plug. As soon as I heard the water gushing I felt better.

The door of the kitchen was open and I saw that there was another path leading to the main road.

And there I was, walking along, not thinking of anything, my eyes fixed on the ground. I walked a long way like that, not looking up, though I passed several people. At last I came to a sign-post. I was on the Cirencester road. Something about the word "miles" written made me feel very tired.

A little farther on the wall on one side of the road was low. It was the same wall on which Marston and I had sat that morning, and he had said, "Do you think we could rest here or will the very stones rise up against us?" I looked round and there was nobody in sight, so I stepped over it and sat down in the shade. It was pretty country, but bare. The white, glaring look was still in the sky.

Close by there was a dove cooing. "Coo away, dove," I thought. "It's no use, no use, still coo away, coo away."

After a while the dazed feeling, as if somebody had hit me on the head, began to go. I thought "Cirencester—and then a train to London. It's as easy as that."

Then I realized that I had left my handbag and money, as well as everything else, in the bedroom at the cottage, but imagining walking back there made me feel so tired that I could hardly put one foot in front of the other.

I got over the wall. A car that was coming along slowed down and stopped and the man driving it said, "Want a lift?"

I went up to the car.

"Where do you want to go?"

"I want to go to London."

"To London? Well, I can't take you as far as that, but I can get you into Cirencester to catch a train if you like."

I said anxiously, "Yes—but I must go back first to the place where I've been staying. It's not far."

"Haven't time for that. I've got an appointment. I'm late already and I mustn't miss it. Tell you what—come along with me. If you'll wait till I've done I can take you to fetch your things."

I got into the car. As soon as I touched him I felt comforted. Some men are like that.

"Well, you look as if you'd lost a shilling and found sixpence."

Again I had to laugh.

"That's better. Never does any good to be down in the mouth."

"We're nearly in Cirencester now," he said after a while. "I've got to see a lot of people. This is market day and I'm a farmer. I'll take you to a nice quiet place where you can have a cup of tea while you're waiting."

He drove to a pub in a narrow street. "This way in." I followed him into the bar.

"Good afternoon, Mrs. Strickland. Lovely day, isn't it? Will you give my friend a cup of tea while I'm away, and make her comfortable? She's very tired."

"I will, certainly," Mrs. Strickland said, with a swift glance up and down. "I expect the young lady would like a nice wash too, wouldn't she?" She was dark and nicely got up, but her voice had a tinny sound.

"Oh, I would."

I looked down at my crumpled white dress. I touched my face for I knew there must be a red mark where I had lain with it pressed against the ground.

"See you later," the farmer said.

There were brightly polished taps in the ladies' room and a very clean red and black tiled floor. I washed my hands, tried to smooth my dress, and powdered my face—Poudre Nildé basanée—but I did it without looking in the glass.

Tea and cakes were laid in a small, dark, stuffy room. There were three pictures of Lady Hamilton, Johnny Walker advertisements, china bulldogs wearing sailor caps and two calendars. One said January 9th, but the other was right— July 28th, 1914. . . .

"Well, here I am." He sat heavily down beside me. "Did Mrs. Strickland look after you all right?"

"Very well."

"Oh, she's a good sort, she's a nice woman. She's known me a long time. Of course, you haven't, have you? But everything's got to have a start."

Then he said he hadn't done so badly that afternoon and stretched out his legs, looking pleased, looking happy as the day is long.

"What were you thinking about when I came in? You nearly jumped out of your skin."

"I was thinking about the time."

"About the time? Oh, don't worry about that. There's plenty of time."

He produced a large silver case, took out a cigar and lighted it, long and slow. "Plenty of time," he said. "Dark in here, isn't it? So you live in London, do you?"

"Yes."

"I've often thought I'd like to know a nice girl up in London."

His eyes were fixed on Lady Hamilton and I knew he was imagining a really lovely girl—all curves, curls, heart and hidden claws. He swallowed, then put his hand over mine.

"I'd like to feel that when I go up to Town there's a friend I could see and have a good time with. You know. And I could give her a good time too. By God, I could. I know what women like."

"You do?"

"Yes, I do. They like a bit of loving, that's what they like, isn't it? A bit of loving. All women like that. They like it dressed up sometimes—and sometimes not, it all depends. You have to know, and I know. I just know."

"You've nothing more to learn, have you?"

"Not in that way I haven't. And they like pretty dresses and bottles of scent, and bracelets with blue stones in them. I know. Well, what about it?" he said, but as if he were joking.

I looked away from him at the calendar and did not answer, making my face blank.

"What about it?" he repeated.

"It's nice of you to say you want to see me again—very polite."

He laughed. "You think I'm being polite, do you? Well, perhaps—perhaps not. No harm in asking, was there? No offence meant—or taken, I hope. It's all right. I'll take you to get your things and catch your train—and we'll have a bottle of something good before we start off. It won't hurt you. It's bad stuff hurts you, not good stuff. You haven't found that out yet, but you will. Mrs. Strickland has some good stuff, I can tell you—good enough for me, and I want the best."

So we had a bottle of Clicquot in the bar.

He said, "It puts some life into you, doesn't it?"

It did too. I wasn't feeling tired when we left the pub, nor even sad.

"Well," he said as we got into the car, "you've got to tell me where to drive to. And you don't happen to know a little song, do you?"

"That was very pretty," he said when I stopped. "You've got a very pretty voice indeed. Give us some more."

But we were getting near the cottage and I didn't finish the next song because I was nervous and worried that I wouldn't be able to tell him the right turning.

At the foot of the path I thought, "The champagne worked all right."

He got out of the car and came with me. When we reached the gate leading into the garden he stood by my side without speaking.

They were on the verandah. We could hear their voices clearly.

"Listen, fool," Julian was saying, "listen, half-wit. What I said yesterday has nothing to do with what I say today or what I shall say tomorrow. Why should it?"

"That's what you think," Frankie said obstinately. "I don't agree with you. It might have something to do with it whether you like it or not."

"Oh, stop arguing, you two," Marston said. "It's all very well for you, Julian, but I'm worried about that girl. I'm responsible. She looked so damned miserable. Supposing she's gone and made away with herself. I shall feel awful. Besides, probably I shall be held up to every kind of scorn and obloquy—as usual. And though it's all your fault you'll escape scot-free—also as usual."

"Are those your friends?" the farmer asked.

"Well, they're my friends in a way . . . I have to go in to get my things. It won't take me long."

Julian said, "I think, I rather think, Marston, that I hear a female pipe down there. You can lay your fears away. She's not the sort to kill herself. I told you that."

"Who's that?" the farmer said.

"That's Mr. Oakes, one of my hosts."

"Oh, is it? I don't like the sound of him. I don't like the sound of any of them. Shall I come with you?"

"No, don't. I won't be long."

I went round by the kitchen into my room, walking very softly. I changed into my dark dress and then began to throw my things into the suitcase. I did all this as quickly as I could, but before I had finished Marston came in, still wearing his black pyjamas crawling with dragons.

"Who were you talking to outside?"

"Oh, that's a man I met. He's going to drive me to Cirencester to catch the London train."

"You're not offended, are you?"

"Not a bit. Why should I be?"

"Of course, the great Julian can be so difficult," he murmured. "But don't think I didn't stick up for you, because I did. I said to him, 'It's all very well for you to be rude to a girl I bring down, but what about your loathly Frankie, whom you inflict upon me day after day and week after week and I never say a word? I'm never even sharp to her—' What are you smiling at?"

"The idea of your being sharp to Frankie."

"The horrid little creature!" Marston said excitedly, "the unspeakable bitch! But the day will come when Julian will find her out and he'll run to me for sympathy. I'll not give it him. Not after this. . . . Cheer up," he said. "The world is big. There's hope."

"Of course." But suddenly I saw the women's long, scowling faces over their lupins and their poppies, and my room in Torrington Square and the iron bars of my bedstead, and I thought, "Not for me."

"It may all be necessary," he said, as if he were talking to himself. "One has to get an entirely different set of values to be any good."

I said, "Do you think I could go out through the window? I don't want to meet them."

"I'll come to the car with you. What's this man like?"

"Well, he's a bit like the man this morning, and he says he doesn't care for the sound of you."

"Then I think I won't come. Go through the window and I'll hand your suitcase to you."

He leaned out and said, "See you in September, Petronella. I'll be back in September."

I looked up at him. "All right. Same old address."

The farmer said, "I was coming in after you. You're well rid of that lot—never did like that sort. Too many of them about."

"They're all right."

"Well, tune up," he said, and I sang "Mr. Brown, Mr. Brown, Had a violin, Went around, went around, With his violin." I sang all the way to Cirencester.

At the station he gave me my ticket and a box of chocolates.

"I bought these for you this afternoon, but I forgot them. Better hurry—there's not much time."

"Fare you well," he said. "That's what they say in Norfolk, where I come from."

"Good-bye."

"No, say fare you well."

"Fare you well."

The train started.

"This is very nice," I thought, "my first-class carriage," and had a long look at myself in the glass for the first time since it had happened. "Never mind," I said, and remembered Marston saying "Never mind, never mind."

"Don't look so down in the mouth, my girl," I said to myself, "*Look gay.*

"Cheer up," I said, and kissed myself in the cool glass. I stood with my forehead against it and watched my face clouding gradually, then turned because I felt as if someone was staring at me, but it was only the girl on the cover of the chocolate-box. She had slanting green eyes, but they were too close together, and she had a white, square, smug face that didn't go with her slanting eyes. "I bet you could be a rotten, respectable, sneering bitch too, with a face like that, if you had the chance," I told her.

The train got into Paddington just before ten. As soon as I was on the platform I remembered the chocolates, but I didn't go back for them. "Somebody will find you, somebody will look after you, you rotten, sneering, stupid, tight-mouthed bitch," I thought.

London always smells the same. "Frowsty," you think, "but I'm glad to be back." And just for a while it bears you up. "Anything's round the corner," you think. But long before you get round the corner it lets you drop.

I decided that I'd walk for a bit with the suitcase and get tired and then perhaps I'd sleep. But at the corner of Marylebone Road and Edgware Road my arm was stiff and I put down the suitcase and waved at a taxi standing by the kerb.

"Sorry, miss," the driver said, "this gentleman was first."

The young man smiled. "It's all right. You have it."

"*You have it,*" *he said. The other one said,* "*Want a lift?*"

"I can get the next one. I'm not in any hurry."

"Nor am I."

The taxi-driver moved impatiently.

"Well, don't let's hesitate any longer," the young man said, "or we'll lose our taximeter-cab. Get in—I can easily drop you wherever you're going."

"Go along Edgware Road," he said to the driver. "I'll tell you where in a minute."

The taxi started.

"Where to?"

"Torrington Square."

The house would be waiting for me. "When I pass Estelle's door," I thought, "there'll be no smell of scent now." Then I was back in my small room on the top floor, listening to the church clock chiming every quarter-hour. "There's a good time coming for the ladies. There's a good time coming for the girls. . . ."

I said, "Wait a minute. I don't want to go to Torrington Square."

"Oh, you don't want to go to Torrington Square?" He seemed amused and wary, but more wary than amused.

"It's such a lovely night, so warm. I don't want to go home just yet. I think I'll go and sit in Hyde Park."

"Not Torrington Square," he shouted through the window.

The taxi drew up.

"Damn his eyes, what's he done that for."

The driver got down and opened the door.

"Here, where am I going to? This is the third time you've changed your mind since you 'ailed me."

"You'll go where you're damn well told."

"Well where am I damn well told?"

"Go to the Marble Arch."

" 'Yde Park," the driver said, looking us up and down and grinning broadly. Then he got back into his seat.

"I can't bear some of these chaps, can you?" the young man said.

When the taxi stopped at the end of Park Lane we both got out without a word. The driver looked us up and down again scornfully before he started away.

"What do you want to do in Hyde Park? Look at the trees?"

He took my suitcase and walked along by my side.

"Yes, I want to look at the trees and not go back to the place where I live. Never go back."

"I've never lived in a place I like," I thought, "never."

"That does sound desperate. Well, let's see if we can find a secluded spot."

"That chair over there will do," I said. It was away from people under a tree. Not that people mattered much, for now it was night and they are never so frightening then.

I shut my eyes so that I could hear and smell the trees better. I imagined I could smell water too. The Serpentine —I didn't know we had walked so far.

He said, "I can't leave you so disconsolate on this lovely night—this night of love and night of stars." He gave a loud hiccup, and then another. "That always happen when I've eaten quails."

"It happens to me when I'm tight."

"Does it?" He pulled another chair forward and sat down by my side. "I can't leave you now until I know where you're going with that large suitcase and that desperate expression."

I told him that I had just come back after a stay in the country, and he told me that he did not live in London, that his name was Melville and that he was at a loose end that evening.

"Did somebody let you down?"

"Oh, that's not important—not half so important as the

desperate expression. I noticed that as soon as I saw you."

"That's not despair, it's hunger," I said, dropping into the backchat. "Don't you know hunger when you see it?"

"Well, let's go and have something to eat, then. But where?" He looked at me uncertainly. "Where?"

"We could go to the Apple Tree. Of course, it's a bit early, but we might be able to get kippers or eggs and bacon or sausages and mash."

"The Apple Tree? I've heard of it. Could we go there?" he said, still eyeing me.

"We could indeed. You could come as my guest. I'm a member. I was one of the first members," I boasted.

I had touched the right spring—even the feeling of his hand on my arm had changed. *Always the same spring to touch before the sneering expression will go out of their eyes and the sneering sound out of their voices. Think about it—it's very important.*

"Lots of pretty girls at the Apple Tree, aren't there?" he said.

"I can't promise anything. It's a bad time of year for the Apple Tree, the singing and the gold."

"Now what are you talking about?"

"Somebody I know calls it that."

"But you'll be there." He pulled his chair closer and looked round cautiously before he kissed me. "And you're an awfully pretty girl, aren't you? . . . The Apple Tree, the singing and the gold. I like that."

"Better than 'Night of love and night of stars?' "

"Oh, they're not in the same street."

I thought, "How do you know what's in what street?

How do they know who's fifth-rate, who's first-rate and where the devouring spider lives?"

"You don't really mind where we go, do you?" he said.

"I don't mind at all."

He took his arm away. "It was odd our meeting like that, wasn't it?"

"I don't think so. I don't think it was odd at all."

After a silence, "I haven't been very swift in the uptake, have I?" he said.

"No, you haven't. Now, let's be off to the Apple Tree, the singing and the gold."

"Oh, damn the Apple Tree. I know a better place than that."

"I've been persuaded to taste it before," Marston said. *"It tasted exactly as I thought it would."*

And everything was exactly as I had expected. The knowing waiters, the touch of the ice-cold wine glass, the red plush chairs, the food you don't notice, the gold-framed mirror, the bed in the room beyond that always looks as if its ostentatious whiteness hides dinginess. . . .

But Marston should have said, "It tastes of nothing, my dear, it tastes of nothing. . . ."

When we got out into Leicester Square again I had forgotten Marston and only thought about how, when we had nothing better to do, Estelle and I would go to the Corner House or to some cheap restaurant in Soho and have dinner. She was so earnest when it came to food. "You must have one good meal a day," she would say, "it is *necessary*." Escalope de veau and fried potatoes and brussels sprouts, we usually had, and then crème caramel or compôte de fruits. And she seemed to be walking along by my side, wearing her blue suit and her white blouse, her high heels tapping. But as we turned the corner by the Hippodrome she vanished. I thought "I shall never see her again—I know it."

In the taxi he said, "I don't forget addresses, do I?"

"No, you don't."

To keep myself awake I began to sing "Mr. Brown, Mr. Brown, Had a violin..."

"Are you on stage?"

"I was. I started my brilliant and successful career like so many others, in the chorus. But I wasn't a success."

"What a shame! Why?"

"Because I couldn't say 'epigrammatic'."

He laughed—really laughed that time.

"The stage manager had the dotty idea of pulling me out of my obscurity and giving me a line to say. The line was 'Oh, Lottie, Lottie, don't be epigrammatic.' I rehearsed it and rehearsed it, but when it came to the night it was just a blank."

At the top of Charing Cross Road the taxi was held up. We were both laughing so much that people turned round and stared at us.

"It was one of the most dreadful moments of my life, and I shan't ever forget it. There was the stage manager, mouthing at me from the wings—he was the promoter too and he also played a small part, the family lawyer—and there he was all dressed up in grey-striped trousers and a black tail-coat and top hat and silver side-whiskers, and there I was, in a yellow dress and a large straw hat and a green sunshade and a lovely background of an English castle and garden—half ruined and half not, you know—and a chorus of footmen and maids, and my mind a complete blank.

The taxi started again. "Well, what happened?"

"Nothing. After one second the other actors went smoothly on. I remember the next line. It was 'Going to Ascot? Well, if you don't get into the Royal Enclosure when you *are* there I'm no judge of character.' "

"But what about the audience?"

"Oh, the audience weren't surprised because, you see, they had never expected me to speak at all. Well, here we are."

I gave him my latchkey and he opened the door.

"A formidable key! It's like the key of a prison," he said.

Everyone had gone to bed and there wasn't even a ghost of Estelle's scent in the hall.

"We must see each other again," he said. "Please. Couldn't you write to me at—" He stopped. "No, I'll write to you. If you're ever—I'll write to you anyway."

I said, "Do you know what I want? I want a gold bracelet with blue stones in it. Not too blue—the darker blue I prefer."

"Oh, well." He was wary again. "I'll do my best, but I'm not one of these plutocrats, you know."

"Don't you dare to come back without it. But I'm going away for a few weeks. I'll be here again in September."

"All right, I'll see you in September, Petronella," he said chirpily, anxious to be off. "And you've been so sweet to me."

"The pleasure was all mine."

He shook his head. "Now, Lottie, Lottie, don't be epi-grammatic."

I thought, "I daresay he would be nice if one got to know him. I daresay, perhaps . . ." listening to him tapping good-bye on the other side of the door. I tapped back twice and then started up the stairs. Past the door of Estelle's room, not feeling a thing as I passed it, because she had gone and I knew she would not ever come back.

In my room I stood looking out of the window, remembering my yellow dress, the blurred mass of the audience and the face of one man in the front row seen quite clearly, and how I thought, as quick as lightning. "Help me, tell me what I have forgotten." But though he had looked, as it seemed, straight into my eyes, and though I was sure he knew exactly what I was thinking, he had not helped me. He had only smiled. He had left me in that moment that seemed like years standing there until through the dread-ful blankness of my mind I had heard a high, shrill, cock-ney voice say, "Going to Ascot?" and seen the stage man-ager frown and shake his head at me.

"My God, I must have looked a fool," I thought, laugh-ing and feeling the tears running down my face.

"What a waste of good tears!" the other girls had told me when I cried in the dressing-room that night. And I heard myself saying out loud in an affected voice, "Oh, the waste, the waste, the waste!"

But that did not last long.

"What's the time?" I thought, and because I wasn't sleepy any longer I sat down in the chair by the window, waiting for the clock outside to strike.

KATHERINE MANSFIELD

Bliss

Although Bertha Young was thirty she still had moments like this when she wanted to run instead of walk, to take dancing steps on and off the pavement, to bowl a hoop, to throw something up in the air and catch it again, or to stand still and laugh at—nothing—at nothing, simply.

What can you do if you are thirty, turning the corner of your own street, you are overcome, suddenly, by a feeling of bliss—absolute bliss!—as though you'd suddenly swallowed a bright piece of that late afternoon sun and it burned in your bosom, sending out a little shower of sparks into every particle, into every finger and toe? . . .

Oh, is there no way you can express it without being "drunk and disorderly"? How idiotic civilization is! Why be given a body if you have to keep it shut up in a case like a rare, rare fiddle?

"No, that about the fiddle is not quite what I mean," she thought, running up the steps and feeling in her bag for the key—she'd forgotten it, as usual—and rattling the letter-box. "It's not what I mean, because—Thank you, Mary"— she went into the hall. "Is nurse back?"

"Yes, M'm."

"And has the fruit come?"

"Yes, M'm. Everything's come."

"Bring the fruit up to the dining-room, will you? I'll arrange it before I go upstairs."

It was dusky in the dining-room and quite chilly. But all the same Bertha threw off her coat; she could not bear the tight clasp of it another moment, and the cold air fell on her arms.

But in her bosom there was still that bright glowing place —that shower of little sparks coming from it. It was almost unbearable. She hardly dared to breathe for fear of fanning it higher, and yet she breathed deeply, deeply. She hardly dared to look into the cold mirror—but she did look, and it gave her back a woman, radiant, with smiling, trembling lips, with big, dark eyes and an air of listening, waiting for something . . . divine to happen . . . that she knew must happen . . . infallibly.

Mary brought in the fruit on a tray and with it a glass bowl, and a bluish dish, very lovely, with a strange sheen on it as though it had been dipped in milk.

"Shall I turn on the light, M'm?"

"No, thank you. I can see quite well."

There were tangerines and apples stained with strawberry pink. Some yellow pears, smooth as silk, some white grapes covered with a silver bloom and a big cluster of purple ones. These last she had bought to tone in with the new dining-room carpet. Yes, that did sound rather farfetched and absurd, but it was really why she had bought them. She had thought in the shop: "I must have some purple ones to bring the carpet up to the table." And it had seemed quite sense at the time.

When she had finished with them and had made two pyramids of these bright round shapes. she stood away from the table to get the effect—and it really was most curious. For the dark table seemed to melt into the dusky light and the glass dish and the blue bowl to float in the air. This, of course, in her present mood, was so incredibly beautiful. . . . She began to laugh.

"No, no. I'm getting hysterical." And she seized her bag and coat and ran upstairs to the nursery.

Nurse sat at a low table giving Little B her supper after her bath. The baby had on a white flannel gown and a blue woollen jacket, and her dark, fine hair was brushed up into a funny little peak. She looked up when she saw her mother and began to jump.

"Now, my lovey, eat it up like a good girl," said nurse, setting her lips in a way that Bertha knew, and that meant she had come into the nursery at another wrong moment.

"Has she been good, Nanny?"

"She's been a little sweet all the afternoon," whispered Nanny. "We went to the park and I sat down on a chair and took her out of the pram and a big dog came along and put its head on my knee and she clutched its ear, tugged it. Oh, you should have seen her."

Bertha wanted to ask if it wasn't rather dangerous to let her clutch at a strange dog's ear. But she did not dare to. She stood watching them, her hands by her side, like the poor little girl in front of the rich little girl with the doll.

The baby looked up at her again, stared, and then smiled so charmingly that Bertha couldn't help crying:

"Oh, Nanny, do let me finish giving her her supper while you put the bath things away."

"Well, M'm, she oughtn't to be changed hands while she's eating," said Nanny, still whispering. "It unsettles her; it's very likely to upset her."

How absurd it was. Why have a baby if it has to be kept —not in a case like a rare, rare fiddle—but in another woman's arms?

"Oh, I must!" she said.

Very offended, Nanny handed her over.

"Now, don't excite her after her supper. You know you do, M'm. And I have such a time with her after!"

Thank heaven! Nanny went out of the room with the bath towels.

"Now I've got you to myself, my little precious," said Bertha, as the baby leaned against her.

She ate delightfully, holding up her lips for the spoon and then waving her hands. Sometimes she wouldn't let the spoon go; and sometimes, just as Bertha had filled it, she waved it away to the four winds.

When the soup was finished Bertha turned round to the fire.

"You're nice—you're very nice!" said she, kissing her warm baby. "I'm fond of you. I like you."

And, indeed, she loved Little B so much—her neck as she bent forward, her exquisite toes as they shone transparent in the firelight—that all her feelings of bliss came back again, and again she didn't know how to express it— what to do with it.

"You're wanted on the telephone," said Nanny, coming back in triumph and seizing *her* Little B.

Down she flew. It was Harry.

"Oh, is that you, Ber? Look here. I'll be late. I'll take a taxi and come along as quickly as I can, but get dinner put back ten minutes—will you? All right?"

"Yes, perfectly. Oh, Harry!"

"Yes?"

What had she to say? She'd nothing to say. She only wanted to get in touch with him for a moment. She couldn't absurdly cry: "Hasn't it been a divine day!"

"What is it?" rapped out the little voice.

"Nothing. *Entendu,*" said Bertha, and hung up the receiver, thinking how much more than idiotic civilization was.

They had people coming to dinner. The Norman Knights —a very sound couple—he was about to start a theatre, and she was awfully keen on interior decoration, a young man,

Eddie Warren, who had just published a little book of poems and whom everybody was asking to dine, and a "find" of Bertha's called Pearl Fulton. What Miss Fulton did, Bertha didn't know. They had met at the club and Bertha had fallen in love with her, as she always did fall in love with beautiful women who had something strange about them.

The provoking thing was that, though they had been about together and met a number of times and really talked, Bertha couldn't make her out. Up to a certain point Miss Fulton was rarely, wonderfully frank, but the certain point was there, and beyond that she would not go.

Was there anything beyond it? Harry said "No." Voted her dullish, and "cold like all blonde women, with a touch, perhaps, of anæmia of the brain." But Bertha wouldn't agree with him; not yet, at any rate.

"No, the way she has of sitting with her head a little on one side, and smiling, has something behind it, Harry, and I must find out what that something is."

"Most likely it's a good stomach," answered Harry.

He made a point of catching Bertha's heels with replies of that kind . . . "liver frozen, my dear girl," or "pure flatulence," or "kidney disease," . . . and so on. For some strange reason Bertha liked this, and almost admired it in him very much.

She went into the drawing-room and lighted the fire; then, picking up the cushions, one by one, that Mary had disposed so carefully, she threw them back on to the chairs and the couches. That made all the difference; the room came alive at once. As she was about to throw the last one she surprised herself by suddenly hugging it to her, passionately, passionately. But it did not put out the fire in her bosom. Oh, on the contrary!

The windows of the drawing-room opened on to a balcony overlooking the garden. At the far end, against the wall, there was a tall, slender pear tree in fullest, richest bloom; it stood perfect, as though becalmed against the jade-green sky. Bertha couldn't help feeling, even from this distance, that it had not a single bud or a faded petal. Down below, in the garden beds, the red and yellow tulips, heavy with flowers, seemed to lean upon the dusk. A grey cat, dragging its belly, crept across the lawn, and a black one, its shadow, trailed after. The sight of them, so intent and so quick, gave Bertha a curious shiver.

"What creepy things cats are!" she stammered, and she turned away from the window and began walking up and down. . . .

How strong the jonquils smelled in the warm room. Too strong? Oh, no. And yet, as though overcome, she flung down on a couch and pressed her hands to her eyes.

"I'm so happy—too happy!" she murmured.

And she seemed to see on her eyelids the lovely pear tree with its wide open blossoms as a symbol of her own life.

Really—really—she had everything. She was young. Harry and she were as much in love as ever, and they got on together splendidly and were really good pals. She had an adorable baby. They didn't have to worry about money. They had this absolutely satisfactory house and garden. And friends—modern, thrilling friends, writers and painters and poets or people keen on social questions—just the kind of friends they wanted. And then there were books, and there was music, and she had found a wonderful little dress-maker, and they were going abroad in the summer, and their new cook made the most superb omelettes. . . .

"I'm absurd. Absurd!" She sat up; but she felt quite dizzy, quite drunk. It must have been the spring.

Yes, it was the spring. Now she was so tired she could not drag herself upstairs to dress.

A white dress, a string of jade beads, green shoes and stockings. It wasn't intentional. She had thought of this scheme hours before she stood at the drawing-room window.

Her petals rustled softly into the hall, and she kissed Mrs. Norman Knight, who was taking off the most amusing orange coat with a procession of black monkeys round the hem and up the fronts.

". . .Why! Why! Why is the middle-class so stodgy—so utterly without a sense of humour! My dear, it's only by a fluke that I am here at all—Norman being the protective fluke. For my darling monkeys so upset the train that it rose to a man and simply ate me with its eyes. Didn't laugh—wasn't amused—that I should have loved. No, just stared—and bored me through and through."

"But the cream of it was," said Norman, pressing a large tortoiseshell-rimmed monocle into his eye, "you don't mind me telling this, Face, do you?" (In their home and among their friends they called each other Face and Mug.) "The cream of it was when she, being full fed, turned to the woman beside her and said: 'Haven't you ever seen a monkey before?' "

"Oh yes!" Mrs. Norman Knight joined in the laughter. "Wasn't that too absolutely creamy?"

And the funnier thing still was that now her coat was off she did look like a very intelligent monkey—who had even made that yellow silk dress out of scraped banana skins. And her amber ear-rings: they were like little dangling nuts.

"This is a sad, sad fall!" said Mug, pausing in front of Little B's perambulator. "When the perambulator comes into the hall—" and he waved the rest of the quotation away. The bell rang. It was lean, pale Eddie Warren (as usual) in a state of acute distress.

"It *is* the right house, *isn't* it?" he pleaded.

"Oh, I think so—I hope so," said Bertha brightly.

"I have had such a *dreadful* experience with a taxi-man; he was *most* sinister. I couldn't get him to *stop*. The more I knocked and called the *faster* he went. And *in* the moonlight this *bizarre* figure with the *flattened* head *crouching* over the *lit-tle* wheel . . ."

He shuddered, taking off an immense white silk scarf. Bertha noticed that his socks were white, too—most charming.

"But how dreadful!" she cried.

"Yes, it really was," said Eddie, following her into the drawing-room. "I saw myself *driving* through Eternity in a *timeless* taxi."

He knew the Norman Knights. In fact, he was going to write a play for N.K. when the theatre scheme came off.

"Well, Warren, how's the play?" said Norman Knight, dropping his monocle and giving his eye a moment in

which to rise to the surface before it was screwed down
again.

And Mrs. Norman Knight: "Oh, Mr. Warren, what
happy socks?"

"I *am* so glad you like them," said he, staring at his
feet. "They seem to have got so *much* whiter since the moon
rose." And he turned his lean sorrowful young face to
Bertha. "There *is* a moon, you know."

She wanted to cry: "I am sure there is—often—
often!"

He really was a most attractive person. But so was Face,
crouched before the fire in her banana skins, and so was
Mug, smoking a cigarette and saying as he flicked the ash:
"Why doth the bridegroom tarry?"

"There he is, now."

Bang went the front door open and shut. Harry shouted:
"Hullo, you people. Down in five minutes." And they
heard him swarm up the stairs. Bertha couldn't help smiling; she knew how he loved doing things at high pressure.
What, after all, did an extra five minutes matter? But he
would pretend to himself that they mattered beyond measure. And then he would make a great point of coming
into the drawing-room, extravagantly cool and collected.

Harry had such a zest for life. Oh, how she appreciated
it in him. And his passion for fighting—for seeking in
everything that came up against him another test of his
power and of his courage—that, too, she understood. Even
when it made him just occasionally, to other people, who
didn't know him well, a little ridiculous perhaps. . . . For
there were moments when he rushed into battle where no

battle was. . . . She talked and laughed and positively forgot until he had come in (just as she had imagined) that Pearl Fulton had not turned up.

"I wonder if Miss Fulton has forgotten?"

"I expect so," said Harry. "Is she on the 'phone?"

"Ah! There's a taxi now." And Bertha smiled with that little air of proprietorship that she always assumed while her women finds were new and mysterious. "She lives in taxis."

"She'll run to fat if she does," said Harry cooly, ringing the bell for dinner. "Frightful danger for blonde women."

"Harry—don't," warned Bertha, laughing up at him.

Came another tiny moment, while they waited, laughing and talking, just a trifle too much at their ease, a trifle too unaware. And then Miss Fulton, all in silver, with a silver fillet binding her pale blonde hair, came in smiling, her head a little on one side.

"Am I late?"

"No, not at all," said Bertha. "Come along." And she took her arm and they moved into the dining-room.

What was there in the touch of that cool arm that could fan—fan—start blazing—blazing—the fire of bliss that Bertha did not know what to do with?

Miss Fulton did not look at her; but then she seldom did look at people directly. Her heavy eyelids lay upon her eyes and the strange half-smile came and went upon her lips as though she lived by listening rather than seeing. But Bertha knew, suddenly, as if the longest, most intimate look had passed between them—as if they had said to each other: "You, too?"—that Pearl Fulton, stirring the beautiful red soup in the grey plate, was feeling just what she was feeling.

And the others? Face and Mug, Eddie and Harry, their spoons rising and falling—dabbing their lips with their napkins, crumbling bread, fiddling with the forks and glasses and talking.

"I met her at the Alpha show—the weirdest little person. She'd not only cut off her hair, but she seemed to have taken a dreadfully good snip off her legs and arms and her neck and her poor little nose as well."

"Isn't she very *liée* with Michael Oat?"

"The man who wrote *Love in False Teeth?*"

"He wants to write a play for me. One act. One man. Decides to commit suicide. Gives all the reasons why he should and why he shouldn't. And just as he has made up his mind either to do it or not to do it—curtain. Not half a bad idea."

"What's he going to call it—'Stomach Trouble'?"

"I *think* I've come across the *same* idea in a lit-tle French review, *quite* unknown in England."

No, they didn't share it. They were dears—dears—and she loved having them there, at her table, and giving them delicious food and wine. In fact, she longed to tell them how delightful they were, and what a decorative group they made, how they seemed to set one another off and how they reminded her of a play by Tchekof!

Harry was enjoying his dinner. It was part of his—well, not his nature, exactly, and certainly not his pose—his—something or other—to talk about food and to glory in his "shameless passion for the white flesh of the lobster" and "the green of pistachio ices—green and cold like the eyelids of Egyptian dancers."

When he looked up at her and said: "Bertha, this is a

very admirable *soufflé!*" she almost could have wept with child-like pleasure.

Oh, why did she feel so tender towards the whole world to-night? Everything was good—was right. All that happened seemed to fill again her brimming cup of bliss.

And still, in the back of her mind, there was the pear tree. It would be silver now, in the light of poor dear Eddie's moon, silver as Miss Fulton, who sat there turning a tangerine in her slender fingers that were so pale a light seemed to come from them.

What she simply couldn't make out—what was miraculous—was how she should have guessed Miss Fulton's mood so exactly and so instantly. For she never doubted for a moment that she was right, and yet what had she to go on? Less than nothing.

"I believe this does happen very, very rarely between women. Never between men," thought Bertha. "But while I am making the coffee in the drawing-room perhaps she will 'give a sign.' "

What she meant by that she did not know, and what would happen after that she could not imagine.

While she thought like this she saw herself talking and laughing. She had to talk because of her desire to laugh.

"I must laugh or die."

But when she noticed Face's funny little habit of tucking something down the front of her bodice—as if she kept a tiny, secret hoard of nuts there, too—Bertha had to dig her nails into her hands—so as not to laugh too much.

It was over at last. And: "Come and see my new coffee machine," said Bertha.

"We only have a new coffee machine once a fortnight," said Harry. Face took her arm this time; Miss Fulton bent her head and followed after.

The fire had died down in the drawing-room to a red, flickering "nest of baby phœnixes," said Face.

"Don't turn up the light for a moment. It is so lovely." And down she crouched by the fire again. She was always cold . . . "without her little red flannel jacket, of course," thought Bertha.

At that moment Miss Fulton "gave the sign."

"Have you a garden?" said the cool, sleepy voice.

This was so exquisite on her part that all Bertha could do was to obey. She crossed the room, pulled the curtains apart, and opened those long windows.

"There!" she breathed.

And the two women stood side by side looking at the slender, flowering tree. Although it was so still it seemed, like the flame of a candle, to stretch up, to point, to quiver in the bright air, to grow taller and taller as they gazed— almost to touch the rim of the round, silver moon.

How long did they stand there? Both, as it were, caught in that circle of unearthly light, understanding each other perfectly, creatures of another world, and wondering what they were to do in this one with all this blissful treasure that burned in their bosoms and dropped, in silver flowers, from their hair and hands?

For ever—for a moment? And did Miss Fulton murmur: "Yes. Just *that*." Or did Bertha dream it?

Then the light was snapped on and Face made the coffee and Harry said: "My dear Mrs. Knight, don't ask me about my baby. I never see her. I shan't feel the slightest interest in her until she has a lover," and Mug took his eye out of the conservatory for a moment and then put it under glass again and Eddie Warren drank his coffee and set down the cup with a face of anguish as though he had drunk and seen the spider.

"What I want to do is to give the young men a show. I believe London is simply teeming with first-chop, unwritten plays. What I want to say to 'em is: 'Here's the theatre. Fire ahead.' "

"You know, my dear, I am going to decorate a room for the Jacob Nathans. Oh, I am so tempted to do a fried-fish scheme, with the backs of the chairs shaped like frying pans and lovely chip potatoes embroidered all over the curtains."

"The trouble with our young writing men is that they are still too romantic. You can't put out to sea without being seasick and wanting a basin. Well, why won't they have the courage of those basins?"

"A *dreadful* poem about a *girl* who was *violated* by a beggar *without* a nose in a lit-tle wood. . . ."

Miss Fulton sank into the lowest, deepest chair and Harry handed round the cigarettes.

From the way he stood in front of her shaking the silver box and saying abruptly: "Egyptian? Turkish? Virginian? They're all mixed up," Bertha realised that she not only bored him; he really disliked her. And she decided from the way Miss Fulton said: "No, thank you, I won't smoke," that she felt it, too, and was hurt.

"Oh, Harry, don't dislike her. You are quite wrong about her. She's wonderful, wonderful. And, besides, how can you feel so differently about someone who means so much to

me. I shall try to tell you when we are in bed to-night what
has been happening. What she and I have shared."

At those last words something strange and almost terrify-
ing darted into Bertha's mind. And this something blind
and smiling whispered to her: "Soon these people will go.
The house will be quiet—quiet. The lights will be out. And
you and he will be alone together in the dark room—the
warm bed. . . ."

She jumped up from her chair and ran over to the piano.

"What a pity someone does not play!" she cried. "What
a pity somebody does not play."

For the first time in her life Bertha Young desired her
husband.

Oh, she'd loved him—she'd been in love with him, of
course, in every other way, but just not in that way. And
equally, of course, she'd understood that he was different.
They'd discussed it so often. It had worried her dreadfully
at first to find that she was so cold, but after a time it had
not seemed to matter. They were so frank with each other
—such good pals. That was the best of being modern.

But now—ardently! ardently! The word ached in her
ardent body! Was this what that feeling of bliss had been
leading up to? But then, then—

"My dear," said Mrs. Norman Knight, "you know our
shame. We are the victims of time and train. We live in
Hampstead. It's been so nice."

"I'll come with you into the hall," said Bertha. "I loved
having you. But you must not miss the last train. That's
so awful, isn't it?"

"Have a whisky, Knight, before you go?" called Harry.

"No, thanks, old chap."

Bertha squeezed his hand for that as she shook it.

"Good night, good-bye," she cried from the top step, feeling that this self of hers was taking leave of them for ever.

When she got back into the drawing-room the others were on the move.

". . . Then you can come part of the way in my taxi."

"I shall be *so* thankful *not* to have to face *another* drive *alone* after my *dreadful* experience."

"You can get a taxi at the rank just at the end of the street. You won't have to walk more than a few yards."

"That's a comfort. I'll go and put on my coat."

Miss Fulton moved towards the hall and Bertha was following when Harry almost pushed past.

"Let me help you."

Bertha knew that he was repenting his rudeness—she let him go. What a boy he was in some ways—so impulsive —so—simple.

And Eddie and she were left by the fire.

"I *wonder* if you have seen Bilks' *new* poem called *Table d'Hôte*," said Eddie softly. "It's *so* wonderful. In the last Anthology. Have you got a copy? I'd *so* like to *show* it to you. It begins with an *incredibly* beautiful line: 'Why Must it Always be Tomato Soup?' "

"Yes," said Bertha. And she moved noiselessly to a table opposite the drawing-room door and Eddie glided noise-lessly after her. She picked up the little book and gave it to him; they had not made a sound.

While he looked it up she turned her head towards the

hall. And she saw . . . Harry with Miss Fulton's coat in his arms and Miss Fulton with her back turned to him and her head bent. He tossed the coat away, put his hands on her shoulders and turned her violently to him. His lips said: "I adore you," and Miss Fulton laid her moonbeam fingers on his cheeks and smiled her sleepy smile. Harry's nostrils quivered; his lips curled back in a hideous grin while he whispered: "To-morrow," and with her eyelids Miss Fulton said: "Yes."

"Here it is," said Eddie. " 'Why Must it Always be To-mato Soup?' It's so *deeply* true, don't you feel? Tomato soup is so *dreadfully* eternal."

"If you prefer," said Harry's voice, very loud, from the hall, "I can 'phone you a cab to come to the door."

"Oh, no. It's not necessary," said Miss Fulton, and she came up to Bertha and gave her the slender fingers to hold.

"Good-bye. Thank you so much."

"Good-bye," said Bertha.

Miss Fulton held her hand a moment longer.

"Your lovely pear tree!" she murmured.

And then she was gone, with Eddie following like the black cat following the grey cat.

"I'll shut up shop," said Harry, extravagantly cool and collected.

"Your lovely pear tree—pear tree—pear tree!"

Bertha simply ran over to the long windows.

"Oh, what is going to happen now?" she cried.

But the pear tree was as lovely as ever and as full of flower and as still.

CARSON McCULLERS

A Domestic Dilemma

On Thursday Martin Meadows
left the office early enough to make the first express
bus home. It was the hour when the evening lilac glow was
fading in the slushy streets, but by the time the bus had left
the mid-town terminal the bright city night had come. On
Thursdays the maid had a half-day off and Martin liked
to get home as soon as possible, since for the past year
his wife had not been—well. This Thursday he was very
tired and, hoping that no regular commuter would single
him out for conversation, he fastened his attention to the
newspaper until the bus had crossed the George Washington Bridge. Once on 9-W Highway Martin always felt that

the trip was halfway done; he breathed deeply, even in cold weather when only ribbons of draught cut through the smoky air of the bus, confident that he was breathing country air. It used to be that at this point he would relax and begin to think with pleasure of his home. But in the last year nearness brought only a sense of tension and he did not anticipate the journey's end. This evening Martin kept his face close to the window and watched the barren fields and lonely lights of passing townships. There was a moon, pale on the dark earth and areas of late, porous snow; to Martin the countryside seemed vast and somehow desolate that evening. He took his hat from the rack and put his folded newspaper in the pocket of his overcoat a few minutes before time to pull the cord.

The cottage was a block from the bus stop, near the river but not directly on the shore; from the living-room window you could look across the street and opposite yard and see the Hudson. The cottage was modern, almost too white and new on the narrow plot of yard. In summer the grass was soft and bright and Martin carefully tended a flower border and a rose trellis. But during the cold, fallow months the yard was bleak and the cottage seemed naked. Lights were on that evening in all the rooms in the little house and Martin hurried up the front walk. Before the steps he stopped to move a wagon out of the way.

The children were in the living room, so intent on play that the opening of the front door was at first unnoticed. Martin stood looking at his safe, lovely children. They had opened the bottom drawer of the secretary and taken out the Christmas decorations. Andy had managed to plug in the

Christmas tree lights and the green and red bulbs glowed with out-of-season festivity on the rug of the living room. At the moment he was trying to trail the bright cord over Marianne's rocking horse. Marianne sat on the floor pulling off an angel's wings. The children wailed a startling welcome. Martin swung the fat little baby girl up to his shoulder and Andy threw himself against his father's legs.

"Daddy, Daddy, Daddy!"

Martin set down the little girl carefully and swung Andy a few times like a pendulum. Then he picked up the Christmas tree cord.

"What's all this stuff doing out? Help me put it back in the drawer. You're not to fool with the light socket. Remember I told you that before. I mean it, Andy."

The six-year-old child nodded and shut the secretary drawer. Martin stroked his fair soft hair and his hand lingered tenderly on the nape of the child's frail neck.

"Had supper yet, Bumpkin?"

"It hurt. The toast was hot."

The baby girl stumbled on the rug and, after the first surprise of the fall, began to cry; Martin picked her up and carried her in his arms back to the kitchen.

"See, Daddy," said Andy. "The toast—"

Emily had laid the children's supper on the uncovered porcelain table. There were two plates with the remains of cream-of-wheat and eggs and silver mugs that had held milk. There was also a platter of cinnamon toast, untouched except for one tooth-marked bite. Martin sniffed the bitten piece and nibbled gingerly. Then he put the toast into the garbage pail. "Hoo-phui— What on earth!"

Emily had mistaken the tin of cayenne for the cinnamon.

"I like to have burnt up," Andy said. "Drank water and ran outdoors and opened my mouth. Marianne didn't eat none."

"Any," corrected Martin. He stood helpless, looking around the walls of the kitchen. "Well, that's that, I guess," he said finally. "Where is your mother now?"

"She's up in you alls' room."

Martin left the children in the kitchen and went up to his wife. Outside the door he waited for a moment to still his anger. He did not knock and once inside the room he closed the door behind him.

Emily sat in the rocking chair by the window of the pleasant room. She had been drinking something from a tumbler and as he entered she put the glass hurriedly on the floor behind the chair. In her attitude there was confusion and guilt which she tried to hide by a show of spurious vivacity.

"Oh, Marty! You home already? The time slipped up on me. I was just going down——" She lurched to him and her kiss was strong with sherry. When he stood unresponsive she stepped back a pace and giggled nervously.

"What's the matter with you? Standing there like a barber pole. Is anything wrong with you?"

"Wrong with *me?*" Martin bent over the rocking chair and picked up the tumbler from the floor. "If you could only realize how sick I am—how bad it is for all of us."

Emily spoke in a false, airy voice that had become too familiar to him. Often at such times she affected a slight English accent, copying perhaps some actress she admired.

"I haven't the vaguest idea what you mean. Unless you are referring to the glass I used for a spot of sherry. I had a finger of sherry—maybe two. But what is the crime in that, pray tell me? I'm quite all right. Quite all right."

"So anyone can see."

As she went into the bathroom Emily walked with careful gravity. She turned on the cold water and dashed some on her face with her cupped hands, then patted herself dry with the corner of a bath towel. Her face was delicately featured and young, unblemished.

"I was just going down to make dinner." She tottered and balanced herself by holding to the door frame.

"I'll take care of dinner. You stay up here. I'll bring it up."

"I'll do nothing of the sort. Why, whoever heard of such a thing?"

"Please," Martin said.

"Leave me alone. I'm quite all right. I was just on the way down——"

"Mind what I say."

"Mind your grandmother."

She lurched toward the door, but Martin caught her by the arm. "I don't want the children to see you in this condition. Be reasonable."

"Condition!" Emily jerked her arm. Her voice rose angrily. "Why, because I drink a couple of sherries in the afternoon you're trying to make me out a drunkard. Condition! Why, I don't even touch whiskey. As well you know. *I* don't swill liquor at bars. And that's more than you can say. I don't even have a cocktail at dinnertime. I only sometimes have a glass of sherry. What, I ask you, is the disgrace of that? Condition!"

Martin sought words to calm his wife. "We'll have a quiet supper by ourselves up here. That's a good girl." Emily sat on the side of the bed and he opened the door for a quick departure. "I'll be back in a jiffy."

As he busied himself with the dinner downstairs he was lost in the familiar question as to how this problem had come upon his home. He himself had always enjoyed a good drink. When they were still living in Alabama they had served long drinks or cocktails as a matter of course. For years they had drunk one or two—possibly three—drinks before dinner, and at bedtime a long nightcap. Evenings before holidays they might get a buzz on, might even become a little tight. But alcohol had never seemed a problem to him, only a bothersome expense that with the increase in the family they could scarcely afford. It was only after his company had transferred him to New York that Martin was aware that certainly his wife was drinking too much. She was tippling, he noticed, during the day.

The problem acknowledged, he tried to analyze the source. The change from Alabama to New York had somehow disturbed her; accustomed to the idle warmth of a small Southern town, the matrix of the family and cousinship and childhood friends, she had failed to accommodate herself to the stricter, lonelier mores of the North. The duties of motherhood and housekeeping were onerous to her. Homesick for Paris City, she had made no friends in the suburban town. She read only magazines and murder books. Her interior life was insufficient without the artifice

of alcohol. The revelations of incontinence insidiously undermined his previous conceptions of his wife. There were
times of unexplainable malevolence, times when the alcoholic fuse caused an explosion of unseemly anger. He en-
countered a latent coarseness in Emily, inconsistent with her
natural simplicity. She lied about drinking and deceived him
with unsuspected stratagems.

Then there was an accident. Coming home from work
one evening about a year ago, he was greeted with screams
from the children's room. He had found Emily holding the
baby, wet and naked from her bath. The baby had been
dropped, her frail, frail skull striking the table edge, so that
a thread of blood was soaking into the gossamer hair. Emily
was sobbing and intoxicated. As Martin cradled the hurt
child, so infinitely precious at that moment, he had an af-
frighted vision of the future.

The next day Marianne was all right. Emily vowed that
never again would she touch liquor, and for a few weeks
she was sober, cold and downcast. Then gradually she began—not whisky or gin—but quantities of beer, or sherry,
or outlandish liqueurs; once he had come across a hatbox
of empty crême de menthe bottles. Martin found a depend-
able maid who managed the household competently. Virgie
was also from Alabama and Martin had never dared tell
Emily the wage scale customary in New York. Emily's
drinking was entirely secret now, done before he reached
the house. Usually the effects were almost imperceptible—a
looseness of movement or the heavy-lidded eyes. The times
of irresponsibilities, such as the cayenne-pepper toast, were
rare, and Martin could dismiss his worries when Virgie was

at the house. But, nevertheless, anxiety was always latent, a threat of indefined disaster that underlay his days.

"Marianne!" Martin called, for even the recollection of that time brought the need for reassurance. The baby girl, no longer hurt, but no less precious to her father, came into the kitchen with her brother. Martin went on with the preparations for the meal. He opened a can of soup and put two chops in the frying pan. Then he sat down by the table and took his Marianne on his knees for a pony ride. Andy watched them, his fingers wobbling the tooth that had been loose all that week.

"Andy-the-candyman!" Martin said. "Is that old critter still in your mouth? Come closer, let Daddy have a look."

"I got a string to pull it with." The child brought from his pocket a tangled thread. "Virgie said to tie it to the tooth and tie the other end of the doorknob and shut the door real suddenly."

Martin took out a clean handkerchief and felt the loose tooth carefully. "That tooth is coming out of my Andy's mouth tonight. Otherwise I'm awfully afraid we'll have a tooth tree in the family."

"A what?"

"A tooth tree," Martin said. "You'll bite into something and swallow that tooth. And the tooth will take root in poor Andy's stomach and grow into a tooth tree with sharp little teeth instead of leaves."

"Shoo, Daddy," Andy said. But he held the tooth firmly between his grimy little thumb and forefinger. "There ain't any tree like that. I never seen one."

"There *isn't* any tree like that and I never *saw* one."

Martin tensed suddenly. Emily was coming down the stairs. He listened to her fumbling footsteps, his arm embracing the little boy with dread. When Emily came into the room he saw from her movements and her sullen face that she had again been at the sherry bottle. She began to yank open drawers and set the table.

"Condition!" she said in a furry voice. "You talk to me like that. Don't think I'll forget. I remember every dirty lie you say to me. Don't you think for a minute that I forget."

"Emily!" he begged. "The children——"

"The children—yes! Don't think I don't see through your dirty plots and schemes. Down here trying to turn my own children against me. Don't think I don't see and understand."

"Emily! I beg you—please go upstairs."

"So you can turn my children—my very own children ——" Two large tears coursed rapidly down her cheeks. "Trying to turn my little boy, my Andy, against his own mother."

With drunken impulsiveness Emily knelt on the floor before the startled child. Her hands on his shoulders balanced her. "Listen, my Andy—you wouldn't listen to any lies your father tells you? You wouldn't believe what he says? Listen, Andy, what was your father telling you before I came downstairs?" Uncertain, the child sought his father's face. "Tell me. Mama wants to know."

"About the tooth tree."

"What?"

The child repeated the words and she echoed them with unbelieving terror. "The tooth tree!" She swayed and renewed her grasp on the child's shoulder. "I don't know what you're talking about. But listen, Andy, Mama is all right, isn't she?" The tears were spilling down her face and Andy drew back from her, for he was afraid. Grasping the table edge, Emily stood up.

"See! You have turned my child against me."

Marianne began to cry, and Martin took her in his arms.

"That's all right, you can take *your* child. You have always shown partiality from the very first. I don't mind, but at least you can leave me my little boy."

Andy edged close to his father and touched his leg. "Daddy," he wailed.

Martin took the children to the foot of the stairs. "Andy, you take up Marianne and Daddy will follow you in a minute."

"But Mama?" the child asked, whispering.

"Mama will be all right. Don't worry."

Emily was sobbing at the kitchen table, her face buried in the crook of her arm. Martin poured a cup of soup and set it before her. Her rasping sobs unnerved him; the vehemence of her emotion, irrespective of the source, touched in him a strain of tenderness. Unwillingly he laid his hand on her dark hair. "Sit up and drink the soup." Her face as she looked up at him was chastened and imploring. The boy's withdrawal or the touch of Martin's hand had turned the tenor of her mood.

"Ma-Martin," she sobbed. "I'm so ashamed."

"Drink the soup."

Obeying him, she drank between gasping breaths. After a second cup she allowed him to lead her up to their room.

She was docile now and more restrained. He laid her night-gown on the bed and was about to leave the room when a fresh round of grief, the alcoholic tumult, came again.

"He turned away. My Andy looked at me and turned away."

Impatience and fatigue hardened his voice, but he spoke warily. "You forget that Andy is still a little child—he can't comprehend the meaning of such scenes."

"Did I make a scene? Oh, Martin, did I make a scene before the children?"

Her horrified face touched and amused him against his will. "Forget it. Put on your nightgown and go to sleep."

"My child turned away from me. Andy looked at his mother and turned away. The children——"

She was caught in the rhythmic sorrow of alcohol. Martin withdrew from the room saying: "For God's sake go to sleep. The children will forget by tomorrow."

As he said this he wondered if it was true. Would the scene glide so easily from memory—or would it root in the unconscious to fester in the after-years? Martin did not know, and the last alternative sickened him. He thought of Emily, foresaw the morning-after humiliation: the shards of memory, the lucidities that glared from the obliterating darkness of shame. She would call the New York office twice—possibly three or four times. Martin anticipated his own embarrassment, wondering if the others at the office could possibly suspect. He felt that his secretary had di-vined the trouble long ago and that she pitied him. He suf-fered a moment of rebellion against his fate; he hated his wife.

Once in the children's room he closed the door and felt

secure for the first time that evening. Marianne fell down on the floor, picked herself up and calling: "Daddy, watch me," fell again, got up and continued the falling-calling routine. Andy sat in the child's low chair, wobbling the tooth. Martin ran the water in the tub, washed his own hands in the lavatory, and called the boy into the bathroom.

"Let's have another look at that tooth." Martin sat on the toilet, holding Andy between his knees. The child's mouth gaped and Martin grasped the tooth. A wobble, a quick twist and the nacreous milk tooth was free. Andy's face was for the first moment split between terror, astonishment, and delight. He mouthed a swallow of water and spat into the lavatory. "Look, Daddy! It's blood. Marianne!"

Martin loved to bathe his children, loved inexpressibly the tender, naked bodies as they stood in the water so exposed. It was not fair of Emily to say that he showed partiality. As Martin soaped the delicate boy-body of his son he felt that further love would be impossible. Yet he admitted the difference in the quality of his emotions for the two children. His love for his daughter was graver, touched with a strain of melancholy, a gentleness that was akin to pain. His pet names for the little boy were the absurdities of daily inspiration—he called the little girl always Marianne, and his voice as he spoke it was a caress. Martin patted dry the fat baby stomach and the sweet little genital fold. The washed child faces were radiant as flower petals, equally loved.

"I'm putting the tooth under my pillow. I'm supposed to get a quarter."

"What for?"

"You know, Daddy. Johnny got a quarter for his tooth."

"Who puts the quarter there?" asked Martin. "I used to think the fairies left it in the night. It was a dime in my day, though."

"That's what they say in kindergarten."

"Who does put it there?"

"Your parents," Andy said. "You!"

Martin was pinning the cover on Marianne's bed. His daughter was already asleep. Scarcely breathing. Martin bent over and kissed her forehead, kissed again the tiny hand that lay palm-upward, flung in slumber beside her head.

"Good night, Andy-man."

The answer was only a drowsy murmur. After a minute Martin took out his change and slid a quarter underneath the pillow. He left a night light in the room.

As Martin prowled about the kitchen making a late meal, it occurred to him that the children had not once mentioned their mother or the scene that must have seemed to them incomprehensible. Absorbed in the instant—the tooth, the bath, the quarter—the fluid passage of child-time had borne these weightless episodes like leaves in the swift current of a shallow stream while the adult enigma was beached and forgotten on the shore. Martin thanked the Lord for that.

But his own anger, repressed and lurking, arose again. His youth was being frittered by a drunkard's waste, his very manhood subtly undermined. And the children, once the immunity of incomprehension passed—what would it be like in a year or so? With his elbows on the table he ate his food brutishly, untasting. There was no hiding the truth —soon there would be gossip in the office and in the town;

his wife was a dissolute woman. Dissolute. And he and his children were bound to a future of degradation and slow ruin.

Martin pushed away from the table and stalked into the living room. He followed the lines of a book with his eyes but his mind conjured miserable images: he saw his children drowned in the river, his wife a disgrace on the public street. By bedtime the dull, hard anger was like a weight upon his chest and his feet dragged as he climbed the stairs.

The room was dark except for the shafting light from the half-opened bathroom door. Martin undressed quietly. Little by little, mysteriously, there came in him a change. His wife was asleep, her peaceful respiration sounding gently in the room. Her high-heeled shoes with the carelessly dropped stockings made to him a mute appeal. Her underclothes were flung in disorder on the chair. Martin picked up the girdle and the soft, silk brassière and stood for a moment with them in his hands. For the first time that evening he looked at his wife. His eyes rested on the sweet forehead, the arch of the fine brow. The brow had descended to Marianne, and the tilt at the end of the delicate nose. In his son he could trace the high cheekbones and pointed chin. Her body was full-bosomed, slender and undulant. As Martin watched the tranquil slumber of his wife the ghost of the old anger vanished. All thoughts of blame or blemish were distant from him now. Martin put out the bathroom light and raised the window. Careful not to awaken Emily he slid into the bed. By moonlight he watched his wife for the last time. His hand sought the adjacent flesh and sorrow paralleled desire in the immense complexity of love.

NANCY HALE

The Bubble

Now when Eric was born in Washington, D.C., I was eighteen, and most people thought I was too young to be having a baby.

I went down there two months before it was going to come, to stay at my mother-in-law's house. She was crazy for the baby to be born in Washington, and I was just as glad to get away from New York. My father had been divorced from my mother, and she had gone abroad, and he was getting married to Estrella, so I couldn't go *there,* and I had got so I couldn't stand that first awful little apartment, with the ivory woodwork and a red sateen sofa; I didn't know how to make it look attractive, and it depressed me. Tom, Eric's father, stayed on in it after I went to his mother's; I remember he used to work in a bond house.

It felt strange, staying with my mother-in-law. She had a big house, right opposite the old British Embassy. That makes you realize how long ago this was, and yet I am still, all these years later, wondering about why it was the way it was. Mrs. Tompkins' house was a real house, with five stories and four servants, and meals at regular times and a gong that the colored butler rang to call you to them. I had never lived in a real house. My father always had apartments with day beds in them, so we could open the whole place up for parties, and we ate any time. My father was an art critic on the *Tribune*. Nobody remembers who he was any more; everybody forgets things so fast.

My room in Washington was in the front, on the top floor, looking out at the rambling, old, mustard-yellow Embassy. Sometimes at night I would lean on the window sill and watch the cars draw up and the people in evening dress get out and walk up the strip of crimson carpet they rolled out across the sidewalk for the Embassy parties. And I would weep, up there on the fourth floor, because I was so big and clumsy, and I felt as if I would never, never go dancing again, or walk along a red carpet, or wear a low-cut dress. The last time I had was one night when I went dancing at the old Montmartre with Tom and Eugene—I was in love with Eugene—and I had seen myself in a long mirror dancing and realized how fat I looked, and that was another reason I wanted to get away from New York and go and have it in Washington. I had two black dresses—one plain wool and the other with an accordion-pleated crêpe skirt—and one velours hat, and I wore them and wore them and wore them all those last weeks, and I swore to myself that when it was born I would burn them in the fireplace in my room there. But I never did.

I used to live in a kind of fever for the future, when the baby would have come and I would look nice again and go back to New York and see Eugene. I took regular walks along the Washington streets—N Street, and Sixteenth Street, and Connecticut Avenue with all the attractive people going into restaurants to lunch—in my shapeless black dress and my velours hat, dreaming of the day when I would be size 12 and my hair would curl again and I would begin to have fun. All those days before Eric was born were aimed frontward, hard; I was just getting through them for what it would be like afterward.

My mother-in-law was the one who was really having the baby; she was full of excitement about it, and used to take me to Washington shops to buy baby clothes. Looking back all these years later, I remember those sunny afternoons in late winter, and the little white dresses and embroidered caps and pink sweaters spread out on the counter, and stopping to have tea and cinnamon toast at the Mayflower, with the small orchestra playing hotel music, and they seem beautiful and tranquil, but in those days I was just doing any old thing she suggested, and I was living to get back to New York and begin having fun again.

I remember she gave a ladies' luncheon for me, to meet some of the young mothers she thought I would like to know. I suppose they were a couple of years older than I, but they seemed middle-aged to me and interested in the stupidest things; I wanted to cry because nobody was anything like me.

But now I remember that the luncheon was really beautiful. The dining room was big and long, and on the sideboard was Mrs. Tompkins' silver *repoussé* tea service. The table was laid with a huge white damask cloth, and the napkins had lace inserts. It was a real ladies' lunch party, with twelve ladies and a five-course luncheon; I had never been to one before in my life, and I seldom have since. I remember the first course was shrimp cocktails in glasses set in bowls filled with crushed ice. And for dessert there was a special confection, which had been ordered from Demonet's, the famous Washington caterer; it was a monument of cake and ice cream and whipped cream and cherries and angelica. But all I could think about was how food bored me and how I wanted to get back and begin living again. I felt in such a hurry.

Later that day, Mrs. Tompkins gave me a lot of her linens. It was before dinner. We used to sit in the small library and listen to Amos and Andy every night at seven. And this night she brought in a great armful of linens to show me, and everything I admired she would give me. There were damask tablecloths with borders of iris and borders of the Greek key, and round embroidered linen tea cloths, and dozens and dozens of lace and net doilies to go under finger bowls, and towels of the finest huck with great padded monograms embroidered on them. "Dear child," she said, "I want for you to have everything nice." I ended up with a whole pile of things. I wonder what ever became of them. I remember imagining what my father would have thought if he could have seen me with a lot of tablecloths and towels in my lap. "The purchase money of the Philistines," he might have said. But I have no idea what happened to all that linen, and my father is dead long ago and nobody remembers him any more. I remember when I went up to my room to change into my other dress for dinner I wept, because I was so big and ugly and all surrounded with lace doilies and baby clothes and Eugene might fall in love with somebody else before I could get back to New York.

That was the night the baby started to come.

It began about ten o'clock, just before bedtime, and when I told my mother-in-law her face lit up. She went and telephoned to the doctor and to the nurse, and then came back and told me the doctor said I was to rest quietly at home until the pains started to come every fifteen minutes, and that the nurse, Miss Hammond, would be right over. I went up to my room and lay down. It didn't hurt too much. When Miss Hammond arrived, she stood by my bed and smiled at me as if I were wonderful. She was tall and thin with sallow hair, an old-maid type.

About one o'clock, Mrs. Tompkins telephoned the doctor again, and he said to take me to the hospital. Mrs. Tompkins told me she had wired Tom to take the midnight down, but I didn't care; I was having pains regularly, and the difference had begun, the thing I have always wondered about.

We all got in a taxi, Mrs. Tompkins and Miss Hammond and I, there in the middle of the night, and drove through the dark Washington streets to the hospital. It was portentous, that drive, significant; every minute, I mean every present minute, seemed to matter. I had stopped living ahead, the way I had been doing, and was living in right now. That is what I am talking about.

I hadn't worn my wedding ring since I fell in love with Eugene. I'd told my mother-in-law that I didn't like the feeling of the ring, which was true. But in the taxi, in the darkness, she took off her own wedding ring and put it on my finger. "Dear child," she said, "I just won't have you going to the hospital with no ring." I remember I squeezed her hand.

I was taken at once to my room in the hospital, where they "prepared" me, and then almost immediately to the delivery room, because they thought the baby was coming right away. But then the pains slowed down, and I stayed in the delivery room for a long time, until the sun began to stream through the east window. The doctor, a pleasant old man with a Southern accent, had come, and he sat in the sunshine reading the morning newspaper. As I lay on my back on the high, narrow delivery cot, the pains got steadily harder, but I remember thinking, There's nothing scary about this. It just feels natural. The pains got harder and harder.

There was the doctor, and a nurse, and my own Miss Hammond, whom I felt I had known forever; occasionally she would wipe my forehead with a cool, wet cloth. I felt gay and talkative. I said, "I know what this pain feels like. It feels as if I were in a dark tunnel that was too small for me, and I were trying to squeeze through it to get to the end, where I can see a little light."

The doctor laughed. "That's not what you're doin'," he said. "That's what that baby's doin'."

But that was the way it felt, all the same.

"Let me know when you need a little somethin'," he said.

After a while I said, "This is *bad*." And instantly he was at my side with a hypodermic needle, which he thrust into my arm, and the pain was blunted for a time.

"Let me know when you need a little somethin'," he said again.

But I was feeling very strong and full of power. I was working my way down that long, dark tunnel that was too tight for me, down toward the little light that showed at the far end. Then I had a terrible pain. That's all I'm going to stand, I thought calmly. Deliberately I opened my mouth and screamed.

At once, they put a mask over my face, and the doctor's voice said, "Breathe deeply."

And I was out.

I would come back into the brilliant sunshine of the room and the circle of faces around me, and smile up at them, and they would smile back. And then a fresh pain would approach, and I would say, "Now."

"Bear down," the doctor's voice said as the mask covered my face and I faded away from the room. "Bear down."

So I would bear down, and be gone.

Back into the sunny room and out again, several times, I went. And then, on one of the returns, to my astonishment, I heard a small, high wail that I nevertheless knew all about. Over to one side of me stood a crib on stilts; it had been standing there all along, but now above its edge I could see two tiny blue things waving faintly.

"It's a boy," I heard my darling Miss Hammond's voice saying. "You've got a beautiful boy, Mrs. Tompkins."

And then I felt a fearful pain coming. They put the mask over my face for the last time, and I went completely out.

When I woke up, it was in my own room. Mrs. Tompkins was there, and Miss Hammond, and Tom. They kissed me, and beamed at me, and Tom kept pressing my hand. But I was immune from them all.

I was inwardly enthroned. Seated on a chair of silver, sword in hand, I was Joan of Arc. I smiled at them all, because I might as well, but I needed nobody, nothing. I was the meaning of achievement, here, now, in the moment, and the afternoon sun shone proudly in from the west.

A nurse entered bearing a pale-blue bundle and put it in my arms. It was Eric, of course, and I looked down into his minute face with a feeling of old familiarity. Here he was. Here we were. We were everything.

"Your father's come," Mrs. Tompkins said.

My father's head appeared round the door, and then he came in, looking wry, as he did when people not his kind were around. He leaned down to kiss me.

"Brave girl," he whispered. "You fooled 'em."

That was right. I had fooled them, fooled everybody. I had the victory, and it was here and now.

Then the nurse took the baby away, and Miss Hammond brought a big tray of food and cranked my bed up for me to eat it. I ate an enormous dinner, and then fell asleep and did not wake up for fifteen hours.

When I woke, it was the middle of the night, and the hospital was silent around me. Then, faintly, from somewhere down the corridor, although the month was February, someone began to sing "Silent Night." It was eerie, in my closed room, to hear singing in the darkness. I looked at where the windows showed pale gray and oblong. Then I realized what the tune was that was being sung, and felt horribly embarrassed. I could hear my father saying, "These good folk with their sentimental religiosity." Then the sound of the singing disappeared, and I was never sure where it had come from, or, indeed, whether I had really heard it or not.

Next morning, bright and early, a short, thin man with gray curly hair walked into my hospital room and said, "What's all this nonsense about your not wanting to nurse your baby? I won't have it. You *must* nurse your child." He was the pediatrician, Dr. Lawford.

Nobody had ever given me an order before. My father believed in treating me as if I were grown-up. I stared at the strange man seating himself by the window, and burst into tears.

"I'll tell you what, my dear little girl," he said after a few moments. "I'll make a bargain with you. I believe you have to go back to New York and take up your life in six weeks. Nurse your baby until you have to go, and then you can wean him."

I nodded. I didn't know anything about any of it—only what older women had said to me, about nursing ruining your figure—and all of that seemed in another life now.

Flowers began to arrive, great baskets of them from all Mrs. Tompkins' friends, and they filled my room until it looked like a bower. Telegrams arrived. A wire came, late one day, from Eugene. It read, "AREN'T YOU SOMETHING."

But Eugene no longer seemed quite real, either.

I would lie in that hospital bed with the baby within my arm, nursing him. I remember it with Dr. Lawford sitting in the chair by the window and tall, old-maidish Miss Hammond standing beside my bed, both of them watching me with indulgent faces. I felt as though they were my father and mother, and I their good child. But that was absurd, because if they were taking care of anybody, it was Eric.

I stayed in the hospital ten days. When we went home to Mrs. Tompkins', it was spring in Washington, and along every curb were barrows of spring flowers—daffodils and hyacinths and white tulips.

Miss Hammond and Eric had the room next to mine on the fourth floor. Miss Hammond did what was called in those days eighteen-hour duty, which meant she slept there with the baby and went off for a few hours every afternoon. It was Mrs. Tompkins' delight, she said, to look after the baby while Miss Hammond was out. Those afternoons, I would take a long nap, and then we would go out and push the baby in his father's old perambulator along the flower-lined streets, to join the other rosy babies in Dupont Circle, where the little children ran about in their matching coats and hats of wool—pink, lavender, yellow, and pale green.

It was an orderly, bountiful life. Breakfast was at eight, and Mrs. Tompkins dispensed the coffee from the silver *repoussé* service before her, and herself broke the eggs into their cups to be handed by the butler to Miss Hammond and me. We had little pancakes with crisp edges, and the cook sent up rich, thick hot chocolate for me to drink, because I had not yet learned to like coffee. In those days, a thing

like that did nothing to my figure. When we had gone upstairs, I would stand in front of the mahogany mirror in
my bedroom, sidewise, looking at my new, thin shape,
flat as a board again, and then I would go in to watch Miss
Hammond perform the daily ceremony of the baby's bath
—an elaborate ritual involving a rubber tub, toothpicks
with a cotton swab on the end of them, oil, powder, and
specially soft towels—and the whole room was filled with
the smell of baby. Then it would be time for me to nurse
Eric.

I used to hold him in my arm, lying on my bed, and it
was as though he and I were alone inside a transparent
bubble, an iridescent film that shut everything else in the
world out. We were a whole, curled together within the
tough and fragile skin of that round bubble, while outside,
unnoticed, time passed, plans proceeded, and the days
went by in comfortable procession. Inside the bubble, there
was no time.

Luncheon was at one-thirty, Amos and Andy was at
seven, dinner was at seven-thirty, bedtime was at ten-thirty,
in that house. The servants made excuses to come up to the
fourth floor and look at the baby, and lent unnecessary helping hands when the butler lifted the perambulator down the
steps to the street for our afternoon walk among the flowers.
The young mothers I had met came to see the baby, and
Mrs. Tompkins ordered tea with cinnamon toast served to
us in the drawing room afterward; they talked of two-o'clock
feedings, and the triangular versus square folding of diapers,
and of formulas, and asked me to lunch at the Mayflower,
early, so that I could get home for the early-afternoon
feeding. But the young mothers were still strangers to me—

older women. I did not feel anything in common with their busy domestic efficiency.

The spring days passed, and plans matured relentlessly, and soon it was time for me to go home to New York with the baby, to the new apartment Tom had taken and the new nurse he had engaged that Mrs. Tompkins was going to pay for. That was simply the way it was, and it never occurred to me that I could change the plans. I wonder what would have happened if a Dr. Lawford had marched in and given me an order. . . . But after all, I did have to go back; New York was where I lived; so it's not that I mean. I really don't understand what I do mean. I couldn't have stayed at my mother-in-law's indefinitely.

I don't remember starting to wean Eric. I remember an afternoon when I had missed several feedings, and the physical ache was hard, and Mrs. Tompkins brought the baby in for me to play with.

I held him in my arms, that other occupant of the fractured bubble, and suddenly I knew that he and I were divided, never to be together again, and I began to cry.

Mrs. Tompkins came and took the baby away from me, but I could not stop crying, and I have never again cried so hard. It never occurred to me that anything could be done about it, but we were separated, and it was cruel, and I cried for something. I wish I could remember exactly what it was I did cry for. It wasn't for my baby, because I still had my baby, and he's grown up now and works in the Fifth Avenue Bank.

After that, time changed again for me. It flowed backward, to the memory of the bubble and to the first high moment in the hospital when I was Joan of Arc. We left Washington on a morning with the sun shining and barrows of flowers blooming along the curb as we went out the front door and the servants lined up on the steps to say goodbye. Eric was in a pink coat and a pink cap to match, with lace edging. But he didn't really belong to me any more—not the old way. I remember Mrs. Tompkins had tears in her eyes when she kissed us goodbye in the Union Station. But I felt dry-eyed and unmoved, while time flowed backward to that night we drove to the hospital in the middle of the night and she put her ring on my finger.

Of course, when we got back, New York looked marvellous. But even while I was beginning to feel all its possibilities again, time still flowed backward for me. I remember when it was that it stopped flowing backward. I was in someone's room in the St. Regis, where a lot of people were having a drink before going on to dance. I sat on the bed. A young man I had never seen before sat beside me. He said, "Where have you been all my life?"

And I said, "I've been having a baby."

He looked at me with the shine gone out of his eyes, and I realized that there were no possibilities in a remark like mine. I laughed, and reached out my glass to whoever the host was, and said something else that made the young man laugh, too. And then time stopped flowing backward and began once more, and for always, to hurry forward again.

So that is what I wonder about, all these years later. What it is that makes time hurry forward so fast? And what it is that can make it stop, so that you can live in now, in here?

Or even go backward? Because it has never stopped or gone backward for me again.

It isn't having a baby, because I've had four, God help me—two by Tom, counting Eric, and two by Harold, not to mention that miscarriage, and although I hoped it would, time never did anything different again, just hurried on, hurried on.

It isn't, as it occurred to me once that it might be, getting free of men in your life as I was free of them long ago with Mrs. Tompkins. Here I am, rid of my husbands, and the younger children off to school now, in this apartment. It isn't big, but I have day beds in the bedrooms so that every room looks like a sitting room for when I have a party. I'm free, if you want to call it that, and my face isn't what it was, so that I'm not troubled with *that* kind of thing, and yet, when you might think life would slow down, be still, time nevertheless hurries on, hurries on. What do I care about dinner with the Deans tonight? But I have to hurry, just the same. And I'm tired. Sometimes I imagine that if Mrs. Tompkins were still alive, or my father, even . . . But they're dead and nobody remembers them any more, nobody *I* see.

JESSAMYN WEST

The Condemned Librarian

Louise McKay, M.D., the librarian
at Beaumont High School, sent me another card today. It was on the wickerwork table, where Mother puts
my snack, when I got home from teaching. This afternoon
the snack was orange juice and graham crackers, the orange
juice in a plain glass, so that the deepness, the thickness of
the color was almost like a flame inside a hurricane lamp.
The graham crackers were on a blue willowware plate, and
it just so happened that Dr. McKay's card was Van Gogh's
"Sunflowers." It was a perfect still life, the colors increasing
in intensity through the pale sand of the wickerwork table
to the great bong (I want to say), for I swear I could hear

it, of Van Gogh's flaming sunflowers. I looked at the picture Mother had composed for me (I don't doubt) for some time before I read Dr. McKay's card.

Dr. McKay sends me about four cards a year—not at any particular season, Christmas, Easter, or the like. Her sentiments are not suited to such festivals. Usually her message is only a line or two: "Why did you do it?" or "Condemned, condemned, condemned." Something very dramatic and always on a post card, so that the world at large can read it if it chooses. Mother shows her perfect tact by saying nothing if she does read. Perhaps she doesn't; though a single sentence in a big masculine hand is hard to miss. Except for her choice of the Van Gogh print, which showed her malice, Dr. McKay's message this afternoon was very mild—for her. "I am still here, which will no doubt make you happy."

Apart from the fact that anyone interested in the welfare of human beings generally would want her there (or at least not practicing in a hospital), it does make me happy. This evening when I pulled down the flag, I was somehow reassured, standing there in the schoolyard with the cold north wind blowing the dust in my face, to think that over there on the other side of the mountains Louise McKay was ending her day, too. Take away the mountains and fields and we might be gazing into each other's eyes.

I sat down in my room with the juice my mother had squeezed—we hate substitutes—and looked at the card and remembered when I had first seen that marching handwriting. Everything else about her has changed, but not that. I saw it first on the card she gave me telling me of my next date with her. From the moment I arrived at Oakland State, I started hearing about Dr. Louise McKay. She was a real campus heroine, though for no real reason. Except that at a teachers college, with no football heroes, no faculty members with off-campus reputations, the craving for superiority must satisfy itself on the material at hand, however skimpy. And for a student body made up of kids and middle-aged teachers come to Oakland from the lost little towns of mountain and desert, I suppose it was easy to think of Dr. McKay as heroic or fascinating or accomplished.

I was different, though. I was neither middle-aged nor a kid. I was twenty-six years old and I had come to Oakland expecting something. I had had choices. I had made sacrifices to get there, sacrifices for which no "heroic" lady doctor, however "fascinating," "well dressed" (I can remember all the phases used about her now), could be a substitute.

I had a very difficult time deciding to go to Oakland State. I had taught at Liberty School for six years and I loved that place. It was "beautiful for situation," as the Bible says, located ten miles out of town in the rolling semi-dry upland country where the crop was grain, not apricots and peaches. It was a one-room school, and I was its only teacher. It stood in the midst of this sea of barley and oats like an island. In winter and spring this big green sea of ripening grain rolled and tossed about us—all but crested and broke—all but, though never quite. In a way, this was irritating.

For half the year at Liberty there were no barley waves to watch, only the close-cut stubble of reaped fields and the enormous upthrust of the San Jacinto Mountains beyond. Color was my delight then. I used to sit out in the schoolyard at noon or recess and paint. A former teacher had discarded an old sleigh-back sofa, had it put out in the yard halfway between the school and the woodshed. It stood amidst the volunteer oats and mustard like a larger growth. It seemed planted in earth. In the fall when Santa Anas blew, tumbleweeds piled up about it. I don't know how long it had been there when I arrived, but it had taken well to its life in the fields; its legs balanced, its springs stayed inside the upholstery, and the upholstery itself still kept some of its original cherry tones. There I sat—when I wasn't playing ball with the kids—like a hunter, hidden in a game blind; only my game wasn't lions and tigers, it was the whole world, so to speak: the mountains, the grain fields, the kids, the schoolhouse itself. I sat there and painted.

Oh, not well. I've never said that, ever. Never claimed that for a minute. And it's easy to impress children and country people who think it's uncanny if you can draw an apple that looks like an apple. And I could do much more than that. I could make mountains that looked like mountains, children who looked like children. How that impressed the parents! So I had gotten in the habit of being praised, though from no one who counted, no one who knew. I had been sensibly brought up by my mother, taught to evaluate these plaudits rightly. I understood that my schoolyard talent didn't make me a Bonheur or Cassatt. Even so, there was nothing else I had ever wanted to do. This schoolteaching was just a way of making money, of helping my mother, who was a widow.

So, because of the time I had for painting and because of the gifts Liberty School had for my eyes, I had six happy years. I sat like a queen on that sofa in the grass while the meadowlarks sang and the butcherbirds first caught their lunches, then impaled their suppers, still kicking, on the barbed-wire fence. I didn't paint all the time, of course. Kids learned to read there. At the end of the sixth year there was only one eighth grader who could beat me in mental arithmetic. I was the acknowledged champion at skin-the-cat and could play adequately any position on the softball team.

There was not much left to learn at Liberty, and I began, I don't know how, to feel that learning, not teaching, was my business.

In the middle of my sixth year I had to put a tarpaulin over the sofa. A spring broke through the upholstery, a leg crumbled. After that I had to prop it on a piece of stove wood. That spring I noticed for the first time that the babies of age six I had taught my first year were developing Adam's apples or busts. Girls who had been thirteen and fourteen my first year came back to visit Liberty School, married and with babies in their arms.

"You haven't changed," they would tell me. "Oh, it's a real anchor to find you here, just the same."

Their husbands, who were often boys my own age, twenty-four or twenty-five, treated me like an older woman. I might have been their mother, or mother-in-law. I was the woman who had taught their wives. I don't think I looked so much old then as ageless. I've taken out some of the snaps of that year, pictures taken at school. My face, in a way, looks as young as my pupils'; in other ways, as old as Mt. Tahquitz. It looks back at me with the real stony innocence of a face in a coffin—or cradle.

At Thanksgiving time I was to be out of school three days before the holiday, so that I could have a minor operation. When I left school on Friday, Mary Elizabeth Ross, one of my fourth graders, clasped me fondly and said, "May I be the first to hold your baby when you get back from the hospital?"

She wouldn't believe it when I told her I was going to the hospital because I was sick, not to get a baby, and she cried when I came back to school empty-armed.

That I noticed these things showed my restlessness. It might have passed, I might have settled into a lifetime on that island, except that at Christmas I hung some of my paintings with my pupils' pictures at the annual Teachers' Institute exhibit. They caused a stir, and I began foolishly to dream of painting full time, of going to a big city, Los Angeles or San Francisco, where I would take a studio and have lessons. I didn't mention the idea to anyone, scarcely to myself. When anyone else suggested such a thing to me, I pooh-poohed it. "Me, paint? Don't be funny."

But I dreamed of it; the less I said, the more I dreamed; and the more I dreamed, the less possible talking became. I didn't paint much that winter, but I moved through those months with the feel of a paintbrush in my hand. I could feel, way up in my arm, the strokes I would need to make to put Tahquitz, dead white against the green winter sky, on canvas, put it there so people could see how it really floated, that great peak, was hung aloft there like a giant ship against the sky. But I didn't say a word to anyone about my plans, not even to the School Board when I handed in my resignation at Easter. I hadn't lost my head entirely. I told them I was going to "study." I didn't say what. They thought education, of course.

The minute I had resigned, I was filled with fear. I sat on my three-legged sofa amidst the waves of grain that never crested and shivered until school was out. I had undoubtedly been a fool; not only was I without money, but where would I find anything as good as what I had? Everything began to say "stay." I would enter my room at night (the one in which I now write), which my mother kept so exquisitely, books ranged according to size and color, the white bedspread at once taut and velvety, the blue iris in a fan-shaped arc in a brown bowl—and I was a part of that composition. If I walked out, the composition collapsed. And outside, I, too, was a fragment. I would stand there asking myself, "Where will you find anything better?"

There was never any answer.

I could only find something different, and possibly worse. So why go? I had seen myself as a lady Sherwood Anderson, locking the factory door behind me and walking down the tracks toward freedom and self-expression. I could dream that dream but I was afraid to act it. I would stand in my perfectly neat bedroom and frighten myself with pictures of my next room, far away, sordid, with strangers on each side. Fear was in my chest like a stone that whole spring. I had no talent, I was gambling everything on an egotistical attention-seeking whim. It was perfectly natural to have done so, but my misery finally drove me to talking

with my mother. It was perfectly natural, she assured me,
to want a change of scene and occupation. Who didn't
occasionally? But why run away to big cities and studios?
Why wouldn't the perfectly natural, perfectly logical thing
(since I'd already resigned) be to go to Oakland State and
study for my Secondary Credential? The minute I, or
Mother—I don't remember which of us—thought of this
way out, I was filled with bliss, real bliss. I would get away,
go to a real city, be surrounded with people devoted to
learning, but not risk everything.

I heard about Dr. Louise McKay from the minute I
arrived on the campus. She was, as I've said, a kind of college heroine, though it was hard to understand why. What
had she done that was so remarkable? She had been a high-
school librarian, and had become a doctor. What's so extraordinary about that? The girls, and by that I mean the
women students—for many of them were teachers themselves, well along in their thirties and forties, or even
fifties—the girls always spoke about Louise McKay's change
of profession as if it were a Lazaruslike feat; as if she had
practically risen from the dead. People are always so romantic about doctors, and it's understandable, I suppose,
dealing as they do with life and death. But Louise McKay!
The girls talked about her as if what she'd done had been
not only romantic, but also heroic.

In the first place, they emphasized her age. Forty-two!
To me at twenty-six that didn't, of course, seem young.
Still, it was silly to go on about her as if she were a Grand-
ma Moses of medicine—and as if medicine itself were not,
quite simply, anything more than doctoring people; saying,

"This ails you" and "I think this pill will help you." They spoke of doctoring as if it were as hazardous as piloting a jet plane. And they spoke of Louise McKay's size, "that tiny, tiny thing," as if she'd been a six-year-old, praising her for her age and her youth at one and the same time. Her size, they said, made it seem as if the child-examining-doll game were reversed; as if doll took out stethoscope and examined child. She was that tiny and dainty, they said, that long-lashed and pink-cheeked. They exclaimed over her clothes, too. They were delightful in themselves, but particularly so because they emphasized the contrast between her profession and her person. She was a scientist and might have been expected to wear something manly and practical—or something dowdy. She did neither. They'd all been to her for their physical examinations—somehow I'd never been scheduled for that—and could give a complete inventory of her chic wardrobe. I saw her only once before I called on her professionally in December. I didn't see many people, as a matter of fact, at Oakland State, in any capacity, except professional.

True, I was studying. Not that the work was difficult—or interesting either. History of Education, Principles of Secondary Education, Classroom Management, Curriculum Development. But the books were better than the people. Had I lived out there on my three-legged sofa with children and nature too long? Or was there something really wrong with the people in teachers colleges? Anyway, I had no friends, and the nearer I got to a Secondary Credential, the less I wanted it. But I wanted something—miserably, achingly, wretchedly, I wanted something. Whether or not this longing, this sense of something lost, had anything to do with the illness that came upon me toward the end of December, I don't know. I attributed this illness at first to the raw damp bay weather after my lifetime in the warmth and dryness of the inland foothills; I thought that my lack of routine, after days of orderly teaching, might be responsible, and, finally, after I had adopted a routine and had stayed indoors out of the mists and fogs and the discomfort persisted, I told myself that everyone as he grew older lost some of his early exuberant health. I was no longer in my first youth, and thus, "when my health began to fail"—I thought of it in that way rather than as having any specific ailment—accounted for my miseries. I had always been impatient with the shufflings and snuffings, the caution on stairs and at the table of the no-longer-young. I thought they could do better if they tried. Now I began to understand that they couldn't do better and that they probably were trying. I was trying. I couldn't do better. I panted on the hills and puffed on the library steps. I leaned against handrails, I hawked and spat and harrumphed like any oldster past his prime. I did what I could to regain the well-being of my youth. I took long walks to get back my lost wind, ate sparingly, plunged under tingling showers.

By the end of December I felt so miserable I decided to see Dr. McKay at the infirmary. So many new things had been discovered about glands and vitamins, about toxins and antitoxins, that one pill a day was possibly all that stood between me and perfect health. I had the feeling, as people do who have always been well, that a doctor commands a kind of magic—can heal with a glance. Even Dr. McKay, this little ex-librarian, a doll of a woman, with her big splashy earrings and high-heeled shoes and expensive perfumes, could cast a spell of health upon me.

That was the first time I'd ever seen Louise McKay close. My first thought was, She looks every inch her age. She had dark hair considerably grayed, there were lines about her eyes, and her throat muscles were somewhat slack. My second thought was, Why doesn't she admit it? I was dressed more like a middle-aged woman than she. Of course, since she had on a white surgeon's coat, all that could be seen of her "personal attire" was the three or four inches of brown tweed skirt beneath it. But she wore red, very high-heeled shell pumps. Her hair was set in a modified page boy, ends turned under in a soft roll, with a thick, rather tangly fringe across her forehead. It was a somewhat advanced hair style for that year—certainly for a middle-aged doctor. Her eyebrows, which were thick and dark, had been obviously shaped by plucking, and her fingernails were painted coral. She was smiling when I came in. She had considerable color in her face for a dark-haired woman, and she sat at a desk with flowers and pictures on it—not family pictures, but little prints of famous paintings.

She said, looking at her appointment calendar, which had my name on it, "Miss McCullars?"

I said, "Yes."

Then she said, "I see we have something in common." She meant our Scotch names of course, but out of some contrariness which I find hard to explain now, I pretended not to understand, so that she had to explain her little joke to me. But then, it wasn't very funny. She discovered, in looking through her files, that I hadn't had the usual physical examination on entering college.

"Why not?" she asked.

"I didn't get a notice to come," I said, "so I just skipped it."

"It would've helped," she told me, "to have that record now to check against. Just what seems to be the trouble?"

"It's probably nothing. I'm probably just the campus hypochondriac."

"That role's already filled."

I didn't feel well even then, though the stimulation of the talk and of seeing the famous Dr. McKay did make me forget some of my miseries. So I began that afternoon what I always continued in her office—an impersonation of high-spirited, head-tossing health. I don't know why. It wasn't a planned or analyzed action. It just happened that the minute I opened her office door I began to act the part of a person bursting with vitality and health. There I was, practically dying on my feet, as it was later proved, but hiding the fact by every device I could command. What did I think I was doing? The truth is, I wasn't thinking at all.

"I must say you don't look sick," she admitted. Then she began to ask me about my medical history.

"I don't have any medical history. Except measles at fifteen."

"Was there some specific question you wanted to ask me? Some problem?"

So she thought I was one of those girls? Or one of her worshipers just come in to marvel.

"I don't feel well."

"What specifically?"

"Oh—aches and pains."

"Where?"

"Oh—here, there, and everywhere."

"We'll run a few tests, and I'll examine you. The nurse will help you get undressed."

When it was over, she said, "Is your temperature ordinarily a little high?"

"I don't know. I never take it."

"You have a couple of degrees now."

"Above or below normal?"

A little of her school-librarian manner came out. "Are you trying to be funny?"

I wasn't in the least.

"A fever is always above normal."

"What does it mean to have a fever?"

"An infection of some sort."

"It could be a tooth? A tonsil?"

"Yes, it could be. I want to see you tomorrow at ten."

I remember my visit next morning very well. The acacia trees were in bloom, and Dr. McKay's office was filled with their dusty honeybee scent. Dr. McKay was still in street clothes—a blouse, white, high-necked, but frothy with lace and semitransparent, so that you saw more lace beneath. As if she were determined to have everything, I thought: age and youth, practicality and ornamentation, science and femininity. You hero of the campus, I thought, ironically. But she rebuked us schoolteachers by the way she dressed and held herself—and lived, I expected; she really did. And I, I rebuked her in turn, for our hurt honor.

"How do you feel this morning?" she asked.

What did she think to uncover in me? A crybaby and complainer, she standing there in her lovely clothes and I in my dress sun-faded from the Liberty schoolyard?

"Fine," I told her, "I feel fine."

How I felt was her business to discover, wasn't it, not mine to tell? If I knew exactly how I felt, and why, what would've been the use of seeing a doctor? Besides, once again in her office I was stimulated by her presence so that my miseries when not there seemed quite possibly something I had imagined.

"I wanted to check your temperature this morning," she told me.

She sat me down on a white stool, put a thermometer in my mouth, then, while we waited, asked me questions which she thought I could answer with a nod of the head.

"You like teaching? You want to go on with it? You have made friends here?"

She was surprised when she took the thermometer from my mouth. After looking at it thoughtfully, she shook it down and said, "Morning temperature, too."

"You didn't expect that?"

"No, frankly, I didn't."

"Why not?"

"In the kind of infection I suspected you had, a morning temperature isn't usual."

I didn't ask what infection she suspected. I had come to her office willing to be thumped, X-rayed, tested in any way she thought best. I was willing to give her samples of sputum or urine, to cough when told to cough, say ahhh or hold my breath while she counted ten. Whatever she told me to do I would do. But she had turned doctor, not I. If she was a doctor, not a librarian, now was her chance to prove it. Here I was with my fever, come willingly to her office. Let her tell me its cause.

For the next month, Dr. McKay lived, so far as I was concerned, the life of a medical detective, trying to find the villain behind the temperature. The trouble was that the villain's habits differed from day to day. It was as if a murderer had a half-dozen different thumbprints, and left now one, now another, behind him, One day much temperature, the next day none. Dr. McKay eliminated villain after villain: malaria, tonsillitis, rheumatic fever, infected teeth. And while she found disease after disease which I did not have, I grew steadily worse. By May about the only time I ever felt well was while I was in Dr. McKay's office. Entering it was like going onto a stage. However near I might have been to collapse before that oak door opened, once inside it I was to play with perfect ease my role of health. I was unable, actually, to do anything else. I assumed health when I entered her office, as they say Dickens, unable to stand without support, assumed health when he walked out before an audience.

It was nothing I planned. I couldn't by an act of will have feigned exuberance and well-being, gone to her office day after day consciously to play the role of Miss Good Health of 1940, could I? No, something unconscious happened the minute I crossed that threshold, something electric—and ironic. I stood, sat, stooped, reclined, breathed soft, breathed hard, answered questions, flexed my muscles, exposed my reflexes for Dr. McKay with vigor and pleasure—and irony. Especially irony. I was sick, sick, falling apart, crumbling dying on my feet, and I knew it. And this woman, this campus hero whose province it was to know it, was ignorant of the fact. I didn't know what ailed me and wasn't supposed to. She was. It was her business to know.

In the beginning, tuberculosis had been included among the other suspected diseases. But the nontubercular fever pattern, the absence of positive sputum, the identical sounds of the lungs when percussed all had persuaded Dr. McKay that the trouble lay elsewhere. I did not speculate at all about my sickness. I had never been sick before, or even, for that matter, known a sick person. For all I knew, I might have elephantiasis or leprosy, and when Dr. McKay began once again to suspect tuberculosis, I was co-operative and untroubled. She was going to give me what she called a "patch test." Whether this is still used, I don't know. The test then consisted of the introduction of a small number of tubercle bacilli to a patch of scraped skin. If, after a day or two, there was no "positive" reaction, no inflammation of the skin, one was thought to have no tubercular infection.

On the day Dr. McKay began this test she used the word "tuberculosis" for the first time. I had experienced when I entered her office that afternoon my usual heightening of well-being, what amounted to a real gaiety.

"So you still don't give up?" I asked when she announced her plan for the new test. "Still won't admit that what you have on your hands is a hypochondriac?"

It was a beautiful afternoon in late May. School was almost over for the year. Students drifted past the window walking slowly homeward, relishing the sunshine and the blossoming hawthorn, their faces lifted to the light. Cubberly and Thorndyke and Dewey given the go-by for an hour or two. Some of this end-of-the-year, lovely-day quiet came into my interview with Dr. McKay. Though it had started with my usual high-spirited banter, I stopped that. It seemed inappropriate. I experienced my usual unusual well-being, but there was added to it that strange, quiet, listening tenderness which marks the attainment of a pinnacle of some kind.

Dr. McKay stood before her window, her surgeon's jacket off—I was her last patient for the day—in her usual frothy blouse, very snow-white against the rose-red of the hawthorn trees.

She turned away from the window and said to me, "You aren't a hypochondriac."

She shook her head. "I don't know." Then she explained the patch test to me.

"Tuberculosis?" I asked. "And no hectic flush, no graveyard cough, no skin and bones?"

The words were still bantering, possibly, but the tone had changed, tender, tender, humorous, and fondling; the battle—if there had been one—over; and the issue, whatever it was, settled. "In spite of all that, this test?"

"In spite of all that," she said.

She did the scraping deftly. I watched her hands, and while I doubt that there is any such thing as a "surgeon's hands," Dr. McKay's didn't look like a librarian's either, marked by fifteen years of mucilage pots, library stamps, and ten-cent fines. I could smell her perfume and note at close range the degree to which she defied time and the expected categories.

"Come back Monday at the same time," she told me when she had finished.

"What do you expect Monday?" I asked.

"I'm no prophet," she answered. "If I were . . ." She didn't finish her sentence.

We parted like comrades who have been together on a long and dangerous expedition. I don't know what she felt or thought—that she had really discovered, at last, the cause of my illness, perhaps. What I felt is difficult to describe. Certainly my feelings were not those of the usual patient threatened with tuberculosis. Instead, I experienced a tranquillity I hadn't known for a long time. I felt like a lover and a winner, triumphant but tranquil. I knew there would be no positive reaction to the skin test. Beyond that I didn't think.

I was quite right about the reaction. Dr. McKay was completely professional Monday afternoon; buttoned up in her jacket, stethoscope hanging about her neck. I entered her office feeling well, but strange. My veins seemed bursting with blood or triumph. I looked out the window and remembered where I had been a year ago. Breathing was difficult, but in the past months I had learned to live without breathing. I wore a special dress that afternoon because I thought the occasion special. I wouldn't be seeing Dr. McKay again. It was made of white men's-shirting Madras and had a deep scooped neckline, bordered with a ruffle.

"How do you feel?" Dr. McKay asked, as she always did, when I entered.

"Out of this world," I told her.

"Don't joke," she said.

"I wasn't. It's the truth. I feel wonderful."

"Let's have a look at the arm."

"You won't find anything."

"How do you know? Did you peek?"

"No, I didn't, but you won't find anything."

"I'll have a look anyway."

There was nothing, just as I'd known. Not a streak of pink even. Nothing but the marks of the adhesive tape to distinguish one arm from the other. Dr. McKay looked and looked. She touched the skin and pinched it.

"Okay," she said, "you win."

"What do you mean I win? You didn't want me to be infected, did you?"

"Of course not."

"I told you all along I was a hypochondriac."

"Okay, Miss McCullars," she said again, "you win." She sat down at her desk and wrote something on my record sheet.

"What's the final verdict?" I asked.

She handed the sheet to me. What she had written was "TB patch test negative. Fluctuating temperature due to neurotic causes."

"So I won't need to come back?"

"No."

"Nor worry about my lungs?"

"No."

Then with precise timing, as if that were the cue for which for almost six months I had been waiting, I had, there in Dr. McKay's office, my first hemorrhage. A hemorrhage from the lungs is always frightening, and this was a very bad one and my first. They got me to the infirmary at once, but there behind me in Dr. McKay's office was the card stained with my blood and saying that nothing ailed me. I was not allowed to speak for twenty-four hours, and my thought, once the hemorrhaging had stopped, was contained in two words, which ran through my mind, over and over again. "I've won. I've won." What had I won? Well, for one thing, I'd won my release from going on with my work for that Secondary Credential. All that could be forgotten, and forgotten also the need to leave Liberty at all. I could go back there, back to my stranded sofa and the school library and the mountains, blue over the green barley.

When at the end of twenty-four hours I was permitted to whisper, Dr. Stegner, the head physician at Oakland State, came to see me.

"When did you first see Dr. McKay?" he asked.

"In December."

"What course of treatment did she prescribe?"

"Not any. She didn't know what was wrong with me."

"Did she ever X-ray you?"

"No."

This, I began to learn, was the crux of the case against Dr. McKay. For there was one. She should have X-rayed me. She should have known that in cases of far advanced tuberculosis, and that was what I had, the already deeply infected system pays no attention to the introduction of one or two more bacilli. All of its forces are massed elsewhere—there are no guards left to repulse border attacks of unimportant skirmishers. But by this time my mother had arrived, alert, knowledgeable, and energetic.

"My poor little girl," she said, "this woman doctor has killed you."

I wasn't dead yet, but as I heard the talk around me I

began to understand that in another year or two I might very well be so. And listening to my mother's talk, I began to agree with her. Dr. McKay had robbed me not only of health, but also of a promising career—I had been poised upon the edge of something unusual. I was training myself for service. I had remarkable talents. And now all was denied me, and for this denial I could blame Dr. McKay. I did. She had cut me down in mid-career through her ignorance. What did the campus think of its hero now? For the campus had heard of Dr. McKay's mistake. And the Board of Regents! My mother said it was her duty; that she owed the steps she was taking to some other poor girl who might suffer as I had through Dr. McKay's medical incompetence. I thought it was a matter for her to decide, and besides, I was far too ill to have or want any say in such decisions. I was sent, as soon as I was able to be moved, to a sanatorium near my home in Southern California.

I had been there four months when I saw Dr. McKay again. At the beginning of the visiting hour on the first Saturday in October, the nurse on duty came to my room.

"Dr. McKay to see you," she said.

I had no chance to refuse to see her—though I don't know that I would have refused if I'd had the chance—for Dr. McKay followed the nurse into the room and sat down by my bed.

She had changed a good deal; she appeared little, nondescript, and mousy. She had stopped shaping her eyebrows and painting her nails. I suppose I had changed, too. With the loss of my fever, I had lost also all my show of exuberance and life. I lay there in the hospital bed looking, I knew, as sick as I really was. We stared at each other without words for a time.

Then I said, to say something, for she continued silent, "How are things at Oakland State this year?"

"I'm not at Oakland State. I was fired."

I hadn't known it. I was surprised and dismayed, but for a heartbeat—in a heartbeat—I experienced a flash of that old outrageous exultation I had known in her office. I was, in spite of everything, for a second, well and strong and tender in victory. Though what my victory was, I sick and she fired, I couldn't have told.

"I'm sorry," I said. I was. It is a pitiful thing to be out of work.

"Don't lie," she said.

"I am not lying," I told her.

She didn't contradict me. "Why did you do it?" she asked me.

"Do what?" I said, at first really puzzled. Then I remembered my mother's threats. "I had nothing to do with it. Even if I'd wanted to, I was too sick. You know that. I had no idea you weren't in Oakland this year."

"I don't mean my firing—directly. I mean that long masquerade. I mean that willingness to kill yourself, if necessary, to punish me. I tell you a doctor of fifty years' experience would've been fooled by you. Why? I'd never seen you before. I wanted nothing but good for you. Why did you do it? Why?"

"I don't know what you mean."

"What had I ever done to you? Lost there in that dark library, dreaming of being a doctor, saving my money and finally escaping. How had I harmed or threatened you that you should be willing to risk your life to punish me?"

Dr. McKay had risen and was walking about the room, her voice, for one so small, surprisingly loud and commanding. I was afraid a nurse would come to ask her to be quiet. Yet I hesitated myself to remind her to speak more quietly.

"Well," she said, "you have put yourself in a prison, a fine narrow prison. Elected it of your own free will. And that's all right for you, if you wanted a prison. But you had no right to elect it for me, too. That was murderous. Really murderous." I began to fear that she was losing control of herself, and tried to ask questions that would divert her mind from the past.

"Where are you practicing, now?" I asked.

She stopped her pacing and stood over me. "I am no longer in medicine," she said. "I'm the librarian in the high school at Beaumont."

"That's not where you were before?"

"No, it's much smaller and hotter."

"It's only thirty miles—as the crow flies—from Liberty, where I used to teach. I'm going back there as soon as I'm well. It was a mistake to leave it." She said nothing.

"I really love Liberty," I said, "and teaching. The big fields of barley, the mountains. There was an old sofa in the schoolyard, where I used to sit. It was like a throne. I thought for a while I wanted to get away from there and try something else. But that was all a crazy dream. All I want to do now is get back."

"I wish you could have discovered that before you came to Oakland."

I ignored this. "Don't you love books?"

"I had better love books," she said, and left the room.

As it happened, I've never seen her again, though I get these cards. I didn't go back to Liberty four years later—when I was able again to teach. I got this other school, but somehow the magic I had felt earlier with the children, I felt no longer. An outdated little schoolroom with the windows placed high so that neither teacher nor pupils could see out; a dusty schoolyard; and brackish water. The children I teach now look so much like their predecessors that I have the illusion of living in a dream, of being on a treadmill teaching the same child the same lesson through eternity. Outside on the school grounds, my erstwhile throne, the sofa, does not exist. The mountains, of course, are still there—a great barrier at the end of the valley.

Just across the mountains are Beaumont and Dr. McKay; and I am sometimes heartened, standing on the packed earth of the schoolyard in the winter dusk, as she suggested, to think of her reshelving her books, closing the drawer of her fine-till, at the same hour. We can't all escape; some of us must stay home and do the homely tasks, however much we may have dreamed of painting or doctoring. "You have company," I tell myself, looking toward her across the mountains. Then I get into my car to drive into town, where my mother has all this loveliness waiting for me; a composition, once again, that really includes me.

Our Friend Judith

I stopped inviting Judith to meet people when a Canadian woman remarked, with the satisfied fervour of one who has at last pinned a label on a rare specimen: "She is, of course, one of your typical English spinsters."

This was a few weeks after an American sociologist, having elicited from Judith the facts that she was fortyish, unmarried, and living alone, had enquired of me: "I suppose she has given up?" "Given up what?" I asked; and the subsequent discussion was unrewarding.

Judith did not easily come to parties. She would come after pressure, not so much—one felt—to do one a favour, but in order to correct what she believed to be a defect in her character. "I really ought to enjoy meeting new people more than I do," she said once. We reverted to an earlier pattern of our friendship: odd evenings together, an occasional visit to the cinema, or she would telephone to say: "I'm on my way past you to the British Museum. Would you care for a cup of coffee with me? I have twenty minutes to spare."

It is characteristic of Judith that the word spinster, used of her, provoked fascinated speculation about other people. There are my aunts, for instance: aged seventy-odd, both unmarried, one an ex-missionary from China, one a retired matron of a famous London hospital. These two old ladies live together under the shadow of the cathedral in a country town. They devote much time to the Church, to good causes, to letter writing with friends all over the world, to the grandchildren and the great-grandchildren of relatives. It would be a mistake, however, on entering a house in which nothing has been moved for fifty years, to diagnose a condition of fossilized late-Victorian integrity. They read every book reviewed in the *Observer* or the *Times,* so that I recently got a letter from Aunt Rose enquiring whether I did not think that the author of *On the Road* was not—perhaps?—exaggerating his difficulties. They know a good deal about music, and write letters of encouragement to young composers they feel are being neglected—"You must understand that anything new and original takes time to be understood." Well-informed and critical Tories, they are as likely to dispatch telegrams of protest to the Home Secretary as letters of support. These ladies, my aunts Emily and Rose, are surely what is meant by the phrase *English spinster*. And yet, once the connection has been pointed out, there is no doubt that Judith and they are spiritual cousins, if not sisters. Therefore it follows that one's pitying admiration for women who have supported manless and uncomforted lives needs a certain modification?

One will, of course, never know; and I feel now that it is entirely my fault that I shall never know. I had been Judith's friend for upwards of five years before the incident occurred which I involuntarily thought of—stupidly enough —as "the first time Judith's mask slipped."

A mutual friend, Betty, had been given a cast-off Dior dress. She was too short for it. Also she said: "It's not a dress for a married woman with three children and a talent for cooking. I don't know why not, but it isn't." Judith was the right build. Therefore one evening the three of us met by appointment in Judith's bedroom, with the dress. Neither Betty nor I were surprised at the renewed discovery that Judith was beautiful. We had both too often caught each other, and ourselves, in moments of envy when Judith's calm and severe face, her undemonstratively perfect body, succeeded in making everyone else in a room or a street look cheap.

Judith is tall, small-breasted, slender. Her light brown hair is parted in the centre and cut straight around her neck. A high straight forehead, straight nose, a full grave mouth are setting for her eyes, which are green, large and prominent. Her lids are very white, fringed with gold, and moulded close over the eyeball, so that in profile she has the look of a staring gilded mask. The dress was of dark green glistening stuff, cut straight, with a sort of loose tunic. It opened simply at the throat. In it Judith could of course evoke nothing but classical images. Diana, perhaps, back from the hunt, in a relaxed moment? A rather intellectual wood nymph who had opted for an afternoon in the British Museum reading room? Something like that. Neither Betty nor I said a word, since Judith was examining herself in a long mirror, and must know she looked magnificent.

Slowly she drew off the dress and laid it aside. Slowly she put on the old cord skirt and woollen blouse she had taken off. She must have surprised a resigned glance between us, for she then remarked, with the smallest of mocking smiles: "One surely ought to stay in character, wouldn't you say so?" She added, reading the words out of some invisible book, written not by her, since it was a very vulgar book, but perhaps by one of us: "It does everything *for* me, I must admit."

"After seeing you in it," Betty cried out, defying her, "I can't bear for anyone else to have it. I shall simply put it away." Judith shrugged, rather irritated. In the shapeless skirt and blouse, and without makeup, she stood smiling at us, a woman at whom forty-nine of fifty people would not look twice.

A second revelatory incident occurred soon after. Betty telephoned me to say that Judith had a kitten. Did I know that Judith adored cats? "No, but of course she would," I said.

Betty lived in the same street as Judith and saw more of her than I did. I was kept posted about the growth and habits of the cat and its effect on Judith's life. She remarked for instance that she felt it was good for her to have a tie and some responsibility. But no sooner was the cat out of kittenhood than all the neighbours complained. It was a tomcat, ungelded, and making every night hideous. Finally the landlord said that either the cat or Judith must go, unless she was prepared to have the cat "fixed." Judith wore herself out trying to find some person, anywhere in Britain, who would be prepared to take the cat. This person would, however, have to sign a written statement not to have the cat "fixed." When Judith took the cat to the vet to be killed, Betty told me she cried for twenty-four hours.

"She didn't think of compromising? After all, perhaps the cat might have preferred to live, if given the choice?"

"Is it likely I'd have the nerve to say anything so sloppy to Judith? It's the nature of a male cat to rampage lustfully about, and therefore it would be morally wrong for Judith to have the cat fixed, simply to suit her own convenience."

"She said that?"

"She wouldn't have to *say* it, surely?"

A third incident was when she allowed a visiting young American, living in Paris, the friend of a friend and scarcely known to her, to use her flat while she visited her parents over Christmas. The young man and his friends lived it up for ten days of alcohol and sex and marijuana, and when Judith came back it took a week to get the place clean again and the furniture mended. She telephoned twice to Paris, the first time to say that he was a disgusting young thug and if he knew what was good for him he would keep out of her way in the future; the second time to apologise for losing her temper. "I had a choice either to let someone use my flat, or to leave it empty. But having chosen that you should have it, it was clearly an unwarrantable infringement of your liberty to make any conditions at all. I do most sincerely ask your pardon." The moral aspects of the matter having been made clear, she was irritated rather than not to receive letters of apology from him—fulsome, embarrassed, but above all, baffled.

It was the note of curiosity in the letters—he even suggested coming over to get to know her better—that irritated her most. "What do you suppose he means?" she said to me. "He lived in my flat for ten days. One would have thought that should be enough, wouldn't you?"

The facts about Judith, then, are all in the open, unconcealed, and plain to anyone who cares to study them; or, as it became plain she feels, to anyone with the intelligence to interpret them.

She has lived for the last twenty years in a small two-roomed flat high over a busy West London street. The flat is shabby and badly heated. The furniture is old, was never anything but ugly, is now frankly rickety and fraying. She has an income of £200 a year from a dead uncle. She lives on this and what she earns from her poetry, and from lecturing on poetry to night classes and extramural university classes.

She does not smoke or drink, and eats very little, from preference, not self-discipline.

She studied poetry and biology at Oxford, with distinction.

She is a Castlewell. That is, she is a member of one of the academic upper-middle-class families, which have been producing for centuries a steady supply of brilliant but sound men and women who are the backbone of the arts and sciences in Britain. She is on cool good terms with her family who respect her and leave her alone.

She goes on long walking tours, by herself, in such places as Exmoor or West Scotland.

Every three or four years she publishes a volume of poems.

The walls of her flat are completely lined with books. They are scientific, classical and historical; there is a great deal of poetry and some drama. There is not one novel. When Judith says: "Of course I don't read novels," this does not mean that novels have no place, or a small place, in literature; or that people should not read novels; but that it must be obvious she can't be expected to read novels.

I had been visiting her flat for years before I noticed two long shelves of books, under a window, each shelf filled with the works of a single writer. The two writers are not, to put it at the mildest, the kind one would associate with Judith. They are mild, reminiscent, vague and whimsical. Typical English belles-lettres, in fact, and by definition abhorrent to her. Not one of the books in the two shelves has been read; some of the pages are still uncut. Yet each book is inscribed or dedicated to her: gratefully, admiringly, sentimentally and, more than once, amorously. In short, it is open to anyone who cares to examine these two shelves, and to work out dates, to conclude that Judith from the age of fifteen to twenty-five had been the beloved young companion of one elderly literary gentleman, and from twenty-five to thirty-five the inspiration of another.

During all that time she had produced her own poetry, and the sort of poetry, it is quite safe to deduce, not at all likely to be admired by her two admirers. Her poems are always cool and intellectual; that is their form, which is contradicted or supported by a gravely sensuous texture. They are poems to read often; one has to, to understand them.

I did not ask Judith a direct question about these two eminent but rather fusty lovers. Not because she would not have answered, or because she would have found the question impertinent, but because such questions are clearly unnecessary. Having those two shelves of books where they are, and books she could not conceivably care for, for their own sake, is publicly giving credit where credit is due. I can imagine her thinking the thing over, and deciding it was only fair, or perhaps honest, to place the books there; and this despite the fact that she would not care at all for the same attention to be paid to her. There is something almost contemptuous in it. For she certainly despises people who feel they need attention.

For instance, more than once a new emerging wave of "modern" young poets have discovered her as the only "modern" poet among their despised and well-credited elders. This is because, since she began writing at fifteen, her poems have been full of scientific, mechanical and chemical imagery. This is how she thinks, or feels.

More than once has a young poet hastened to her flat, to claim her as an ally, only to find her totally and by instinct unmoved by words like modern, new, contemporary. He has been outraged and wounded by her principle, so deeply rooted as to be unconscious, and to need no expression but a contemptuous shrug of the shoulders, that publicity seeking or to want critical attention is despicable. It goes without saying that there is perhaps one critic in the world she has any time for. He has sulked off, leaving her on her shelf, which she takes it for granted is her proper place, to be read by an appreciative minority.

Meanwhile she gives her lectures, walks alone through London, writes her poems, and is seen sometimes at a concert or a play with a middle-aged professor of Greek who has a wife and two children.

Betty and I had speculated about this professor, with such remarks as: Surely she must sometimes be lonely? Hasn't she ever wanted to marry? What about that awful moment when one comes in from somewhere at night to an empty flat?

It happened recently that Betty's husband was on a business trip, her children visiting, and she was unable to stand the empty house. She asked Judith for a refuge until her own home filled again.

Afterwards Betty rang up to report:

"Four of the five nights Professor Adams came in about ten or so."

"Was Judith embarrassed?"

"Would you expect her to be?"

"Well, if not embarrassed, at least conscious there was a situation?"

"No, not at all. But I must say I don't think he's good enough for her. He can't possibly understand her. He calls her Judy."

"Good God."

"Yes. But I was wondering. Suppose the other two called

her Judy—'little Judy'—imagine it! Isn't it awful? But it does rather throw a light on Judith?"

"It's rather touching."

"I suppose it's touching. But *I* was embarrassed—oh, not because of the situation. Because of how she was, with him. 'Judy, is there another cup of tea in that pot?' And she, rather daughterly and demure, pouring him one."

"Well yes, I can see how you felt."

"Three of the nights he went to her bedroom with her— very casual about it, because she was being. But he was not there in the mornings. So I asked her. You know how it is when you ask her a question. As if you've been having long conversations on that very subject for years and years, and she is merely continuing where you left off last. So when she says something surprising, one feels such a fool to be surprised?"

"Yes. And then?"

"I asked her if she was sorry not to have children. She said yes, but one couldn't have everything."

"One can't have everything, she said?"

"Quite clearly feeling she *has* nearly everything. She said she thought it was a pity, because she would have brought up children very well."

"When you come to think of it, she would, too."

"I asked about marriage, but she said on the whole the role of a mistress suited her better."

"She used the word mistress?"

"You must admit it's the accurate word."

"I suppose so."

"And then she said that while she liked intimacy and sex

and everything, she enjoyed waking up in the morning alone and *her own person*."

"Yes, *of course*."

"Of course. But now she's bothered because the professor would like to marry her. Or he feels he ought. At least, he's getting all guilty and obsessive about it. She says she doesn't see the point of divorce, and anyway, surely it would be very hard on his poor old wife after all these years, particularly after bringing up two children so satisfactorily. She talks about his wife as if she's a kind of nice old charwoman, and it wouldn't be *fair* to sack her, you know. Anyway. What with one thing and another, Judith's going off to Italy soon in order *to collect herself*."

"But how's she going to pay for it?"

"Luckily the Third Programme's commissioning her to do some arty programmes. They offered her a choice of The Cid—El Thid, you know—and the Borgias. Well, the Borghese, then. And Judith settled for the Borgias."

"The Borgias," I said, "*Judith?*"

"Yes, quite. I said that too, in that tone of voice. She saw my point. She says the epic is right up her street, whereas the Renaissance has never been on her wave length. Obviously it couldn't be, all the magnificence and cruelty and *dirt*. But of course chivalry and a high moral code and all those idiotically noble goings-on are right on her wave length."

"Is the money the same?"

"Yes. But is it likely Judith would let money decide? No, she said that one should always choose something new, that isn't up one's street. Well, because it's better for her character, and so on, to get herself unsettled by the Renaissance. She didn't say *that,* of course."

"Of course not."

Judith went to Florence; and for some months postcards informed us tersely of her doings. Then Betty decided she must go by herself for a holiday. She had been appalled by the discovery that if her husband was away for a night she couldn't sleep; and when he went to Australia for three weeks, she stopped living until he came back. She had discussed this with him, and he had agreed that, if she really felt the situation to be serious, he would dispatch her by air, to Italy, in order to recover her self-respect. As she put it.

I got this letter from her: "It's no use, I'm coming home. I might have known. Better face it, once you're really married you're not fit for man nor beast. And if you remember what I used to be like! *Well!* I moped around Milan. I sunbathed in Venice, then I thought my tan was surely worth something, so I was on the point of starting an affair with another lonely soul, but I lost heart, and went to Florence to see Judith. She wasn't there. She'd gone to the Italian Riviera. I had nothing better to do, so I followed her. When I saw the place I wanted to laugh, it's so much not Judith, you know, all those palms and umbrellas and gaiety at all costs and ever such an ornamental blue sea. Judith is in an enormous stone room up on the hillside above the sea, with grape vines all over the place. You should see her, she's got beautiful. It seems for the last fifteen years she's been going to Soho every Saturday morning to buy food at an Italian shop. I must have looked surprised, because she explained she liked Soho. I suppose because all that dreary vice and nudes and prostitutes and everything prove how right she is to be as she is? She told the people in the shop she was going to Italy, and the *signora* said, what a coincidence, she was going back to Italy too, and she did hope an old friend like Miss Castlewell would visit her there. Judith said to me: 'I felt lacking, when she used the word friend. Our relations have always been formal. Can you understand it?' she said to me. 'For fifteen years,' I said to her. She said: 'I think I must feel it's a kind of imposition, don't you know, expecting people to feel friendship for one.' *Well.* I said: 'You ought to understand it, because you're like that yourself.' 'Am I?' she said. 'Well, think about it,' I said. But I could see she didn't want to think about it. Anyway, she's here, and I've spent a week with her. The widow Maria Rineiri inherited her mother's house, so she came home, from Soho. On the ground floor is a tatty little *rosticcerìa* patronised by the neighbours. They are all working people. This isn't tourist country, up on the hill. The widow lives above the shop with her little boy, a nasty little brat of about ten. Say what you like, the English are the only people who know how to bring up children. I don't care if that's insular. Judith's room is at the back, with a balcony. Underneath her room is the barber's shop, and the barber is Luigi Rineiri, the widow's younger brother. Yes, I was keeping him until the last. He is about forty, tall dark handsome, a great *bull,* but rather a sweet fatherly bull. He has cut Judith's hair and made it lighter. Now it looks like a sort of gold helmet. Judith is all brown. The widow Rineiri has made her a white dress and a green dress. They fit, for a change. When Judith walks down the street to the lower town, all the Italian males take one look at the golden girl and melt in their own oil like ice cream. Judith takes all this in her stride. She sort of acknowledges the homage. Then she strolls into the sea and vanishes into the foam. She swims five miles every day. *Naturally*. I haven't asked Judith whether she has collected herself, because you can see she hasn't. The widow Rineiri is matchmaking. When I noticed this I wanted to laugh, but luckily I didn't because Judith asked me, really wanting to know: 'Can you see me married to an Italian barber?' (Not being snobbish, but stating the position, so to speak.) 'Well, yes,' I said, 'you're the only woman I know who I can see married to an Italian barber.' Because it wouldn't matter who she married, she'd always be her *own person*. 'At any rate, for a time,' I said. At which she said, asperously: 'You can use phrases like for a time in England but not in Italy.' Did you ever see England, at least London, as the home of licence, liberty and free love? No, neither did I, but of course she's right. Married to Luigi it would be the family, the neighbours, the church and the *bambini*. All the same she's thinking about it, believe it or not. Here she's quite different, all relaxed and free. She's melting in the attention she gets. The widow mothers her and makes her coffee all the time, and listens to a lot of good advice about how to bring up that nasty brat of hers. Unluckily she doesn't take it. Luigi is crazy for her. At mealtimes she goes to the *trattoria* in the upper square and all the workmen treat her like a goddess. Well, a film star then. I said to her, you're mad to come home. For one thing her rent is ten bob a week, and you eat *pasta*

and drink red wine till you bust for about one and sixpence.
No, she said, it would be nothing but self-indulgence to
stay. Why? I said. She said, she's got nothing to stay for.
(Ho ho.) And besides, she's done her research on the Borghese, though so far she can't see her way to an honest
presentation of the facts. What made these people tick? she
wants to know. And so she's only staying because of the
cat. I forgot to mention the cat. This is a town of cats. The
Italians here love their cats. I wanted to feed a stray cat
at the table, but the waiter said no, and after lunch, all the
waiters came with trays crammed with leftover food and
stray cats came from everywhere to eat. And at dark when
the tourists go in to feed and the beach is empty—you know
how empty and forlorn a beach is at dusk?—well, cats appear from everywhere. The beach seems to move, then you
see it's cats. They go stalking along the thin inch of grey
water at the edge of the sea, shaking their paws crossly at
each step, snatching at the dead little fish, and throwing
them with their mouths up on to the dry sand. Then they
scamper after them. You've never seen such a snarling and
fighting. At dawn when the fishing boats come in to the
empty beach, the cats are there in dozens. The fishermen
throw them bits of fish. The cats snarl and fight over it.
Judith gets up early and goes down to watch. Sometimes
Luigi goes too, being tolerant. Because what he really likes
is to join the evening promenade with Judith on his arm
around the square of the upper town. Showing her off. Can
you *see* Judith? But she does it. Being tolerant. But she
smiles and enjoys the attention she gets, there's no doubt
of it.

"She has a cat in her room. It's a kitten really, but it's pregnant. Judith says she can't leave until the kittens are born. The cat is too young to have kittens. Imagine Judith. She sits on her bed in that great stone room, with her bare feet on the stone floor and watches the cat, and tries to work out why a healthy uninhibited Italian cat always fed on the best from the *rosticceria* should be neurotic. Because it is. When it sees Judith watching it gets nervous and starts licking at the roots of its tail. But Judith goes on watching, and says about Italy that the reason why the English love the Italians is because Italians make the English feel superior. They have no discipline. And that's a despicable reason for one nation to love another. Then she talks about Luigi and says he has no sense of guilt, but a sense of sin; whereas she has no sense of sin but she has guilt. I haven't asked her if this has been an insuperable barrier, because judging from how she looks, it hasn't. She says she would rather have a sense of sin, because sin can be atoned for, and if she understood sin, perhaps she would be more at home with the Renaissance. Luigi is very healthy, she says, and not neurotic. He is a Catholic of course. He doesn't mind that she's an atheist. His mother has explained to him that the English are all pagans, but good people at heart. I suppose he thinks a few smart sessions with the local priest would set Judith on the right path for good and all. Meanwhile the cat walks nervously around the room, stopping to lick, and when it can't stand Judith watching it another second, it rolls over on the floor, with its paws tucked up, and rolls up its eyes, and Judith scratches its lumpy pregnant stomach and tells it to relax. It makes *me* nervous to see her, it's not like her, I don't know why. Then Luigi shouts up from the barber's shop, then he comes up and stands at the door laughing, and Judith laughs, and the widow says: Children, enjoy yourselves. And off they go, walking down to the town eating ice cream. The cat follows them. It won't let Judith out of its sight, like a dog. When she swims miles out to sea, the cat hides under a beach hut until she comes back. Then she carries it back up the hill, because that nasty little boy chases it. *Well.* I'm coming home tomorrow thank God, to my dear old Billy, I was mad ever to leave him. There is something about Judith and Italy that has upset me, I don't know what. The point is, what on earth can Judith and Luigi *talk* about? Nothing. How can they? And of course it doesn't matter. So I turn out to be a prude as well. See you next week."

It was my turn for a dose of the sun, so I didn't see Betty. On my way back from Rome I stopped off in Judith's resort and walked up through narrow streets to the upper town, where, in the square with the vine-covered *trattoria* at the corner, was a house with ROSTICCERIA written in black paint on a cracked wooden board over a low door. There was a door curtain of red beads, and flies settled on the beads. I opened the beads with my hand and looked in to a small dark room with a stone counter. Loops of salami hung from metal hooks. A glass bell covered some plates of cooked meats. There were flies on the salami and on the glass bell. A few tins on the wooden shelves, a couple of pale loaves, some wine casks and an open case of sticky pale green grapes covered with fruit flies seemed to be the only stock. A single wooden table with two chairs stood in a corner, and two workmen sat there, eating lumps of sausage and bread. Through another bead curtain at the back came a short, smoothly fat, slender-limbered woman with greying hair. I asked for Miss Castlewell, and her face changed. She said in an offended, offhand way: "Miss Castlewell left last week." She took a white cloth from under the counter, and flicked at the flies on the glass bell. "I'm a friend of hers," I said, and she said: "*Si,*" and put her hands palm down on the counter and looked at me, expressionless. The workmen got up, gulped down the last of their wine, nodded and went. She *ciao*'d them; and looked back at me. Then, since I didn't go, she called: "Luigi!" A shout came from the back room, there was a rattle of beads, and in came first a wiry sharp-faced boy, and then Luigi. He was tall, heavy-shouldered, and his black rough hair was like a cap, pulled low over his brows. He looked good-natured, but at the moment uneasy. His sister said something, and he stood beside her, an ally, and confirmed: "Miss Castlewell went away." I was on the point of giving up, when through the bead curtain that screened off a dazzling light eased a thin tabby cat. It was ugly and it walked uncomfortably, with its back quarters bunched up. The child suddenly let out a "Ssssss" through his teeth, and the cat froze. Luigi said something sharp to the child, and something encouraging to the cat, which sat down, looked straight in front of it, then began frantically licking at its flanks. "Miss Castlewell was offended with us," said Mrs. Rineiri suddenly, and with dignity. "She left early one morning. We did not expect her to go." I said, "Perhaps she had to go home and finish some work."

Mrs. Rineiri shrugged, then sighed. Then she exchanged a hard look with her brother. Clearly the subject had been discussed, and closed forever.

"I've known Judith a long time," I said, trying to find the right note. "She's a remarkable woman. She's a poet." But there was no response to this at all. Meanwhile the child, with a fixed bared-teeth grin, was starting at the cat, narrowing his eyes. Suddenly he let out another "Sssssss" and added a short high yelp. The cat shot backwards, hit the wall, tried desperately to claw its way up the wall, came to its senses and again sat down and began its urgent, undirected licking at its fur. This time Luigi cuffed the child, who yelped in earnest, and then ran out into the street past the cat. Now that the way was clear the cat shot across the floor, up onto the counter, and bounded past Luigi's shoulder and straight through the bead curtain into the barber's shop, where it landed with a thud.

"Judith was sorry when she left us," said Mrs. Rineiri uncertainly. "She was crying."

"I'm sure she was."

"And so," said Mrs. Rineiri, with finality, laying her hands down again, and looking past me at the bead curtain. That was the end. Luigi nodded brusquely at me, and went into the back. I said goodbye to Mrs. Rineiri and walked back to the lower town. In the square I saw the child, sitting on the running board of a lorry parked outside the *trattoria,* drawing in the dust with his bare toes, and directing in front of him a blank, unhappy stare.

I had to go through Florence, so I went to the address Judith had been at. No, Miss Castlewell had not been back. Her papers and books were still here. Would I take them back with me to England? I made a great parcel and brought them back to England.

I telephoned Judith and she had already written for the papers to be sent, but it was kind of me to bring them. There had seemed to be no point, she said, in returning to Florence.

"Shall I bring them over?"

"I would be very grateful, of course."

Judith's flat was chilly, and she wore a bunchy sage-green woollen dress. Her hair was still a soft gold helmet, but she looked pale and rather pinched. She stood with her back to a single bar of electric fire—lit because I demanded it—with her legs apart and her arms folded. She contemplated me.

"I went to the Rineiris' house."

"Oh. Did you?"

"They seemed to miss you."

She said nothing.

"I saw the cat too."

"Oh. Oh, I suppose you and Betty discussed it?" This was with a small unfriendly smile.

"Well, Judith, you must see we were likely to?"

She gave this her consideration and said: "I don't understand why people discuss other people. Oh—I'm not criticising you. But I don't see why you are so interested. I don't understand human behavior and I'm not particularly interested."

"I think you should write to the Rineiris."

"I wrote and thanked them, of course."

"I don't mean that."

"You and Betty have worked it out?"

"Yes, we talked about it. We thought we should talk to you, so you should write to the Rineiris."

"Why?"

"For one thing, they are both very fond of you."

"Fond," she said smiling.

"Judith, I've never in my life felt such an atmosphere of being let down."

Judith considered this. "When something happens that shows one there is really a complete gulf in understanding, what is there to say?"

"It could scarcely have been a complete gulf in understanding. I suppose you are going to say we are being interfering?"

Judith showed distaste. "That is a very stupid word. And it's a stupid idea. No one can interfere with me if I don't let them. No, it's that I don't understand people. I don't understand why you or Betty should care. Or why the Rineiris should, for that matter," she added with the small tight smile.

"Judith!"

"If you've behaved stupidly, there's no point in going on. You put an end to it."

"What happened? Was it the cat?"

"Yes, I suppose so. But it's not important." She looked at me, saw my ironical face, and said: "The cat was too young to have kittens. That is all there was to it."

"Have it your way. But that is obviously not all there is to it."

"What upsets me is that I don't understand at all why I was so upset then."

"What happened? Or don't you want to talk about it?"

"I don't give a damn whether I talk about it or not. You really do say the most extraordinary things, you and Betty. If you want to know, I'll tell you. What does it matter?"

"I would like to know, of course."

"*Of course!*" she said. "In your place I wouldn't care. Well, I think the essence of the thing was that I must have had the wrong attitude to that cat. Cats are supposed to be independent. They are supposed to go off by themselves to have their kittens. This one didn't. It was climbing up onto my bed all one night and crying for attention. I don't like cats on my bed. In the morning I saw she was in pain. I stayed with her all that day. Then Luigi—he's the brother, you know."

"Yes."

"Did Betty mention him? Luigi came up to say it was time I went for a swim. He said the cat should look after itself. I blame myself very much. That's what happens when you submerge yourself in somebody else."

Her look at me was now defiant; and her body showed both defensiveness and aggression. "Yes. It's true. I've always been afraid of it. And in the last few weeks I've behaved badly. It's because I let it happen."

"Well, go on."

"I left the cat and swam. It was late, so it was only for a few minutes. When I came out of the sea the cat had followed me and had had a kitten on the beach. The little beast Michele—the son, you know?—well, he always teased the poor thing, and now he had frightened her off the kitten. It was dead, though. He held it up by the tail and waved

it at me as I came out of the sea. I told him to bury it.
He scooped two inches of sand away and pushed the kitten
in—on the beach, where people are all day. So I buried it
properly. He had run off. He was chasing the poor cat.
She was terrified and running up the town. I ran too. I
caught Michele and I was so angry I hit him. I don't believe
in hitting children. I've been feeling beastly about it ever
since."

"You were angry."

"It's no excuse. I would never have believed myself ca-
pable of hitting a child. I hit him very hard. He went off,
crying. The poor cat had got under a big lorry parked in
the square. Then she screamed. And then a most remarkable
thing happened. She screamed just once, and all at once
cats just materialised. One minute there was just one cat,
lying under a lorry, and the next, dozens of cats. They sat
in a big circle around the lorry, all quite still, and watched
my poor cat."

"Rather moving," I said.

"Why?"

"There is no evidence one way or the other," I said in
inverted commas, "that the cats were there out of concern
for a friend in trouble."

"No," she said energetically. "There isn't. It might have
been curiosity. Or anything. How do we know? However, I
crawled under the lorry. There were two paws sticking out
of the cat's back end. The kitten was the wrong way round.
It was stuck. I held the cat down with one hand and I
pulled the kitten out with the other." She held out her long
white hands. They were still covered with fading scars and
scratches. "She bit and yelled, but the kitten was alive. She

left the kitten and crawled across the square into the house. Then all the cats got up and walked away. It was the most extraordinary thing I've ever seen. They vanished again. One minute they were all there, and then they had vanished. I went after the cat, with the kitten. Poor little thing, it was covered with dust—being wet, don't you know. The cat was on my bed. There was another kitten coming, but it got stuck too. So when she screamed and screamed I just pulled it out. The kittens began to suck. One kitten was very big. It was a nice fat black kitten. It must have hurt her. But she suddenly bit out—snapped, don't you know, like a reflex action, at the back of the kitten's head. It died, just like that. Extraordinary, isn't it?" she said, blinking hard, her lips quivering. "She was its mother, but she killed it. Then she ran off the bed and went downstairs into the shop under the counter. I called to Luigi. You know, he's Mrs. Rineiri's brother."

"Yes, I know."

"He said she was too young, and she was badly frightened and very hurt. He took the alive kitten to her but she got up and walked away. She didn't want it. Then Luigi told me not to look. But I followed him. He held the kitten by the tail and he banged it against the wall twice. Then he dropped it into the rubbish heap. He moved aside some rubbish with his toe, and put the kitten there and pushed rubbish over it. Then Luigi said the cat should be destroyed. He said she was badly hurt and it would always hurt her to have kittens."

"He hasn't destroyed her. She's still alive. But it looks to me as if he were right."

"Yes, I expect he was."

"What upset you—that he killed the kitten?"

"Oh, no, I expect the cat would if he hadn't. But that isn't the point, is it?"

"What is the point?"

"I don't think I really know." She had been speaking breathlessly, and fast. Now she said slowly: "It's not a question of right or wrong, is it? Why should it be? It's a question of what one is. That night Luigi wanted to go promenading with me. For him, that was *that*. Something had to be done, and he'd done it. But I felt ill. He was very nice to me. He's a very good person," she said, defiantly.

"Yes, he looks it."

"That night I couldn't sleep. I was blaming myself. I should never have left the cat to go swimming. Well, and then I decided to leave the next day. And I did. And that's all. The whole thing was a mistake, from start to finish."

"Going to Italy at all?"

"Oh, to go for a holiday would have been all right."

"You've done all that work for nothing? You mean you aren't going to make use of all that research?"

"No. It was a mistake."

"Why don't you leave it a few weeks and see how things are then?"

"Why?"

"You might feel differently about it."

"What an extraordinary thing to say. Why should I? Oh, you mean, time passing, healing wounds—that sort of thing? What an extraordinary idea. It's always seemed to me an extraordinary idea. No, right from the beginning I've felt ill at ease with the whole business, not myself at all."

"Rather irrationally, I should have said."

Judith considered this, very seriously. She frowned while she thought it over. Then she said: "But if one cannot rely on what one feels, what can one rely on?"

"On what one thinks, I should have expected you to say."

"Should you? Why? Really, you people are all very strange. I don't understand you." She turned off the electric fire, and her face closed up. She smiled, friendly and distant, and said: "I don't really see any point at all in discussing it."

BIOGRAPHICAL NOTES

HORTENSE CALISHER was born in New York City in 1911. She graduated from Barnard College during the Depression, became a social worker, married and had two children; not until she was well into her thirties did she begin writing seriously. Her first collection of stories, *In the Absence of Angels,* was published in 1951, and her first novel, *False Entry,* ten years later. Since then she has written eight novels, among them *Journal from Ellipsia, The New Yorkers* and *Standard Dreaming,* as well as an autobiography, *Herself.*

MAVIS GALLANT was born in Canada and attended seventeen different schools there, beginning with a convent school at the age of four. Her first job was with a newspaper in Montreal; since then she has spent most of her adult life in Europe, and now lives in Paris. She is the author of four highly regarded books: two novels, *Green Water, Green Sky* and *A Fairly Good Time;* and two collections of short stories, *The Other Paris* and *My Heart Is Broken.*

NANCY HALE was born in Boston in 1908, and her first story appeared in the *Boston Herald* when she was eleven. After going to New York in 1928, she worked on the staffs of *Vogue* and *Vanity Fair,* and then became the first woman reporter for *The New York Times,* where she remained until 1936. Meanwhile, magazines began publishing her short stories, and in 1942 *The Prodigal Women,* a novel, was her first bestseller. She has gone on to write over fifteen books of fiction and criticism, including such novels as *The Sign of Jonah* and *Secrets,* and collections of short stories such as *Between the Dark and the Daylight* and *The Pattern of Perfection.*

DORIS LESSING was born of British parents in Persia in 1919, and moved with her family to Southern Rhodesia when she was five years old. In 1949, she went to England, where she has lived ever since. Her first novel, *The Grass Is Singing,* appeared in 1955, and was followed by a collection of short stories, *This Was the Old Chief's Country.* Both these books had African settings, but soon Doris Lessing's fiction was to reflect more cosmopolitan themes as she gave brilliant expression to the major ideological, psychological and sexual dilemmas of our time in such major works as *The Golden Notebook* and the five novels that comprise the *Children of Violence* series, as well as other novels, short stories, plays and poetry. Her most recent novel is the highly acclaimed *The Summer Before the Dark.*

CARSON MCCULLERS was born in Georgia in 1917. In 1936, she arrived in New York to study music, lost her tuition money in the subway and turned to writing instead. She was twenty-three when her first novel, *The Heart Is a Lonely Hunter,* was recognized as an achievement of the first rank. This initial success was followed and enhanced by *Reflections in a Golden Eye, The Member of the Wedding* (first a novel, then a play), *The Ballad of the Sad Cafe,* and *Clock Without Hands.* After a long and gallant struggle against a debilitating illness, Carson McCullers died in 1967.

KATHERINE MANSFIELD was the pseudonym of Kathleen Beauchamp, born in New Zealand in 1888. Her writing talent early manifested itself; her first story was published in a local magazine when she was nine. In 1902, she went to London, where she studied music and became an accomplished cellist. Returning to New Zealand in 1906, she found herself unhappy in its provincial atmosphere, and soon went back to England. There she entered into an abortive short marriage, then an unhappy love affair, which was followed by an illegitimate pregnancy terminating with a stillborn child in a German spa. From her stay in Germany came her first collection of stories, *In a German Pension* (1911). It was only when she met and later married the critic J. Middleton Murry that she was able to devote full energy to her writing. Her stories won ever-widening recognition; and with *Bliss and Other Stories* in 1920 her artistry was universally acclaimed. Her last years were spent in intense creative activity and an equally intense battle against the inroads of the ill health that had always plagued her. Katherine Mansfield died in January, 1923, while seeking physical and spiritual regeneration through following the doctrines of the Russian mystic Gurdjieff in his institute near Paris.

KATHERINE ANNE PORTER was born in Indian Creek, Texas, in 1894. She was raised in Texas and later sojourned in New Orleans, New York, Mexico, Europe and numerous other places.

Until the publication of her first and only novel, *Ship of Fools,* in 1962 brought her popular success and financial security, she eked out a bare living through journalism, teaching and other activities while devoting her primary energies to the writing of fiction. These efforts resulted in three slender volumes of novellas and short stories—*Flowering Judas and Other Stories, Pale Horse, Pale Rider* and *The Leaning Tower and Other Stories*—that rank with the finest writing of our time. She is also the author of a collection of essays, *The Days Before.*

JEAN RHYS was born in Dominica, West Indies, in 1894. When she was sixteen, shortly before the outbreak of World War I, she went to London, where she found employment in stage productions of musical comedies. She went to Europe after the war, and in Paris, with the encouragement of the novelist Ford Madox Ford, she began to write. *The Left Bank,* a collection of short stories, appeared in 1927, and was followed by the novels *Postures* (1928), which was published in America (1929) as *Quartet, Voyage in the Dark* (1934), *After Leaving Mr. Mackenzie* (1937) and *Good Morning, Midnight* (1939). During the following twenty years, Jean Rhys vanished from the literary scene, but in 1958, she began to publish new stories, and in 1966 her most recent novel, *Wide Sargasso Sea,* appeared. Since then, all her previous novels have been republished, and stories from *The Left Bank* have appeared with her later stories in *Tigers Are Better-Looking.*

CHRISTINA STEAD was born in Australia in 1902 and was educated at Sydney University. She arrived in Europe in the 1920s, worked in London and Paris and then came to the United States during the following decade. She taught at New York University and worked in Hollywood before going to live in England after World War II. Her first published fiction was a volume of short stories, *The Salzburg Tales,* in 1934. She went on to write ten novels, including *House of All Nations, Dark Places of the Heart,* and the novel generally regarded as her masterpiece, *The Man Who Loved Children. The Puzzleheaded Girl,* a collection of four novellas, appeared in 1968.

JESSAMYN WEST was born in Indiana in 1907 of Quaker parents. When she was six, she moved with her family to California, and has lived in that state ever since. Her first novel, *The Friendly Persuasion* (1945), was an immense success. Since then, she has enjoyed a notable career as a novelist, short story writer, screenwriter, teacher and lecturer. Her many books include *The Witch Diggers, Love, Death and the Ladies' Drill Team, To See the Dream, South of the Angels* and *Leafy Rivers.*

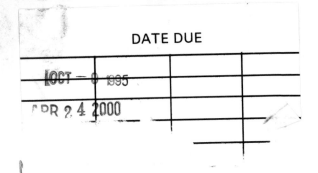